Georgia

A Trilogy

Part One

Michael Boylan

PWI Books

Bethesda, Maryland

Published in the United States of America

ISBN-13: 978-0692752548 (PWI Books)

ISBN-10: 0692752544

Library of Congress Control Number: 2016947112

Copy edited by Joanna Jensen
Proof read by Lydia Johnson

The Archē Novels

Naked Reverse

Georgia (A Trilogy)

T-Rx: The History of a Radical Leader

The Long Fall of the Ball from the Wall

Book One

A New Suit of Clothes

Or

The Author's Introduction to the Work

It might be suggested that the twelve books that follow are, in certain respects, individual dramas with events transpiring and characters entering and exiting before the reader. As in any good drama, there is some considerable attention given to the costumes and scenery used. And much pain has been devoted to the construction of sets that are, to a degree, imitative of scenes which we see every day in life, though of course, being only a drama, these scenes are illusions meant to be constructed more fully in the reader's imagination. To be vital, this machinery must be embellished by the theater-goer's mind so that he or she sees it in a unique manner. Stage scenery can have little actual depth because of the physical limitations of the stage, but the members of the audience can add the necessary depth in their minds so that they can "see" the depth that is not objectively there. There is no deception involved on the part of the set designer. He only wishes that the individual pieces be suggestive so that the rest of the audience's job of construction may be easier and more enjoyable.

Now, I know little of these matters, personally, as my profession is that of costumes. Little need be said of the costumes of the characters, except that the same principle established above is in effect. However, I am often besieged with requests about what to wear to the theater. This is a very difficult question to answer, for there are many answers depending on what effect one wishes to achieve. For example, some come to the theater simply to witness a good story. For these patrons, I suggest buying the cheapest seats in the gallery and wearing nothing more than what they might wear to their respective places of employment.

There is a sense in which every theater-goer wishes to be entertained, and certainly if the theater does not entertain, then the entire enterprise is a failure. However, there are those who come to the theater and know the story already. They do not come to hear a tale which they have never heard before, but perhaps wish to see how the company does the play--in other words to compare how the present players perform a piece that they saw performed by someone else. To these patrons, I suggest seats in the dress circle and that they wear dark conservative clothes that display their more sedate participation. Particularly striking on men is an oxford grey two button with contrasting vest.

Now there are those who may have seen the play (or read it) before and also take a particular interest in drama as a composite activity; that is, a group effort of set designers, director, actors, and costume makers. These patrons take particular delight in how different parts fit together to form a whole and are conscious of the many elements working within the structure of the story to produce a final product which depends upon a myriad of mediums for its desired effect. To these patrons I suggest seats in the Royal Circle or Rear Stalls. Ladies of this type might enjoy long evening dresses with a low neck and some jewelry. Men should wear black tie and tux.

Finally, for those who are so intrigued by the story, component parts, and interpretations of the various artists involved that they feel compelled to return to several performances in order to more fully understand by repetition the exact sense of each source of input as well as the varying nuances in tone and rhetoric, I must insist that they purchase front stalls or rear boxes while attiring themselves in full dress.

For the patrons of this drama, I have selected several suits of clothing which I have sewn from the finest cloth. Only the patron of the latter class will choose all of the items to wear, for they require additional time and expense. At the other end there will be those who wish only to read and enjoy the story wearing only what they ordinarily wear every day (I must confess that I often attend dramas in this fashion for relaxation). To these gentle people, I bid equally fond wishes. No group is better than the other. They merely wish to experience something slightly different. For the patrons in the groups between the extremes, I suggest that you dip into this display of clothing and pick what you like and leave the rest behind. One may purchase any variety of ticket for this drama, but should take pains that he or she dress appropriately. And now, before the curtain rises I shall bid you farewell until the beginning of the next play, where I shall have prepared some different attire for your pleasure. One mustn't dress in exactly the same manner throughout an entire dramatic season!

Here, for your considered judgment, are synthetic delights in both poetry and prose--both in fiction and non-fiction--whatever suits the fancy or stimulates the imagination.

Exhibits:

A double tale will I tell: at one time it grew to be one only from many, at another it divided again to be many from one. There is a double coming into being of mortal things and a double passing away. One is brought about and again destroyed, by the coming together of all things, the other grows up and is scattered as things are again divided. And these things never cease from continual shifting, at one time all coming together, through Love into one, at another each borne apart from others through Strife. (So, in so far as they have learnt to grow into one from many) and again, when the one is sundered and once more many, thus far they come into being and they have no lasting life; but in so far as they never cease from continual interchange of places, thus far are they ever Changeless in the cycle.

Empedocles, (DK 158) tr. G. S. Kirk and J.E. Raven.

Oh Shamash, why did you give this restless heart to Gilgamesh, my son; why did you give it? You have moved him and now he sets out on a long journey to the land of Humbaba, to travel an unknown road and fight a strange battle. Therefore from the day that he goes till the day he returns, until he reaches the cedar forest, until he kills Humbaba and destroys the evil thing which you, Shamash, abhor, do not forget him; but let the dawn, Aya, your dear bride, remind you always, and when day is done give him to the watchman of the night to keep him from harm.

The Epic of Gilgamesh, tr. N.K. Sandars

Orestes: On all who act above the law there shall be given justice: justice by killing. This in order that we might have fewer villains.

Sophocles, *Electra*, my tr.

The mortal who pleasantly continues to lead straight down the road unbroken by its troubles enjoys a most blessed life indeed.

Euripides, *Electra*, my tr.

For this reason also the question is asked whether happiness is to be acquired by learning or by habituation or some other sort of training or comes in virtue of some divine providence or again by chance. Now if there is any gift of the gods to men, it is reasonable that happiness should be god-given, and most sure god-given of all human things inasmuch as it is the best. But this question would perhaps be more appropriate to another inquiry; happiness seems, however, even if it is not god-sent, but comes as a result of virtue and some process of learning or training, to be among the most god-like things; for that which is the prize and end of virtue seems to be the best thing in the world and something god-like and blessed.

It will also on this view be very generally shared; for all who are not maimed as regards their potentiality for virtue may win it by a certain kind of study and care. But if it is better to be happy thus than by chance, it is reasonable that the facts should be so, since everything that depends on action of nature is by nature as good as it can be, and similarly everything that depends on art or any rational cause, and especially if it depends on the best of all causes. To entrust to chance what is greatest and most noble would be a very defective arrangement.

The answer to the question we are asking is plain also from the definition of happiness; for it has been said to be a virtuous activity of the soul of a certain kind . . . for we stated the end of political science to be the best end, and political science spends most of its pains on making the citizens to be of a certain character, viz., good and capable of noble acts.

> Aristotle, *Ethica Nicomachea*, 1099b 8-32, tr. W.D. Ross

"To everyone," said Zeus, "and let them all share in them; for cities would not arise if only a few shared in them as in other arts. And by my order he who cannot share in conscience and justice shall be killed as a plague on the state."

> Plato, *Protagoras* 322d 1-5, my tr.

I judge that knowledge can never be evil except if we change the word's meaning and confuse it (*scientia*) with experience (*experientia*). Experience is not always good, as when we experience punishment. Yet how can what is properly and correctly called knowledge be evil since it is acquired by reason and understanding?

> Augustine, *De arbitro libro*, my tr.

The word for 'law' (*lex*) comes from the verb *ligare* (to bind), because it obligates in regard to action. . . Laws that are humanly imposed can either be just or not. If they are just they bind our conscience. . . . If unjust they may be of two varieties: One is in opposition to human welfare. . . . The second way law may be unjust is when it countermands the divine good. Such laws may not be observed at all.

> Thomas Aquinas, *Summa Theologica* I-II, 90-96, my tr.

To this war of every man, against every man, this also is consequent; that nothing can be unjust. The notions of right and wrong, justice and injustice have there no place. Where there is no common power, there is no law: where no law, no injustice. . . . The RIGHT OF NATURE, which writers commonly call *ius naturale*, is the liberty each man hath to use his own power, as he will himself for the preservation of his own nature; that is to say, of his own life; and consequently of doing anything, which in his own judgment, and reason, he shall conceive to be the aptest means thereunto.

Thomas Hobbes, *Leviathan* from ch. 13 & 14.

Men living together according to reason, without a common superior on earth with authority to judge between them, is properly the state of nature. The state of nature has a law of nature to govern it.

John Locke, *The Second Treatise of Civil Government*, from ch. 2 & 3.

It has always been evident that all cases of justice are also cases of expediency: the difference is in the peculiar sentiment which attaches to the former, as contradistinguished from the latter. If this characteristic sentiment has been sufficiently accounted for; if there is no necessity to assume for it any peculiarity of origin; if it is simply the natural feeling of resentment, moralized by being made coextensive with the demands of social good; and if this feeling not only does but ought to exist in all classes of cases to which the idea of justice corresponds; that idea no longer presents itself as a stumbling block to the utilitarian ethics. Justice remains the appropriate name for certain social utilities which are vastly more important. . . .

John Stuart Mill, *Utilitarianism*, ch. 5.

My dearly beloved Brethren and Fellow Citizens: having travelled over a considerable portion of these United States, and having, in the course of my travels, taken the most accurate observations of things as they exist—the truth of my observations has warranted the full and unshaken conviction, that we, (coloured people of these United States), are the most degraded, wretched, and abject set of beings that ever lived since the world began; and I pray God that none like us ever may live again until time shall be no more.

> David Walker, "Preamble to the Coloured Citizens of the World." (Boston, MA, September 28, 1829)

Steal away, steal away, steal away to Jesus,

Steal away, steal away home,

I ain't got long to stay here.

> African American Spiritual.

Our duty therefore can be defined as that action which will cause more good to exist in the Universe than any possible alternative.

> G.E. Moore, *Principia Ethica*.

Aries

Calcination

Chapter 1

"A Short Description of Dorthay Beauchay"

DORTHAY BEAUCHAY WAS ALL ALONE when she packed the last of her cases that she was to take with her to Nice. The sun was slanting through the windows and filled her room with the quiet sadness of late afternoon's slow dissolution. She was taking only seven bags, even though she would be staying for six months or more, because most of her clothes were last season's style; it would be necessary to buy new ones in France if she wanted to venture from her house to anywhere on the Promenade des Anglais or the Quai Des États-Unis. However, this would be a quiet trip: just herself and the Mediterranean sun in the fresh Provence air. As she slid her stationery into the pocket of her petite valise, her thoughts drifted to her first visit to Nice when she had been "taken" by the elegant restaurants, night spots, and the Palais de la Méterranée. They had all rushed by her so quickly, carrying her along in the energetic wave of excitement that Nice offered at night.

Her brother, Samuel, had kept them going at a furious pace. For Nice gets into one's blood easily and quickly speeds the pulse so that one is running on a different tempo than that to which the body is accustomed. Consequently, that which was previously normal became slow and dull in comparison. Yes, Nice was infectious. Samuel had felt it too, though he wouldn't have admitted it. Of course, all the same, when the croupier spun the wheel of chance, even Samuel's heart outraced the flying metal ball.

This trip, however, would be different. It was ten years later, and what time hadn't deadened, familiarity *would*. It had been three months since he had left. He was a plain man with nothing to commend him except a swarthy complexion. It was surprising how she could have felt tenderness for him. A drummer by trade, he had traveled about living by his wit and charm, which, as she thought back on it, she now judged to be quite minimal. "If that's all he has to keep himself alive, I think he'll soon starve," she said aloud. She could imagine him traveling to the North, having no one succumb to his sales pitch, and then being left to the elements: no food, little warm clothing. . . *Ha!* she said to herself, *it would serve him right: He that liveth by the wit shall die by the wit"* (he'll probably lie *half-frozen in a cold Wisconsin winter, his blackness covered with white)*. Dorthay kept this image of his dying a while longer before hearing Billy Williams calling the workers from the fields. Theirs (her and her brother's) was a prosperous plantation (for she never referred to it as a farm, even though, strictly speaking, that's exactly what it was—or perhaps, more charitably, an estate). They didn't require many share-croppers, except on the soybean fields (because soybeans didn't bring in enough money to be worked by the hired hands). And though she had no personal memory of her father, Jacques Beauchay, or of Laura Vanderkamp Beauchay, her mother (who had lived on a real plantation complete with nearly three hundred slaves), she could imagine from stories her brother would relate to her or from stories that old Colonel Rutherford would spin about how it used to be in the grand old days when life was fair and pure among the fine families of Georgia.

Yes, those were wonderful years to think back upon; the grand balls where one's dance card would be filled until the wee hours of the morning with the names of handsome young gentlemen full of the finest graces and breeding. The memory of the gaiety and excitement of life as it must have been *before* always brought that sad longing for those carefree days of grace and splendor. Why had she been born too late for the life she longed to live? Why had she been born into an era in which those scores of eligible young gentlemen callers never came because they had been killed— massacred by those barbarous, savage northerners who had no respect for human life? It was like the fall of Rome to the savages from the North, who completely destroyed a high level of life that they could not possibly understand. These modern Goths razed an era into oblivion because they were totally unable to recognize beauty or culture when they saw it starkly revealed in a highly evolved civilization.

And yet, she was thirty-four years old and in all likelihood would never be married. Though, she reminded herself, there were exceptions to this general rule. Why, hadn't Cindy Lou Rutherford been over thirty when she married (though she had been engaged before the war)? Still, Dorthay had ceased waiting for her gentlemen callers, who she knew would never come. She sat alone, looking after her brother (because his fragile wife didn't have a grain of sense or will power, being confined to bed so often due to "sickness" as she liked to call it). Dorthay thought that it was a sign of decay when the best families, like the Beauchays, started taking in sickly women like her sister-in-law, who couldn't stay out of bed long enough to look after her own household. *If I weren't here,* she thought, *this whole place would run down in a year's time.* No, she reminded herself, she must strive to return in six months.

After she snapped her case shut, Dorthay sat on the edge of the bed and looked about the room. Her bags were ready for the trip. Things would become quiet again in Nice. She would leave tomorrow on the train for the coast. Dorthay quickly looked about the room and decided to take a walk before supper.

On the floor and next to her bed was a soiled, white blouse that she'd forgotten to put away.

Chapter 2

"An Incident between Samuel Beauchay and Jefferson"

SAMUEL BEAUCHAY, slapping a newspaper against his left hand, felt quite alone as he paced his study. "It's incredible," he muttered to himself. "How can cotton prices get any lower? I'm going to have to replant with soybeans or something, because I'm not about to give in to those damn Yankee industrialists who think they can just subject the agricultural production of the South to anything they please. Well they can't! And I'd rather lose money on another crop than give those northern bastards my cotton for nothing!" With that he threw the rolled newspaper against the door. This brought an immediate sound of approaching steps and a knock, "Is everything all right, Mr. Beauchay?"

"Yes, Jefferson, yes--I mean no, god dammit!"

The door opened and a tall, strong black man dressed in casual farm clothes entered and walked over to Mr. Beauchay. "Now calm yourself, Mr. Beauchay, what's the matter?"

As he talked, Jefferson John Brown took Mr. Beauchay's arm and led him over to a chair and sat him down. His voice was calm and deliberate.

"Sit down and tell me about it."

"It's those northern industrialists, they want to push down the price of cotton again. It's all in the paper," Mr. Beauchay looked around to try and spot the messenger of the unfortunate tidings, but it was nowhere in sight. "Now where did I put that blasted thing?" yelled Beauchay, again in a flurry.

"I have it," said Jefferson in his soothing voice that had an infinite patience in its resonance. "I picked it up when I came in." He handed the paper to Mr. Beauchay who tore at the pages, trying to find the financial section on commodities.

"There it is, Jefferson, have a look for yourself."

Jefferson sat down and began to study the paper as if he were a business associate of Mr. Beauchay instead of his ranking employee--though this description was not quite correct either. Jefferson had grown up with Samuel Beauchay (in fact, they had been born only a fortnight apart and were much closer than one usually imagines in a relationship between a white land owner and his black employee).

When Jefferson was fourteen, his father died and as Jefferson didn't get on well with Marcel Beauchay, Samuel Beauchay's uncle, who was running things at the time, Jefferson decided to make an unannounced departure for the North. (I use the term 'unannounced' because even though the Civil War technically was over, Marcel Beauchay ran his farm like a pre-War plantation, and it was still not permissible for anyone to leave, unless they were given permission--which was not likely to be given unless one was a thief.)

So Jefferson ran away to Boston because he had heard that it was a city without prejudice. Jefferson wanted an education but soon found that he was not going to get it in Boston. Indeed, it was hard for him even to get a job in order to eat and to have lodging. No one would hire him for more than a couple weeks at a time, and that was only to do a job for which they would just as soon have hired animals from the stable if the animals had had the required dexterity to handle the task.

But finally, after two years of scrimping and saving (which was not easy when one did not have steady work yet had steady expenses like room, board, and clothing), Jefferson had enough money to stake himself in New York, which, he reasoned because of its size, would not have time to discriminate against him. His ride let him off and he took a ferry to Manhattan and walked about, looking for places which might need someone. One store caught his eye because of its tidy appearance. Like several other windows in the neighborhood, there was a sign posted: MEN WANTED: NO IRISH NEED APPLY. Instead of discouraging him, such signs gave Jefferson some hope. At least in New York, Jefferson thought, people are open about their feelings. I can deal with that. It is when they hide behind masks as they had in Boston that really bothered Jefferson. In Boston, people had kept Jefferson waiting until someone could see him. He would wait for hours before he realized that no one would see him. He was not officially turned down for a job because he was black, but he would have preferred that to wasting a morning or afternoon due to benign neglect.

But perhaps, Jefferson reasoned, things would be different in New York. After all New York hadn't started the Underground Railroad and hadn't been the seat of the abolitionist movement as Boston had been; New York didn't have anything to prove. It could be openly bigoted without having to conform to the mask of phony Christian Brotherhood. So it was that when Jefferson saw this store, he decided to give it a try. He didn't bother to check to see what kind of establishment he was entering. He knew that he couldn't be choosey. After all, a job was a job. Inside he found a dimly lit dusty room with a counter and a small man behind it who absently turned around to face Jefferson when the little bell on the door signaled someone's presence.

"The sign says you needs men."

The man behind the counter looked up at Jefferson's six-foot-one-inch frame and his large muscular shoulders, immediately cleaned his wire rimmed spectacles, and looked again.

"The sign says no Irish needs apply, but as you can see, I ain't Irish."

A high squeaking laugh bubbled out of the little man as he cleaned his glasses yet another time. "No, I can see that." His voice broke out in more laughter. "That's certainly evident; you're not *Irish*. The goons who made me put up that sign can't complain on that count." Then the little man began wiping his hands on the black-stained, full length apron he was wearing. "Give me a hand with this box; I've been trying to lift it all morning, and I'd almost given up hope. I was just about to unload it and put the papers into two boxes when you came in." Jefferson was somewhat surprised by this comment. What he wanted to know was whether he had a job or not. He didn't want to lift heavy boxes, especially if there would be no money for his effort. On the other hand, if he refused, then he knew that he didn't have a job. He lifted the box. "Where does you want it?" asked Jefferson, straining slightly even though the box didn't seem all that heavy. He had certainly lifted much heavier ones earlier in his life with less effort than he was expending at the present moment.

"Over there, in the wagon and then take it around to this address." The little man scribbled something down on a scrap of paper and handed it to Jefferson.

Again Jefferson was surprised. *This must mean that I have the job, but why didn't he say that? This little fellow with the semi-bald head and the squeaky voice is a queer one, but shouldn't I ask him whether I have the job?* This seemed like an important question to ask before one went lugging around a cart of papers. What if this is just an errand for me to run; kind of a little favor for the tiny man: a good turn. Spit on good turns. I need a job, not thanks for running errands. This isn't the South. A black man can ask a white man exactly what terms he has to offer. Then he can accept or reject them as he sees fit. Jefferson repeated this to himself three times. Each succeeding time with slightly less conviction. There weren't too many jobs around and I've only got ten cents. Even if this is just an errand, he'll probably give me some money for it anyway. Sometimes you have to take a chance. He also repeated this for emphasis. But even this phrase had lost almost all of its meaning for him over the past eight months. Jefferson stuffed the paper in his pocket and started out of the door with the cart. When he was half-way out he heard, "Your pay is ten dollars a week and I'll pay you half of your first week's wages tomorrow." When Jefferson heard that he started off at a trot. As he moved, the wagon bounced along the uneven street owing to his spritely pace. Then he suddenly realized that he had no idea where anything in New York was located.

Chapter 3

"Further Incidents Concerning Jefferson and a Certain Errand"

JEFFERSON RETRIEVED THE ADDRESS from his pocket and tried to make it out. The writing was only semi-legible, but it looked as if it was "Number 4, 42nd St." He looked up and saw a sign. He found that he was at Madison Square, but that didn't help him with his address. He wandered aimlessly in the general direction that he remembered the little man had been waving when he had sent Jefferson on his way, but more and more Jefferson was becoming convinced that this course was not the most likely to succeed. The little bald man would expect him back soon and all he would be able to say was that he didn't know New York. But that wouldn't be the thing to say, because then the man would fire him. Nobody wants a delivery man who doesn't even know the city where he is supposed to be making his deliveries! He must come up with another response that didn't imply either that he was unfamiliar with the city or that he had gotten lost. But if he hadn't gotten lost the only excuse Jefferson would have is that he stopped along the way and had a drink or stopped for a rest. Either of these alternatives made him undesirable as a lazy bum or a drunkard. No, he decided, the only way to extricate himself from this situation was to make good on his assigned task and deliver the papers on time-- or better yet, faster than the little bald man had expected. But how fast did he expect Jefferson to deliver the papers?

In the midst of all these questions, Jefferson thought it prudent to stop a man who looked as if he knew what he was about and ask him where Number 4, 42nd Street was.

"Excuse me--" started Jefferson.

"Yes, what is it?" snapped the man impatiently as he stopped immediately and scowled at Jefferson.

"I looking for Number 4, 42nd Street," Jefferson began rather slowly in his normal calm manner of speaking (which he never hurried even when he was excited or upset).

"Don't know it," the man said tersely and resumed his previous brisk pace as if he had never stopped.

Jefferson crumpled up the paper in his hand and held it tightly as he watched the man strut away. Then he jammed the wad into his shirt pocket and picked up the bars of the wagon and began pulling again.

He asked three other people where Number 4, 42nd Street was located and each in his own way went by without stopping to tell Jefferson where it was. One didn't even pause, but simply turned his head away from Jefferson and walked on.

This was somewhat discouraging to Jefferson. After all, if he was to keep his job, he would have to find the proper address. And the only way he was going to find it was if someone gave him directions. Things were looking dim when Jefferson saw a policeman who was walking down the sidewalk, whistling and knocking the lamp posts with his Billy Club. Now certainly a policeman would tell me where to go, thought Jefferson. He won't ignore me like the rest. So Jefferson put down his cart and walked over to the policeman.

"Excuse me, sir," started Jefferson, adding the 'sir' to get on the policeman's good graces. "I've gots ta find Number 4, 42nd Street."

"Well, you're walking in the wrong direction there, boy," the policeman started. He was friendly enough for a policeman, but something about him made Jefferson feel uneasy. "You have to go back to that last block there and turn right and walk for about a mile and you'll be there."

"Thank ya," said Jefferson, starting to turn back to his cart when the policeman said again, "Have you got that straight? Turn right and then follow the street straight on."

"Yes, I gots it," replied Jefferson, who suddenly heard a ripping sound as he spun around and saw three lads about fourteen years old ripping the papers in Jefferson's cart. Instantly Jefferson dashed to the cart and grabbed one of the boys who had taken several of the handbills.

"Give me them," yelled Jefferson as he wrestled the boy to the ground.

"Get away from me, nigger," snarled the boy.

Jefferson got him to the ground and began to squeeze the boy's wrist to get the papers out of his hand when over he rolled--

--*jarring disorientation in a pulsing pain that kept time with the flow of blood through the bulging arteries at the base of his head-- waves of dizziness--pounding--pulsing, a dreaminess, and the feeling that he had to wake up.* For a moment everything seemed as if it were in slow motion. Colors changed as nature followed the waves of dizzy pain. Then his eyes fixed on the policeman standing over him with his club in hand.

"What happened?" Jefferson tried to say, but nothing came out except a gasp of air.

"You watch yourself there, boy, you shouldn't go attacking white folk; that's against the law."

"Well, isn't it 'gainst da law ta steal and ta destroy someone's possessions?"

The policeman either didn't hear or ignored Jefferson; he turned and walked away without answering. Then the defender of rights, New York's finest, pivoted and delivered an admonition, "I'd better not hear about you causing any more trouble, coon, or it will be hard on you, understand?"

Jefferson sat up and brushed off his clothes. The pain was still great. He felt the side of his face and found the lump above his temple. There was only a small cut which would heal by the time he arrived at his destination, Number 4, 42nd Street.

Lifting his load, which was now feeling quite heavy, he made his way to the road that the policeman had directed him towards. The street was foul-smelling and full of mud. *I don't want to walk in that*, he decided at once. He tried walking around the block, but found another street that was just as muddy, so again, he decided to go around the block.

Soon Jefferson was thoroughly lost and decided to stop and sit down. His stomach hurt some because he hadn't eaten in over a day, but most of all, he felt weak. The cut on his face was no longer bleeding, but the surrounding area was still tender. He cleaned off the excess dry blood with his shirt tail, being careful not to re-open the cut. Though the cart hadn't lost much of its cargo, Jefferson had been shaken by the incident, feeling somehow that he had failed his employer.

Down the street, Jefferson saw another black man who was walking along the wooden sidewalk in a costume that resembled a painted Indian. He was stopping men and asking them if they wanted their boots cleaned. One man, after his boots were finished, started to walk away without paying. The boot cleaner went after him, importuning him for the fee that the man owed. The man probably would not have paid any attention to the boot cleaner except that there were lots of people around to censure his action and possibly act in the boot cleaner's behalf. So the "philanthropist" sneered and grudgingly got out five pennies and tossed them onto the sidewalk so that two of them fell between the boards.

Jefferson decided to get up and walk a bit further. He turned right and was on a large street paved with stones and full of people. He saw a surrey that took his fancy, being deep red with silver trim. It was drawn by two smooth, black horses whose coats gleamed and muscles rippled with contained strength.

It was getting late. Jefferson needed directions. But if he had been snubbed in the back alleys of the city, he could certainly not expect better treatment on this elegant boulevard. He put down his load and turned toward the nearest shop. It was number 4. The coincidence was unsettling. Then he saw a street post. He was on 42nd Street.

Chapter 4

"An Account of the Education of Jefferson"

WHEN JEFFERSON RETURNED to the printer's shop the little man looked up and greeted him, "Back so soon?"

Jefferson didn't know how to take this remark so he remained silent.

"You don't know the city, do you?" asked the little man again. Jefferson reluctantly shook his head. "Well, you've done very well. I was testing to see how quick you were. I need someone with a little moxy who can figure out some of the problems that occur here regularly every day. Yes, we have one crisis a day--at least!"

Jefferson sat down and watched the little man move about.

"Are you hungry?"

"Not really," replied Jefferson.

"Well, if you're a stranger and you've been looking for a job, then you must be a little hungry. Here, I saved a piece of bread and a hunk of cheese for you."

Jefferson looked at him. The little man held out the food. "Go ahead, take it. I don't want it and if I leave it around here the rats will get it, or worse yet one of the precinct lieutenants will."

"Precinct lieutenants?" Jefferson repeated, taking the food.

'Yes, the thugs who made me put a restrictive policy on my hiring—you read it: No Irish. . . . Well, that's their doing. They like to keep neighborhoods of Irish, Poles, Jews—you name it--together. They don't like things mixed. That way the precinct lieutenants can register them to vote in blocks which are isolated and thus control their employment. Come Election Day they can demand their votes and collect a 'voluntary' election contribution. That's how they make their living. They squeeze out their share from kick-backs, bribes and voluntary election contributions. I used to run a paper before they shut me down."

"Shuts ya down?"

"Yes," he started, beginning to chuckle again, "sounds kind of funny, eh? I mean this being America, the land of the free and all that. But you see, I've been against them from the start, and I'd get tips from other people who also hated them and their brand of corruption. Well, we weren't much, but I guess they thought we were dangerous enough that they needed to break in here one night and smash my press. They almost murdered one of my two workers."

Jefferson finished the cheese and bread and sat back to listen.

"Here, have some beer; I have a little left in the pail. That is, if you don't mind doing without a glass."

Jefferson took the pail and finished the beer.

"So naturally," the little man continued, "both fellows quit. I don't blame them. I'd probably have done the same myself. But that left me in a bad position. I couldn't run the paper all by myself. I'm not strong enough to do all the work involved in printing and distributing. And I couldn't withstand a beating like they gave my last worker." The little man scratched his sideburn a moment. "I just thought I'd tell you a few things about the place, so that you'd know just what sort of operation I'm running here."

Jefferson felt a little uneasy. This man had certainly been kind to him in offering him a job and some food, but was it worth risking his neck for a few dollars? Indeed not, he thought. "The situation you've walked into. It's not too inviting. But you see, when I saw you walk in here (a man twice my size), well, I sort of started dreaming again. You know, I was dreaming about when I used to run the paper."

The man had certainly been generous, etc., but that didn't obligate Jefferson to die for him. Perhaps it would be best to get out while he could. Jefferson started to rise.

"Oh no, you mustn't think I'm really going to start the paper again. Oh no, it was just a passing fantasy of mine, a fleeting thought you might say." He started to laugh and then began pacing in front of Jefferson so that Jefferson couldn't get up. "No, I'm content in printing hand bills and posters for various companies.

Yes, that's quite sufficient for me. I have no ambitions beyond being a simple printer. I just want to do a modest trade."

The little man rubbed his hands together and returned behind the half-counter that served to separate the printing apparatus from the small reception area. "You need a place to stay?"

Jefferson was surprised by this. He didn't know quite what to say. The little fellow was talking like someone possessed about starting a newspaper again, and then he proclaims that he is happy. Jefferson didn't know whether he liked this very much. But what was he to do? It's getting late and a nice bed would certainly be welcome. He could stay for the night and then leave in the morning if this guy continues in his eccentricity. "Well, for t'night I gots no room or nothin'."

"Fine, splendid! You must come and stay with me. I'll put you up until you decide you want to leave."

This sounded fine. Jefferson extended his hand to the already outstretched hand of the little man.

"By the way," the little fellow started, "my name is Peabody and you're the first Negro I've ever personally known."

Chapter 5

"Introducing the Cats of Peabody and the Roles they
Play"

JEFFERSON FOUND MR. PEABODY to be an even stranger
man than he had first envisioned. For one thing, Mr. Peabody had
four cats who slept in his bed with him and were named Matthew,
Mark, Luke, and John. None of the cats would let Jefferson get close
to them, but Mr. Peabody said that was because they didn't take to
strangers and had to get to know a person before they would let
anyone pet them.

Also, Mr. Peabody would read from the Bible after every
evening meal to the cats who all gathered about and sat quietly
around his feet while he read.

"These cats may look harmless, but believe me, they're not,"
said Mr. Peabody one evening. "They're from Egypt and are vicious.
If someone would break into this place, one of my darlings would
maul him. I mention this from an actual experience garnered from
when I ran the paper. A goon broke in here and Luke took one of his
eyes out." Peabody half-smiled and stroked Luke. Luke then walked
over to Jefferson and allowed him to pet her. "They protect me and I
love them."

"Why did ya names them fo men when they is women?"
"Because the Gospel writers were men and the only safeguards I've
got are the Bible and these cats; it seemed appropriate to combine
them somehow." As Peabody spoke, Luke returned and hopped onto
her master's lap and lay down.

Another strange habit Mr. Peabody had which Jefferson puzzled over was the securing of every door at night with two large bolts as well as similarly securing his barred windows. Jefferson had never seen so much fear over being attacked (and Jefferson's experience included living in the Deep South and witnessing the activities of the Ku Klux Klan). He could not make up his mind whether all this was really necessary or whether Mr. Peabody was just over protective and easily frightened.

***

The one day he had agreed to stay led to a week, and Jefferson had no desire to leave. But he was getting a little curious about a place to go to school, so he decided to ask Peabody about it.

"Oh, very good," Peabody started, somewhat surprised by Jefferson's request. "Does that mean you want to leave?" he said in an altogether tone that Jefferson had never heard him use.

"No, really I sorts of likes it here, but I wants to educate myself, too."

"Well, you know it's difficult to give you a good answer until I know how much schooling you have had?"

Jefferson was silent.

"Have you ever been to school? I mean, you can read. Where did you learn that?"

"I knows a few of my letters from a woman where I was brung up."

"I see. Well, it's necessary to have a firm grasp of English grammar and vocabulary before you can properly start school. I'll tell you what," started Peabody, scratching his sideburn, "I think I can get you an English grammar book to study and if you like, I will help you some. You know, to be in the printing business you have to have impeccable English."

Jefferson looked up at Peabody with a partial smirk and raised eyebrows. He had wanted to go to a school--a regular school and sit at a desk. But this man was trying to deny him this opportunity by telling him that he had to become proficient at reading, writing, and speaking. But what was the use of that? He could speak and people understood well enough what he was saying. Why was it necessary to learn it over again (even if it was the "correct" way)? Would anyone understand him better when he asked what time it was or where the railroad station was located? It defied him to see the direct advantages in undertaking such a difficult and possibly circumventing endeavor in order simply to satisfy the feeble whims of one broken-down, bald, old printer with dreams of saving New York City.

"You don't look too enthusiastic about it. Well, I don't blame you. English isn't one of the most glamorous of academic disciplines. It seems very stuffy to you, I suppose. Well, give it a week. If you don't like it or should I more properly say, if you don't see the purpose in it, then I will return the grammar book and you can try another alternative. Just a week's trial; is it worth a try?"

Again Jefferson was faced with a "give it a chance" line from the old printer. This made him skeptical, but on the other hand there was the possibility that Peabody could be partially correct. Jefferson folded his hands and bit his lower lip.

Chapter 6

"All About the Matriculation of Jefferson"

ON THE FIFTH NIGHT OF HIS TRIAL WEEK, Jefferson was busily locating all of the nouns and the verbs in a particular paragraph when he put down his pen and sighed, "This don't make no sense. It's nonsense."

"What, the lesson? Or can't you make any sense of the difference between a noun and a verb?" replied Peabody.

"Why I 'possed ta do this?"

"Well, for one thing, so that you can be understood."

"But folk understands whats I says."

"You have a most peculiar form of speech, Jefferson," Peabody began. He gave no thought about how his pupil might take this bit of criticism he was administering, but it was a necessary dose, so he continued. "For example, say you were in the newspaper business and you set a story in your present speech patterns. Then when the paper was printed and ready to be distributed, it would only be intelligible to those people who knew your unique expression. And suppose further that one of the papers was lost and found again in one hundred years when your particular style of jargon has completely gone out of common usage. Then no one could understand what the deuce you were trying to communicate."

Jefferson listened attentively, but didn't seem very convinced by these arguments. Why was it necessary to communicate with people one hundred years from now? And besides, what was all this talk about newspapers? They didn't have a newspaper going and, considering the risks involved, Jefferson doubted that he ever wanted to be part of such a dangerous profession. This noun and verb garbage might be necessary for newspaper men (this was a speculation he didn't care to indulge himself in, as it was nihil ad rem), but what was important was how he, Jefferson John Brown, was going to acquire the learning that schools imparted upon people to enable them to be elegant dressers with fine things and red & silver surreys.

"And what's most important," Peabody continued, "is that we think in words and if you don't understand how words are supposed to go together in orderly patterns, then you will never be able to fully experience some of the most complex and interesting ideas that men of genius have authored. So much of the history of ideas will be closed to you if you stop now. Without an understanding of grammar, you can't understand the noblest thoughts of Mankind."

Here Peabody paused for a moment and got up from his chair and walked over to John, who was sleeping on top of the fireplace. He picked her up in his arms and stroked her fur as he walked slowly back towards Jefferson.

"And that, my dear friend, is what education is all about: understanding ideas."

What was this about understanding ideas? All the rich whites in the South would go to school and come back as "gentlemen." There was nothing about *understanding* ideas. What sort of wild notion was he being asked to accept? This man, who talked to his cats and bolted the doors at night and who hummed music and waved his hand in front of him--in short, who was a little on the peculiar side, was asking Jefferson to accept a bill of goods that seemed to be not exactly what he wanted. Education meant being respected as a gentleman. It meant having fine things like surreys and expensive clothes. All one had to do was look the part. Those who were well-to-do had an education. Therefore, it must be that which was the key to the kind of life that Jefferson dreamed of. What, after all, were ideas but formless pictures that were in his head? They didn't get him any closer to having the kinds of things that educated white men in Georgia had.

"All a teacher can do, Jefferson, is to help a pupil understand an idea as accurately as possible. And accuracy is important." Peabody stopped. He saw that he wasn't getting through to his charge, so he decided to switch approaches. He put down the cat and stood beside Jefferson.

"For instance, you are pretty quick, aren't you?"

What does he mean? thought Jefferson. *What's he talking about now? My mind's beginning to get jumbled. I wish he'd stop for a while and let me sort things out.*

"Well, I bet I can beat you."

Jefferson tilted his head and smiled. How could Peabody beat me in any race? I could defeat him running backwards.

"Ready to take me on?--good. Now the race is to see who can get the correct answer first. I'll write in one column on the slate the number of times I go to the storeroom to bring out bundles of paper and in the other column how many bundles I have in each load. The problem is to figure out how many bundles end up on the table. For example, if I go into the storeroom once and bring out two bundles, then there would be a total of two bundles on the table."

This would be easy, Jefferson thought. He did the first two problems rapidly, but then Peabody started using higher numbers and Jefferson had to count on his fingers and Peabody easily out-dueled him. There must have been some catch or trick to it because Peabody had been beaten on the first two exercises; it didn't make sense that when the problems became harder that he would become faster.

"What's da trick?" asked Jefferson intently.

"Ah, so you want to know my secret, eh? You're right; there is a secret. And I'll tell you about it. It's called multiplication."

Jefferson grinned. *Multiplication,* he said to himself. What power he could have if he could *figure* as quickly as Peabody. The thought excited him. "How long does it takes ta learn?"

"Not too long," said Peabody. "You see, there are different levels. What I showed you was merely one of the lowest levels. At higher stages there is almost no limit to the things that you can do."

This thought overwhelmed Jefferson: there were higher levels at which he could do almost *anything.* How fantastic it would be to own these skills and be able to discharge them at will. How glorious it would be to learn the incantations that brought the marvelous multiplication under his power.

"There's one other thing that's important," said Peabody.

"What's that?"

"Often times the directions will be very specific. It will be necessary to continue with your grammar as well."

Jefferson's mouth dropped slightly. He was stunned. What had these numbers to do with those tedious nouns and verbs? The two seemed as separate as day and night.

"You see, it's all interrelated. Once you start in learning, you have to take it all."

Their eyes met for a long interval. There were no knit brows or smirks. Jefferson shrugged his shoulders as Mark jumped into his lap.

Chapter 7

"On Jefferson's Leaving to College and the Surrounding Events"

JEFFERSON PROVED TO BE a fast learner, for after only fifteen months, he had finished the grammar book and was reading novels by Dickens, Austen, and Fielding. He was fascinated at how these various writers would tell a story. The events in the plot (though fictional) often times seemed more real than events in his own life. He had learned how to multiply, divide, and studied some elementary algebra. All this he learned without going to school. He taught himself through the books supplied by Peabody.

Even work was more pleasant because he thought continually about problems and questions which had been stimulated by his reading. These questions would have a great effect on Jefferson. He would become very disturbed by some problem in mathematics or by an ethical problem posed in a textbook on political science. Jefferson was serious about his education.

Life was going along pleasantly until one day Peabody announced, "I've gotten you a place in a school."

Jefferson was stunned. He had discarded the idea of going to school long ago because he had accepted that school was merely a place that helped people learn ideas. And after all, why did he need to go to some special place to do that when he was progressing so well at home? But still, a deep inner spark suddenly kindled when Peabody mentioned *school*. It was as if Jefferson was still charmed somehow at the thought (though he had told himself intellectually that he did not need to go to school). This amused Jefferson. For

Jefferson agreed with Peabody that Man is an animal which may be controlled by his reason. Jefferson fancied himself to be such a man, and yet behind his logic and disciplined exterior he felt a leap of excitement over the prospect of his going to school. This disparity between theory and practice captivated Jefferson (even as it confused him).

"I won't go," said Jefferson.

"Of course you will go. You've always wanted the opportunity. Now don't be foolish. I've already made the arrangements. You're to travel to Ithaca in two weeks and start classes in three."

The journey was an exciting one for Jefferson. He ran over all the events. "You'll have to stay for nine months, after which you'll get a summer holiday. During the nine months you will have several other holidays as well so you shan't be over worked."

He had to leave. Why was Peabody doing this? The only man who had ever shown him any degree of true kindness and friendship was sending him away. Jefferson had never really considered how attached he had become to old Peabody.

"I think you have a lot of potential, Jefferson. You are very bright and I want you to develop that power, that gift. Remember the story of the man with the talents." Peabody was always backing up his statements with stories from the Bible. Jefferson could picture them all sitting around the table (Jefferson and the cats) listening to Peabody's high, strident voice read another story. The cats who were friendly to Jefferson, Luke and Mark, would sometimes lie against his leg while Peabody read. It was always a contented time, a moment when they were all together in peaceful concentration on a single end: the point of the story.

"Your tuition is all taken care of, but I'm afraid you'll have to work for your room and board. I've not a lot of money you know . . . I did the best I could."

The day of departure soon arrived, and Jefferson's things were packed.

"Are you sure that you don't want to come down to the station?" asked Jefferson.

"No, I'm not very good at those sorts of things," Peabody said softly.

Then Peabody handed Jefferson a book, *My Bondage and My Freedom,* by Fredrick Douglas. Opening the front cover once he was underway, Jefferson read the inscription:

To start you along--Peabody.

***

The journey was an exciting one for Jefferson. In his mind he ran over all the events of his life and felt very lucky. He remembered vividly the cruelty of Marcel Beauchay. This led to his exodus and his dream of a new life. Now his dream seemed on the verge of becoming true. He wanted so much to make a good accounting of himself, both for his own pride and because of Peabody. Then a terrible thought hit him. What if Peabody died while he was at school? Peabody was not strong nor was he young and it was conceivable that he could die at any moment. How Jefferson would hate himself if he couldn't help Peabody. The parting words of Peabody replayed themselves in his mind. "I hope you'll write a letter occasionally and feel free to use this place during vacations and holidays if you want."

Peabody's manner had been easy, yet had that *easiness* been put on for his Jefferson's benefit? In parting, the two men had stood locked together, arms outstretched, grasping each other's shoulders and staring intently. They were statues as Matthew slowly rubbed herself against Jefferson's leg.

Chapter 8

"About the Events Prompting Jefferson to Return"

AFTER FOUR YEARS AT COLLEGE, Jefferson began to view reality in a way he never had before. He had majored in philosophy. Now life seemed to be composed of certain large ethical decisions which Man had to answer in order to form a society. He read with much interest the writings of Kant, Frederick Douglas, and John Stuart Mill on ethics. In contrast to much of Mill's work, Jefferson believed in the inviolability of certain human rights. Rights weren't predicated on promoting happiness, but were right in themselves. Thomas Aquinas took this position. This view assured that no man would be treated as a means only as Kant argued. This was how animals were treated and this was the way that blacks throughout the country were being treated. Jefferson agreed with Fredrick Douglas' assessment that there was equally bad racial bigotry in the North as there was in the South. The main difference was that in the South they were more openly demonstrative of their feelings.

Jefferson made up his mind that he was going to go to Baltimore and try to organize former slaves and the children of former slaves so that they could fight for their rights. He chose Baltimore because it was half-way between the South and the North and because it was so close to the nation's capital.

At school he had been the only black in an all-white population of 800. This was confusing both in the way he was treated and in the way it made him feel. Because he was conspicuous, he felt as he imagined a cripple or someone else who was different might feel: *always on display*. He could never really relax because people were always watching him, judging him, waiting for him to make a mistake so that they could throw him out. It might have been his imagination, but he felt that he was expected to do more than anyone else and do it better. For an 'A' he had to perform at a higher level than the other students. It was as if he was always being required to prove himself again and again. But he did it. And he would be graduating ninth in a class of forty.

At times he was caught between desires of trying to be just like his fellows and playing down the difference in color, and urges of flaunting his being *different*. At these times he felt like saying, "Accept me for what I am, because I am not going to be nor am I going to pretend to be white."

It was a difficult task to reconcile these opposing feelings, but in the end Jefferson decided to devote himself to Negro political rights.

Then, three days before Commencement, he received a telegram from New York City:

THE POLITICAL GOONS ARE ON THE RAMPAGE--AM STARTING THE PAPER AGAIN.
--PEABODY.

This news troubled Jefferson. He had passed all his classes. His degree was secure, but then there was the Commencement ceremony. Jefferson had fancied walking across the temporary wooden stage: the first black to graduate from the college. But he also knew that this telegram meant trouble for old Peabody. He wanted to go and help him despite his plans about Baltimore. After all, he said to himself, "What I want to do is to help people and what better way can there be for me to help than by repaying the man who's been almost a father to me?" Jefferson walked to the telegraph office to send his reply.

Chapter 9

"A Crusading Partnership is Formed"

"IT'S REALLY BEYOND BELIEF," began Peabody. "They had a judge who couldn't be bought and he convicted three councilmen for bribery and conspiracy. One week later the decision was reversed by a higher court. Then Judge Mallory wrote the United States Attorney General and made an appeal to the newspapers for someone to print his letter so that everyone could read it. I thought that printing Mallory's letter made good sense because not only would it allow the public to be informed about the details of the case, it would also offer protection for the judge. Because after it was publicized that he was appealing to the Attorney General against City Hall, then the goons wouldn't dare touch him. Well, naturally the big papers wouldn't touch it. They know where their bread is buttered. And so finally I went to see Mallory and offered to print it." Peabody had been pacing about in the print room. Jefferson was sitting in a hard back wooden chair with his legs crossed. The cats were protecting the corners of the room. "Well, Mallory sent down some court clerks to help me and we ran off ten thousand copies and had started distributing them when a gang of thugs stopped us after we'd gotten rid of a few hundred. They confiscated the rest. Luckily I had planned for such an event and had left stacks of fifty circulars near every small store on the east side early that morning. But God only knows how many have gotten out. Well, apparently the hatchet men have been threatening the judge, so he is hiding right now and we've got to carry the case to the people. Are you with us?"

"Let's get the machines moving," said Jefferson.

After two weeks of going out every day and trying to distribute as much material as they could in their campaign to rally public opinion against City Hall, Jefferson and Peabody were honored with a nocturnal visit in which the printing press was damaged, windows were broken, and the front door was smashed.

The next morning, Peabody looked at the shambles with a strange look of satisfaction. "We are getting to them," he said, clearing his glasses.

"It looks to me as if they're getting to us," Jefferson replied.

"They're afraid of what we're doing. We must be reaching somebody." Peabody walked through the rubble towards the press, rubbing his hands together. "Let's try and fix the press this morning and then I'll go visit the judge and tell him the news."

It took them two and one half full days to fix the press and get a new door, which they reinforced. They also began a project to double bar the windows. The materials were largely donated anonymously by friends and sympathizers.

About a week later when Jefferson was nearly done with the last stages of minor repair, Peabody came busting into the office. "Quick, set up the Press for a big story. The Attorney General has personally vowed to talk with Judge Mallory about the case and it will be reviewed."

"We did it!" yelled Jefferson in delight.

"Yes, it certainly looks good," replied Peabody, "but this only means we have to double our efforts at publicity so that this issue doesn't die in some corrupt commission somewhere."

They printed an extra-large edition and when Jefferson went to get their newsboys none were to be found. He went back and told Peabody.

"Yes, their mothers are probably frightened for them. We're a marked paper, Jefferson. We've only got days, probably."

"Nonsense," said Jefferson, trying to cheer up his friend, "we've *almost* won. The Attorney General is going to look into the case, and you *can't* bribe an Attorney General."

But Peabody didn't reply. He only sat rubbing his hands and mumbling quietly to himself.

Chapter 10

"Incidents which Prompted a Disturbance"

THREE DAYS LATER, Jefferson slept late and woke up to find Peabody gone. I'll bet he's already setting the afternoon edition, thought Jefferson. So without eating breakfast, Jefferson went down to the shop and to his surprise found that no one was there. There was, however, a note.

> *All is Lost. Got to confirm. Be back soon.*
> *Peabody*

All is lost? How could that be? Why, they had just won. It was already in writing how the Attorney General was going to review the case. Had he backed down on his promise? *Everything seemed so confusing. It was so different from how he'd imagined ethical systems ought to operate. In every ethical system, one imagines that the agents are rational. But how can these systems be correct when all around he was witnessing the exact opposite: irrational people acting randomly as they chose in a short-sighted manner. But as Plato pointed out, it is not ultimately in their self-interest to act immorally.* The disparity between theory and practice bothered Jefferson so much that he went to the presses and started setting the type for the next edition. These advertisements were becoming fewer and fewer each week. This was evidence of the pressure from the political bosses.

Then the door swung open and in staggered a tired Peabody.

"What's the matter?" started Jefferson. "You look terrible. You need some sleep. When did you last eat?"

"It's lost. It's lost," said Peabody hoarsely as he slumped into a chair. His glasses and face were dusty and his eyes bloodshot. He looked as if he'd been going all night.

"What's lost? What are you talking about?" demanded Jefferson.

"All our efforts finished: everything."

"Come out with it, man, what's happened?"

Peabody took off his hat and tossed it on the floor and said without looking up, "They've found him. Judge Mallory's been murdered. His body was recovered this morning in the East River."

Jefferson was stunned. How could they do this? How could they boldly murder a man who had previously made clear who his antagonists might be? The judge was famous. Didn't they know that this would start an investigation?

"We've got to do something," said Jefferson at once.

"But they've won. There won't be any inquiry now," said Peabody. "If they're bold enough to kill a federal judge, do you think they'd so much as blink twice about eliminating some two-bit paper that is working against them?"

"Well they haven't shut us down yet," said Jefferson.

"They haven't tried," said Peabody.

"Don't you think we ought to make them go through the effort? After all, the place *is* reinforced with iron. It's not going to be child's play."

"So you're in favor of continuing?" asked Peabody as he stood up.

"Yes."

"Good. So am I. But I just want to warn you: it won't be a bright future."

"If we don't try, they're *certain* to win. At least there is a chance if we try."

"Yes, a chance."

They worked all that day on a special edition which they would print later. During dinner, they made plans for distributing the paper in order to get maximum circulation. It was decided that an early morning dispersion and then an evening dispersion to certain key points would reach the maximum number of people.

Afterwards, as Peabody read from the Bible, he suddenly stopped as if he were struck by something. He was just finishing a verse from the Beatitudes: *Blessed are those who hunger and thirst for righteousness, for they shall be satisfied.* Peabody looked over at Jefferson, but Jefferson was stroking Luke.

Chapter 11

"Concerning Matters that Happened on a Very Dark Night"

WHEN DAWN CAME, Peabody and Jefferson, having been up all night printing the paper, were finally ready to take out the initial loads. Peabody kept clearing his glasses. "You need some rest," said Jefferson. "I can finish this alone."

"No, it must come out in an hour or we risk getting our paper confiscated. Remember, they aren't expecting us to deliver in the morning. We're an afternoon paper."

"Well, I can do it. You've been up for two days and you're not as young as you used to be."

"Yes, yes I know that. But just give me a minute to catch my breath and I'll be all right."

They managed to get the paper out in time and went back to print copies for the afternoon distribution. Both men worked like demons to complete the journal before the hour of their planned distribution to the taverns.

"I hope we've reached somebody who's not afraid," said Peabody.

"After they read this, how can anyone simply sit back and do nothing? They'd have to be beasts to ignore a situation like this. I remember when I was growing up on the farm down South and someone started picking on someone that it only took one person to side against the bully. Soon everyone else would come to the aid of the victim. It's the same situation here. You just wait and see."

"Well, needless to say, I hope you are right."

At Peabody's suggestion, Jefferson scouted the streets to see if it was safe to deliver the papers. Everywhere Jefferson saw suspicious people. He reported to Peabody that a night delivery might be better. "Good," said Peabody, "I think I'll get a little rest now. Wake me for the delivery; then we'll have dinner."

When it came time to deliver the papers, Jefferson saw that Peabody was sound asleep with Matthew, Mark, and Luke laying near, guarding him. *I'll let him sleep*, decided Jefferson, *he needs the rest*. So Jefferson went about distributing the papers himself. He encountered little trouble at first, but around nine o'clock he was walking along the street when he saw a flash out of the corner of his eye that made him turn. He was just in time to see a man pointing a pistol at him. Jefferson dove to the ground and rolled under the raised wooden sidewalk.

While Jefferson was in mid-air, the gun went off. The man ran towards Jefferson's wagon and dumped it over. Then the man kneeled down, trying to locate Jefferson, who was hiding in the shadows under the raised wooden sidewalk behind some trash. Suddenly a rat scampered out from under the sidewalk and the man fired twice more. He must be almost out of bullets, thought Jefferson.

Jefferson felt that he needed to draw just one more shot, which he did by tossing some gravel out into the street. The gun went off and Jefferson, who had used the opportunity to roll his body into a position of advantage, made one final roll out into the street, positioned himself into a squat, and lunged out at the man, knocking him backwards. They were tightly gripped together as they rolled over. The two figures were cemented as opposing forces that were seeking to overcome each other. But they were too evenly matched and neither could gain an advantage. Jefferson was straining with his full strength. His muscles ached. Even as they rolled over he tried to draw on some reserves of power, but to no avail. Then the gun went off again. Jefferson's count had been wrong. But Jefferson hadn't been shot.

The other man's grip, which had been overpowering, was instantly weakened and the pair tumbled to the ground. The man raised his gun to batter Jefferson's head when he doubled over in pain and rolled over on his side, bleeding onto the hard earth.

Jefferson grabbed the gun from the dying man and searched his pocket and took out a handful of bullets as he struggled to his feet. Jefferson's head was heavy with a dull emptiness. His body was drained of strength. But still, he mechanically righted the wagon as he doggedly started trotting towards his next and last stack of papers as his attempted assassin gave up the ghost.

Jefferson only went to one more bar on the way and left all his remaining papers that were in the wagon in front of a large store that was quite popular. He had to check on one other stack of papers that he had left about one half mile away. It had been Peabody's idea to leave the papers in stacks that were approximately one half mile apart in case any of the goons happened to hit one stack where they were distributing so there would still be a reserve left.

When Jefferson got to the reserve pile, he found that the twine that bound the papers had been cut. The only explanation was that whoever had tampered with them was waiting for the distributor of the papers to arrive so that he might be disposed of along with his papers. The gun was secure and loaded as Jefferson deliberately set to work, lifting the papers into the cart. Suddenly all his senses were at peak alertness; his body poised for action at any instant.

When the cart was loaded, he gripped the bundles and decided to push the vehicle forward. This allowed him more control over its motion. The old wheels creaked along the still street. The only light was a hidden moon and the reflection of a street lamp, which was a block away. Carefully and steadily he moved along. His body, which hadn't gotten any rest in forty-eight hours, now seemed impervious to the awkward, heavy cart.

Then he heard it.

Perhaps it was a creak of someone stepping on an old board. Jefferson had definitely heard something. This caused him to stop and look around, but all was silent. A certain chill bit into Jefferson and a breeze swept past him, carrying the dust and garbage of the street along. He started again, knowing that the wind would cover the sounds of a slinking sniper. Then he heard it once more. They must be getting into position, he thought. Quickly, his eyes scanned the area around him. It wasn't a particularly advantageous position to be in. Perhaps they have me in a cross-fire, he wondered. About twenty yards ahead was an alley. *If anything happens I'll duck into that alley,* he decided. Again he felt for his gun, but this caused him to slip with the cart. As Jefferson tried to recover, his feet tripped over some refuse in the street and both Jefferson and his cart made a most ill-timed descent to the ground.

Instantly there were shots as the ambuscading shadows became all too real assassins. He was trapped. Jefferson had been saved from that first volley by his cart, but that wouldn't last for long. He sprung up and bolted for the alley. Bullets screamed past his head in insensible rapidity. He felt a stinging in his left hand, but he kept moving through the mud of the dark alley when he saw what he thought was a shape. Jumping headlong at it, he hit the barrel and came down with a resounding jolt as the barrel cracked and some thick fluid came oozing out. Instantly his pant leg was soaked, but when he tried to move he was impeded by the splinters of the barrel. They were firmly embedded in his pant leg. Then a door opened somewhere as the owner of the barrel decided to see what all the commotion was about.

Jefferson pounced on his chance. He jerked his leg forward with lightning speed, ripping his pant leg and thrusting long splinters into his shin as he vaulted over the fallen barrel into the open door. The surprised man gave no resistance as Jefferson pushed him aside.

There was more gunfire as Jefferson raced upstairs and out onto the roof. From the roof he could see that the alley had indeed been a dead end and that his only chance was to try a clothes line that stretched between the building he was standing upon and another about forty feet away. If he could get into the window, he could make it through the building and then to the street a block away.

Leaping onto the balcony where the rope was attached, Jefferson dove off the railing and grabbed the rope, which supported his weight though it sagged so much that Jefferson was afraid that he was going to fall. He quickly made his way hand-over-hand to the other side and then cut the line behind him. Jefferson knelt low in the shadow of the balcony and watched as three men mounted the other roof and looked for him. Finding nothing, they decided that Jefferson had not, in fact, made it to the roof since no man could jump forty feet. After their exit, Jefferson took his knife and forced open a window as cleanly as he could. He then climbed inside the dark apartment. I hope they're out, he thought. Then suddenly a light flashed. Jefferson dove behind a chair. A figure stood in the doorway. "I gots a rifle here that'll kill you certain less you stands up, pronto."

Jefferson stood up to see a middle-aged black man dressed in a night shirt, holding a rifle.

"Over here, boy, and lets me see ya," barked the older man. Jefferson complied. "What you doin' here?"

"Some white men are after me and they want to kill me," Jefferson replied at once.

"What you do?"

"Nothing."

"Tell me what you do," said the old man as he thrust the gun barrel into Jefferson's stomach.

"I was just walking down the street with some newspapers when I saw these men with guns and they started firing."

"You jist walkin'?"

"That's right. Minding my own business when--"

"You're leg's bleeding. Come in and let me wash it," said the man, putting down his gun. "You know jist walkin' was ails they needed to shoots you in Flawida, but I thoughts they'se run things different up here."

"Are you from Florida?" asked Jefferson when they were over to the sink.

The man nodded.

"Well," responded Jefferson, "I'm from Georgia, about twenty miles northwest of Savanna, a little place called Bella County."

"That right? You don't talk like no southern folk I know."

"I've been to school up North. Living here changes the way you talk."

"You's been ta school? I didn't's know that's they lets colored folk into white man's schools."

"Well, I was rather fortunate--" Jefferson began when the older man saw that Jefferson's hand was also bleeding badly.

"I ain't no doctor, but you'se needs some doctoring to your hand. It's can go bad."

"Yes, I know," said Jefferson, looking at his hand. "I'll get it looked after soon. I'm much obliged to you."

The old man finished cleaning the wounds, then wrapped them in clean rags.

Chapter 12

"A Very Short Chapter with a Very Searing Conclusion"

AFTER THANKING THE OLD MAN, Jefferson carefully started making his way back to his home when he heard the aggressive guttural sound of a cat. He stopped and saw John coming out of the shadows. The sight of the cat brought an immediate feeling of relief to Jefferson.

"Hello there, little John."

The cat sprung into Jefferson's arms and made low, vibrating noises deep in her throat. "You're a long way from home," said Jefferson, who suddenly thought it strange that John had been there at all. Though, when he thought back, there had only been three cats sleeping on the bed. Still, Peabody's cats rarely strayed far from the house (though John might be an exception as she was the most secretive and private of the cats). Jefferson smiled. John had never been friendly to Jefferson. But then Jefferson felt a disquiet within his breast. He had been so focused upon his task and staying alive that he had been dead to the world about him. It wasn't until he got within a block of the house that Jefferson understood.

He set down the cat and started running the instant he became aware of the smoke. His mind was racing, he hadn't been alive to the world until the cat brought him back. There was something further that he had to attend to. Jefferson soon reached the place where he had spent so many happy years and found a burnt, feeble skeleton of a house. Around the charred remains was a fire brigade and a small crowd of people. The fire was now merely smoldering.

Jefferson suddenly rushed through the line past restraining hands and into the hot ashes and coals. He lifted up large pieces of debris in his search. Soon he found the charred body of Peabody with his right arm broken and his left arm chained to what had been a post. Jefferson turned to face the mob of people, wanting to tell them that their government did this and everything was being corrupted and anyone who tried to reform it was being killed and if they didn't do something, then they were all guilty of the murder the same as if they had beaten up the poor old man and then burned him alive. But Jefferson didn't say any of this. Instead, he shuffled through the rubble and found the cat, who was still alive and followed him closely as they drifted away from the smoldering ruins.

Book Two

The Role of the Audience

I have often been amazed at how great a power an audience has over drama. There have been many fine plays that have been shut down after only a few showings because they have not been favorably received by the public. This occasions several remarks by the more cynical factions of the profession that when there is a dramatic success everyone seeks to copy it in a lesser style so to share in the success of the profitable production. What the theater section gets is a mass of plays that are popular, but which everyone agrees are decidedly second-rate. Now, there is a problem about this, for I have been using terms that have not been defined very well, but this is because I wish to begin with what one experiences as problems, in a crude form, and move to principles instead of barraging the reader with some theory (for in all honesty I have no theory, but merely a few old saws that I use to cut out my ideas). Nothing that I am saying is new nor do I pretend that it is. I only wish to be allowed to talk about some of these things as many others have done and will do in the future. At any rate, enough of this, you already know that nothing I am going to say is all that profound. But perhaps I may bring up an idea that you have thought about before, but have not had the time to get into shape. As a result of my fumbling, perhaps the reader will be inspired to put some of these questions to the test of hard analysis and answer the enigmas that I can only begin to formulate.

We all complain about the low quality of art, but when an ambitious work comes along many of us would rather just shrug our shoulders and say, "Let someone else support it." I know that I do this with an embarrassing frequency. We like the idea of good art, but then when it comes time to go and to support it with our presence or our money, we develop an excuse. It takes too much trouble to become engaged in something complicated after a hard day's work. We want to sit down and relax in an easy chair or go and see a bawdy musical rather than something that we'd term "artistic." Now perhaps I'm more to blame than my ambitious patrons for this error (for so I always feel that I am in error when I create excuses for myself) and to you who do not reside in this category with me, I most heartily beg your pardon and insist that you skip on to the exhibits at the end of this section. But to the rest of you, I ask that you merely contemplate why we should feel so bad. In other words, to introspect in order to discover the source of our guilt. Now, in my case it runs something like this: I want good art (In my personal worldview I declare that to be a *good*). Thus, I usually enjoy a good, ambitious play when I take the trouble to go and to see one (afterwards I am filled with resolutions to go out thrice a week to *high drama*). But usually once I am at home after a difficult day, I cannot get the resolution to get myself to sit down in front of something which will engage me. Now, I know that Drama is supported in this society by money. Authors need money to eat, and if the best writers are not being supported by money, then they will become something else—such as lawyers or businessmen or (worse yet) bad writers.

This makes me feel guilty for I feel partly responsible for the state of affairs that we are in at present: namely a few good writers presently at work and a low level of art at large.

Now, I have several rationalizations for my lethargy. The best one is that I want to orate about how art should not be dependent upon money and that somehow such an art is corrupt since money itself is evil and creates a perversion, inherently. I can go on and on about how art should not be dependent upon money (more accurately: a particular source of money). To support such a system is to perpetuate an evil which somehow pervades art, making it evil as well.

I always feel good after this attack for I can go and stretch my legs and am content over how I am making a sacrifice by not going to that *excellent play* because to do so is to perpetuate pecuniary evils. However, this good feeling soon wears away when I realize that the play I have just seen and paid my money to experience was not uplifting, but makes me feel worse afterwards than before I entered the theatre. I resolve to see something more ambitious, thinking that it is better to perpetuate corrupt evils that create good plays than the trash that I have just seen. I am going to pay my money anyway, so why not on something that is a good investment, something which is truly entertainment.

Now there are some who will dispute my use of such terms as "good" and "trash." I may have been a little hasty (after all, I am not a professional critic or philosopher). But it seems to me that there is some kind of concurrence about what is truly worthwhile and what is not. This is especially true after a play has been around awhile and the production is labeled a "hit." Contemporary drama that is of a high class or aspires to this position (i.e., of being a "hit" or a "classic") should be patronized. Necessarily, there can be few great writers who will be able to earn a living at their craft. But when we begin thinning out their ranks, we will find a proportional decrease in the number of dramas which are written in the highest, purest form.

I feel convinced that an audience (public-at-large) affects the quality of art in its society. As a part of this audience, I feel a responsibility to do something about this. I am not saying that my behavior will alter radically (musicals are always relaxing), but I do admit some responsibility for the condition of things and, hopefully, will become sufficiently enthusiastic for making the purchase of a ticket that will leave me better for the experience more often than I have previously been. We have got to do something; it is our art and our heritage.

Here are some costumes which may excite enthusiasm for such ventures.

Exhibits:
quod, o patrona virgo, [Oh, Virgin, my patroness]
plus uno maneat perenne saeclo. [may my work last more than a century/ *a definition of a classic work of art*]
> Catullus, I, 9-10.

Here cease, ye Powers, and let your vengeance end. Troy is no more, and can no more offend. And thou, O sacred Maid, inspired to see the event of things in dark futurity. Give me, what Heaven promised to my fate: To conquer and command the Latiun state;

To fix my wandering gods; and find a place for the long exiles of the Trojan race.

Virgil, Aeneid VI (tr. J. Dryden)

The day is coming; I can feel the mood,
When new God Liber, son of Semele
Shall on earth rule. If you honor him not
As you should, you shall be ripped and torn
Into a thousand parts. Your blood will pollute the wood.

Ovid,   "Pentheus   and   Bacchus"   from   the
Metamorphoses (my tr.)

The negative *animus* does not appear only as a death-daemon. In myths and fairy tales he plays the role of robber and murderer. One example is Bluebeard, who secretly kills all his wives in a hidden chamber. In this form the *animus* personifies all those semiconscious, cold, destructive reflections that invade a woman in the small hours, especially when she has failed to realize some obligation of feeling. It is then that she begins to think about the family heritage and matters of that kind--a sort of web of calculating thoughts, filled with malice and intrigue which get her into a state where she even wishes death to others. ("When one of us dies, I'll move to the Riviera," said a woman to her husband when she saw the beautiful Mediterranean coast--a thought that was rendered relatively harmless by the reason of the fact that she said it!) By nursing secret destructive attitudes, a wife can drive her husband and a mother her children into illness, accident or even death.

Carl. G. Jung, Man and His Symbols (1964)

They took John Henry to the river.
         And buried him in the sand
And every locomotive come a-roaring by,
         Says, "There lies that steel-drivin' man,
              Lawd, there lies a steel-drivin' man"

Some say he came from Georgia,
         And some from Alabam.
But it's wrote on the rock at the Big Bend Tunnel,
         That he was an East Virginia man
              Lord, an East Virginia man.
              "John Henry" traditional African American Ballad

Frankie and Johnny were lovers,
      Lordy, how they could love,
Swore to be true to each other,
      True as the stars up above,
         He was her man, but he done her wrong.
         "Frankie and Johnny" traditional African American
         Ballad

Trouble in my mind, I'm blue,
But I won't be blue always,
For the sun will shine in my backdoor someday.

Trouble in my mind, that's true,
I have almost lost my mind;
Life ain't worth livin', feel I could die.

I'm gonna lay my head on some lonesome railroad line:
Let the two-nineteen train ease my troubled mind.
         "Trouble in Mind" Richard M. Jones, 1926.

Taurus

Congelation

Chapter 1

"On Dorthay Beauchay's Return and Subsequent Events"

"YOU SEE WHAT I MEAN?" cried Beauchay. "How can they get away with it if every Southerner stops planting their cotton? Why, in no time at all, they'd be forced to their knees begging for us to plant again. What do you think, Jefferson? You've got a head for figures."

"They have to be stopped somewhere by someone, but the location of that battle is a revelation that has not been divined to me," Jefferson said lazily as if in a dream. Then he turned and faced Beauchay. "You'll never make it alone. They'll snap you in half like a dry twig under a plow. But if you can get others in on it . . . then maybe you will succeed. It's an impossible venture, and the odds are overwhelmingly against you, but with help *perhaps* you'll make it."

"Yes, I think it'll work, too. It's a splendid idea. Show those Northerner's that we have as much fight in us now as we did fifty years ago. Why, I can hardly remember my father, but he used to say that when a man lost his fight, he was as good as dead. Yes, that's what he'd say, 'good as dead.' I've never forgotten those words."

While he was talking, Jefferson put his hand upon an oddly shaped cross that hung on a chain around his neck inside his shirt.

There was a knocking on the door. "What is it?" yelled Beauchay gruffly. Beauchay always yelled when he was excited.

"A letter fo ya Mista Boshay."

"Well, bring it in then. What's holding you back, woman?"

Samuel Beauchay snatched the letter out of her hand and frantically fumbled about, trying to open it.

"Thank you, Maria," said Jefferson to the maid, who turned around and made her exit having unburdened herself of the letter.

After quickly scanning the letter, Beauchay announced, "It's from Dorthay; she's coming home any day now."

"Well, I'll talk to Jackson and Maria and they'll get her room in order," said Jefferson.

"Yes, it's going to be a busy week," murmured Beauchay absently as he picked up the paper in his other hand and walked over to the window, looking out over his fields which still enchanted him as they had when he was a boy.

Chapter 2

"An Odd Accident which Befall Mr. Beauchay"

THAT EVENING BEAUCHAY went to bed rather late, as he was occupied by his troubled mind. There were his crops that must be taken in as well as his decision about the cotton. And there had been some trouble in the fields which he hadn't had time to attend to as yet because of other involvements. Then there was the matter of getting a midwife and doctor for his wife, who was expecting any day. And, of course, his sister was returning from her trip to France: all these things troubled Beauchay as he mechanically got into his night shirt and carried the candle to his bed stand before sliding under the covers. It was going to be a difficult week. It would require all his diligence and presence of mind, he decided, as he blew out the candle and turned over to say good-bye to his troubles and succumb to the peace of sweet sleep, when suddenly his nose touched something warm and soft! It was soft and spongy. Then there was an ear-splitting cry and a noxious smell. It was an infant crying. Immediately, Beauchay started shouting orders to everyone: to servants who were asleep, servants who lived miles away and to servants who had been dead for years. He called his wife, his sister, Jefferson: everybody. All this was done in a clamor to get control of the situation. But getting control of the situation proved to be a difficult matter. In an effort to get his candle, Samuel Beauchay had gotten entangled in the bed clothes. In an effort to extricate himself from the bed clothes, he knocked over the candle.

The candle was finally recovered when Mr. Beauchay stepped on the candle holder. This action caused some pedial discomfort accentuated by the fact that Samuel Beauchay had been thrashing about with some violence. So it was when Maria Dodd opened the door she saw Mr. Beauchay hopping around on one foot and cursing every general in the old Union Army. This tirade was accompanied by the wailings of the unhappy infant.

"Now Mista Boshay, what's da fuss in here?"

When she had freed her employer from his difficulty and Mr. Beauchay had marched over to his armoire to put on a robe, he finally replied, "There's a baby in my bed."

"Gracious," cried Maria, "it's not the missus', is it?"

"Of course not," said Beauchay. "Bring that light over here so that I can see the little beggar's features."

Upon inspection they found that the little child was indeed a boy and quite unhappy at that moment.

"Why, it's an orphan," said Maria, who instantly began to rebuke the baby for disturbing Mr. Beauchay.

Mr. Beauchay (not seeing the twinkle in Maria's eyes as she delivered her diatribe) replied, "Now Maria, don't blame the baby. It's not his fault someone left him here."

"Someone's whose been a playin' with fire and dont's want ta gets burnt. I'se a bets it's from the fields. Why youse oughts ta take this baby und finds out whose youngin' it is and makes them suffa for interuptin ya sleep." As she talked she relieved the baby's damp agitation and bundled him in a clean sheet.

"Now Maria, I think you're being a bit harsh," said Beauchay, who now thought that the baby was rather cute (when he had finished crying). "Someone obviously wanted to give the baby a good home. And what better home is there about these parts than mine?"

"You gots to punish the mama," said Maria gravely.

"It's hardly the child's doing. I think I'll look after the child, at least for the time, until I can decide what to do with him." Maria tried to convince her employer that he was making a mistake in encouraging immorality. But the more she argued, the firmer Samuel Beauchay was in his resolve. He felt that perhaps there was indeed room for one more in their thirty room house.

Chapter 3

"On the Decent Behavior of Myra Dow and
Circumstantial Evidence"

THE NEXT DAY, upon prodding from his wife, who somewhat agreed with Maria, Beauchay called a general meeting of all hands and share croppers to try and determine if the guilty parties could be found. After a thorough interrogation of everyone present, it was thought that possibly Myra had been the guilty party. But Myra was one of the few people not present, so Beauchay could not question her. He gave strict orders that when spotted, she should be brought up to the house immediately.

Now, Myra Dow was the daughter of a mixed-breed sharecropper named Francis Dow, who had never been married (as the father had run away before Francis was in her third month). The father had been white and Myra grew up to have light brown skin. She was mixed race but she was judged to be black according to the standards of the South. She did retain some of the features of her mother, among which were her beautiful brown eyes and smooth, graceful, flat nose which made her one of the most attractive women on the farm. She worked in the store that was run for the workers of the Beauchay and Vanderkamp Farms. Because it was summertime, she had decided to take a trip with her mother to visit her uncle who lived in Savanna.

Myra, through working in the store, had the opportunity to see many of the workers from the two farms. Though one might expect most of the shoppers at the store to have been women, Myra's rare beauty, manner, and charming voice caused many men to stop by the store to see and talk to her. This, of course, didn't make her too popular with many of the wives, who became infuriated when their husbands would come home from the store with some useless item that they had purchased. They would rail at their men for being so foolish in buying something they didn't need, but who they were really upset with was Myra and her power to captivate their mates.

Reportedly, according to gossip in the county, there had been countless cases of indigestion caused by men having to eat burnt meals that their wives had *accidently* left cooking too long on the days when the men were tardy returning from the fields after visiting Myra's store.

Myra was really quite an innocent girl. Only seventeen, she had grown up having to help in the fields and had received a minimal education from her aunt. They were poor, but one day when she was fifteen, Myra's quick wit and· charming personality caught the eye of the manager of the store, and after a year of special favors she was offered the job (which paid good money).

The store keeper tried to win favors from Myra, but was generally unsuccessful as Myra most often kept her full attention upon her work. This did not discourage others from trying their luck with her, however, and she quickly became used to it all and learned how to handle most advances with friendliness but also firm coolness. Myra got on, and countless hands went away discouraged and greeted by a burnt dinner.

Chapter 4

"The Responsibility of Samuel Beauchay to do Something to Myra"

SO IT WAS THAT MYRA was nominated (chiefly by the wives) as the most likely candidate for the mother of this foundling. The fact that Myra had been working in the store up until her trip (which had begun two weeks before) did little to dispel the thought in people's minds. Once the unfortunate Myra's name was mentioned in connection with the child, everyone began fitting pieces together so that it seemed natural that she should be the mother. For example, the fact that she didn't display the usual sign of pregnancy that is quickly recognized even by small children was, the crowd contended, not unusual. First, she always wore an apron behind the counter, which would afford her some camouflage. Second, the baby was reported to be very small and probably wouldn't have made much of an impression because of his miniscule dimensions. In fact, her trip was probably just a ruse to have the baby somewhere else. Then she could return secretly to plant the child in Beauchay's house. Because of his universally acknowledged generous heart, she could be certain he'd keep the baby and bring him up just as if he were a Beauchay. She had always been a sharp little tart, they said, who always seemed to get the best of every situation. Why, just look at how she got her position in the store, and at such a young age! It didn't seem possible for such a young girl to get such a high paying job, unless she . . . (here the story would usually go in several directions which all pointed to some rather intimate liaison). In no time at all, some version of this story had circulated not only around the two farms (Samuel Beauchay's and Charles Vanderkamp's), but also to the far reaches of the county, to the Rutherfords in the West and the Stuarts and the Thompsons in the Northeast.

Inside his house, Samuel Beauchay sat staring out at his fields, thinking about all the decisions he would have to make, when in burst George Washington Clay, the coachman. "You all wants me, sah?"

This speech was managed with the greatest effort, for Clay was not a good talker.

"I called for you an hour ago."

"Yes sah, I means, I is sorry, but I was exercisin' one of ya horses."

"Over talking to that girl at the Stuart's again, eh?"
Clay remained silent and dropped his head.

"Well, don't look down, man, it's the most natural thing in the world-- providing you use restraint, of course."

"Yes sah," began Clay, but Beauchay did not wait for a response and continued.

"Indeed, there has always been a bit too much of that kind of thing with the Stuarts over the years, and if you ask me, it's the reason they've no money. Selling their plantation bit by bit as they've been doing is a disgrace to us all. Too many years without restraint did them in. The South was built on restraint, Clay," said Beauchay as he rose and strode grandly across the room to lift one of the crossed family swords from the wall. These weapons had been used by his father, Jacques Beauchay and his uncle, Marcel Beauchay, during the War between the States.

"Yes, restraint and good breeding, that's what made us great! But now, look about you! All of the fine families are falling apart." As he said these words he gestured with the sword, whose blade was adorned with the stains of human blood. "Too many things are happening too quickly for the old life of gentility. We used to take our time; make decisions slowly. This was the proper method: to weigh all competing factors and then to deliberate in due course (always in due course)--but now?" Beauchay, who seemed to Clay to be lost in a daze, whirled about. "Everything now must be done immediately. Every decision is late and overdue even before the facts are known. It's zip zap, make up your mind, zip zap there's no more time."

As Beauchay recited the words 'zip' and 'zap' he swung the blade he was holding at invisible targets in the air. This behavior, in and of itself, didn't bother Clay. But the coincidence of these invisible targets being located very near to where he, himself, was standing did cause some agitation. When Beauchay 'zapped' once again very near to his coachman, Clay could see very clearly and distinctly the blood stains on the very sharp metal. Immediately, visions of his own blood adorning the sword flashed before him and frightened the young man to such an extent that his legs were allowed to mutiny from their task of physical support, and Clay ended up on the maple floor looking up.

"Clay, are you all right?" said a concerned Samuel Beauchay as he rushed over to his fallen servant. But Clay, whose senses returned just as quickly, wanted no more of this one-sided fencing and scrambled to his feet in the direction of the door.

"I slipped on da floor. Dids I break anything?"

"You *break* anything? Of course not. The only thing damaged was my story, young man--and your tail bone. But I'm certain both will stand the fall all right." Beauchay put the sword down on his desk and seated himself.

"What I want you to do," started Beauchay, "is to ride into town and send this telegram for me." He scribbled some things on a paper. "Check to see if there is any further word from my sister and deliver this letter to Charles Vanderkamp, will you. Mind you, give it to him personally."

"Yes sah," said Clay, backing out of the door as he restrained the urge to bolt away to freedom. Almost as he was out, before the door was fully closed, Mrs. Beauchay came in looking anxious and worried.

"I don't know when you are going to bring that Dow girl in," she started.

"Why?" asked Beauchay, who, in all truth, had forgotten who Myra Dow was.

"It's a travesty how you allow this sinful creature to go unpunished when she's been involved with that fellow who minds the tenant's store."

"I wish I knew what--" began Beauchay again, but to no avail. His wife kept up her accusations, so Beauchay decided that he best sit down and listen.

"What's to stop all the girls from doing the same when they see that not only are they not punished for it, but they're rewarded by getting a first-class upbringing in a fine home for the litter of their ill-conceived union?"

Then there was a brief silence which was soon broken by Mrs. Beauchay, "Well, are you going to do something?"

"My dear Mary Lou," started Beauchay, sensing it was his turn to talk. "I shall have the rascal whipped, of course, but who are you talking about and what is all this nonsense?"

"Why the baby, of course."

"You mean the foundling?"

"That's exactly whom I mean."

"But before I do anything I have to find the mother and then (hopefully) the father."

"Samuel Beauchay, does everything have to fall on your head in order for you to understand what's going on? They found the mother long ago."

"When, where—who is she?" he asked, slightly confused, as he started shuffling papers randomly into little piles on his desk.

"Her name's Myra Dow and she clerks in the worker's store."

"But how did you find out that she's the mother; did she confess?"

"Confess! That type never confesses. It's common knowledge that she is a loose woman who entices men at the store where she works. It's probably impossible to determine who the father is at all."

"Well," said Beauchay in a low voice as he straightened his tie. This sort of thing happened with a certain amount of regularity, even in Bella County. Samuel Beauchay was a little perplexed that this particular case should bring out the puritanical natures of so many people. If this sort of thing had been accepted at the Stuarts for years, why should anyone make a fuss over a farm hand (to whom Samuel imagined this kind of accident regularly occurred)? "I'll have to look into this," was the only reply that he could manage. "Look into!" exclaimed his frantic wife. "Why, it seems very simple to me what you should do." By this time Mary Lou Vanderkamp Beauchay was almost screaming at her husband, who was rather perplexed at his wife's emotional behavior which he generally attributed to the Stuart blood on her mother's side.

"Please dear, the servants will hear," said Samuel Beauchay in lieu of anything pertinent to say.

"I don't care if they do hear. Let everyone hear; I don't care. What I want is for you to take action against that woman."

"Now, Mary Lou, calm yourself. I'll do what I think will be best."

This seemed to be the appropriate response, Samuel Beauchay thought. He was neither agreeing with his wife nor disagreeing. Instead, his sole objective was to pacify his pregnant spouse.

He went to her and held her as she sobbed.

"Oh Samuel, when I dream of our baby who's soon to be born and how beautiful he will be, I feel so happy that I tingle inside. But when I think of that--that illegitimate child in the same house--I just want to cry."

Samuel held his wife and was not really listening to her speech. She was hysterical and would exaggerate everything out of proportion. This was not his wife talking. She was a compassionate woman.

Then the clincher came, "Because, dear," she continued, "people will talk and well, even though I know that it is rubbish, people might start claiming wild things about why you're keeping the child."

Samuel was startled, but his wife quickly added, "I know that there's not an ounce of truth in it, but still-- it might be better if you found this woman and returned the child to her."

"Yes, but--" began Beauchay again, but his wife kept on. "I know how it sounds cruel, tossing a child into the world in which he may starve or worse, but really, don't you think you have an obligation to your unborn son and to me? Think of your good name. Please darling, get rid of this little brat as soon as possible. You know babies are like puppies. If you keep them for only a few days, you never want to give them up." She paused as Samuel felt a seething anger inside of him. How could she infer that the name of Beauchay was so fragile that he had to be on guard every second to protect it against false charges and malicious slander? People whose respect dropped because of silly rumors weren't very valuable in any case. The name of Beauchay was a far more respected name than that of Vanderkamp, who had married Stuarts, Rutherfords, and other declining families.

How could she question the honor of the Beauchays, who had served with the highest honor in the War Between the States and before that had had the grandest plantation for miles and miles? Her very tone implied an intention to bully and speed up what must be, by its very nature, a full investigation into the facts.

Why, these sorts of things happened all the time. What made this case unusual was that the baby had been deposited in Samuel Beauchay's bed. This made him an interested party. As such he would act with due care. A child's life was at stake and he must act with deliberation. Anyone who found fault with this did not respect the very principles upon which the sovereign state of Georgia was founded.

"Yes, darling. We both want the same thing. I'll make everything right in the end. Don't worry," said Beauchay as he stroked his wife's soft, long hair.

Chapter 5

"A Less than Heralded Return"

AMIDST THIS CONFUSION, the return of Dorthay Beauchay received considerably less fanfare than might otherwise have been the case. When she arrived by coach at Varner's Junction, the village that was only seven miles from her brother's farm, she waited and waited for some reception, but none was forthcoming. This was because Clay had strayed on his mission to the telegraph office and had only gotten as far as the local saloon in which he had soon forgotten about any and all charges that Beauchay had entrusted him to dispose. As a result, this left dear Dorthay sitting in the dirty station for a full hour before angrily sending for a carriage from the livery stable to drive her out to her brother's estate.

To the saving fortune of Samuel Beauchay, who was on his afternoon ride, Dorthay's coach was spotted before it entered the estate and Beauchay instantly recognized his sister (even though the distance was a good hundred and fifty yards).

Samuel approached on his horse, "Why sister, we didn't expect you today."

Dorthay, who was more upset than her normal strict disposition allowed, did not respond at first. She had to repress the cholē which was running through her veins. After a moment when her sanguineous humor had regained control, she tilted her head and replied tersely, "I sent a telegram three days ago."

"Why that's impossible," said Beauchay, who hardly knew what he was saying since he had certainly noticed his sister's temper. He was prudent enough not to cross a lady in her anger. But he failed to see how he could have been in the wrong. He had sent someone to the telegraph office only yesterday.

"I assure you, Samuel, it is not only possible, but as a matter of fact it is an actuality! I have the receipts in my bag to prove it."

"But just yesterday I sent someone to check."

"Well, I suggest your messenger became distracted."

Beauchay saw immediately what had happened. Clay had stopped by to the Stuarts or to get in on some betting pool or to tip a few at the saloon. It was Beauchay's fault, of course, for a commander must accept full responsibility for the actions of his troops. "Of course, Dorthay, I'm terribly sorry for this inconvenience. But what's more important is that we will have a welcome home celebration."

Dorthay sat back in her seat and so indicated to her brother that she felt that this response was satisfactory. He would ride ahead and she would direct the coachman to drive slowly. She would be paid her proper due.

Chapter 6

"On Dinner at the Beauchay Estate"

DURING ALL THIS CLAMOR over Dorthay's return, there was little notice of another woman also returning to the estate: Myra Dow. She was traveling mostly on foot with her mother, but occasionally they would be lucky enough to obtain a ride from some kind soul on the back of his cart or wagon. These rides lasted only a few miles at most, but still they served to break the monotony of walking. They wanted to get back as soon as they could. Though they enjoyed their sojourn, both were anxious to return home.

Meanwhile, Dorthay was having a most sumptuous dinner after an afternoon tea featuring sweet cakes and cream. Mrs. Beauchay was not present for dinner, but then a woman who is about to deliver is not required to keep to any particular schedule. No one thought that it was odd that Mrs. Beauchay did not attend Dorthay's reception. No one, that is, except Dorthay.

Dorthay had never been close to her sister-in-law. In fact, Dorthay had always felt that Mary Lou resented her staying on the estate after Samuel's marriage. Dorthay imagined that Mary Lou thought her an unnecessary and unpleasant distraction to daily life. That Vanderkamp has always been such a possessive woman. She wanted to fully consume Samuel. She didn't understand that a southern gentleman must be allowed his freedom, for that is what had established the Beauchays. Mary Lou had to allow her husband privacy. For without privacy, the marriage state is unbearable. All this Dorthay knew. For the sake of her family, she could not leave Samuel to that woman.

It might seem strange for a woman who has never been married to make these pronouncements with such conviction, but that was Dorthay's nature. She felt a responsibility to educate her brother on the marriage state. He must learn to subdivide his personality. One plot should be allotted to the marriage self. It would be that part of himself which he shared with his wife. They would cultivate it together. It was the territory of husband and wife. The other parts of the soul were to be kept separate.

These would be his centers of power from which he would continue in the line of Beauchays and make his mark. But this Mary Lou Stuart wanted all the sides to herself. She wanted to dominate Samuel. Indeed, such an all-consuming relationship, Dorthay thought, would destroy the existing individuals and create a gradual dissolution of the spirit until one party had been depleted by the other. Thus, instead of a common plot from which each party could personally prosper, instead there was a poisonous insular bond which had to be fatal to one of them. Dorthay knew that if Mary Lou won this battle, her next target would be Dorthay herself.

"Would you pass the beans, please?" asked Dorthay in a soft, southern drawl. "You know, it's a shame that Mary Lou couldn't come down for supper."

"Well, she isn't feeling well," replied Samuel.

"Has she been sick? I hope not; she's not a very strong sort of woman."

"No. It's just the excitement."

"Oh dear me, I wouldn't want to have been the cause for that frail woman to become ill. God knows she'll have it hard enough when her time comes. She's so small, you know."

"Well, it's not just you, Dorthay." Samuel launched into an explanation of the foundling and the suspected mother, Myra Dow.

"My, that is the strangest thing I think I've ever heard. It's shocking that she would have had the nerve to bring it to the house. Have you found the little slut and beaten her?"

Samuel was amazed at how vocal the women were against Myra. Of course he didn't condone illegitimate births, but what could you do? The offspring were not consulted. And no matter how much moralizing went on at the Baptist Church on Sunday morning there would still be young people rolling in the hay Sunday afternoon.

Samuel felt rather sorry for Myra. She had been wronged by some villain who used her and then departed when he could no longer get what he wanted. But Beauchay did not feel anger as these women did. He was upset, but this stemmed from pity and empathy with the impotence we all feel over our destiny.

"Yes, it's a nasty affair," replied Samuel. "But tell me, do you like the wine?"

Strangely, Dorthay was not at all offended at the turn of the conversation and eagerly tasted the imported vintage.

Chapter 7

"Myra Leaves Bella County"

AT THE INSISTENCE of the whole farm in general, Mr. Beauchay summoned Myra Dow to see him when it was known that she had returned. Myra had heard the stories that were flying about concerning her and was at first quite vocal in her strenuous objections to them. This seemed to confirm the General Opinion that she was guilty. Then she stopped defending herself from the stories and off-hand remarks. By simply ignoring them, most people declared that she had finally given up denying them and that an innocent person would persist in defending herself. In short, Myra didn't know what to do when she first came before Mr. Beauchay.

"Myra," started Mr. Beauchay somberly from behind his dark mahogany desk, "you know what people have been saying about you. Are you the mother of the child left in my house a fortnight ago?" But instead of an answer, Myra broke out in a wailing flood of tears and sobs such that Beauchay became quite confused and called his sister Dorthay (who just happened to be nearby) to look after the girl until she was able to speak to him again.

Myra and Dorthay talked for some time in another room and when Myra finally returned, her talk had done much to compose her.

"Now, as I started to say before, Myra, it is a serious thing to beget a child out of wedlock, you understand." This time, Beauchay decided to start immediately with the facts. "Now if all women went out and did what you did the country would come to ruin in *this* world and be punished severely in the *next*." It might have seemed incongruous to some that Beauchay spoke to Myra about hell and punishment since he himself had a hard time believing in them. But sometimes a man finds himself in a role in which the lines are written for him. In such situations, one only has the choice of how one is to deliver the lines. It was not the case that Beauchay was an atheist. No, he went to church every so often. And if questioned, he'd certainly classify himself as a Christian, but his notions on all of these things were rather fuzzy. He lived in an empirical world and so most of his thoughts were concretely directed.

"Man and woman were made to be joined together as husband and wife in the solemn act of holy matrimony, which is flagrantly assaulted when women allow themselves to violate its dictums."

This admonition to women in general must have been a slip of the tongue, for certainly Beauchay was only addressing one woman. And contrary to many southern gentlemen, he held that men were to some degree responsible as well (though the extent of this responsibility was not sharply resolved).

"So it is with the greatest seriousness that I consider an action which so intimately affects our general society, yea, the welfare of mankind and the entire South--as acts of this kind most certainly do. They affect the very purity of our race!" By race it must be assumed that Beauchay meant the race of Man, for he could have no other meaning.

"And so Myra, it is not without good reason that our institutions are established, for so they exist among all civilized people alike and a violation of those solemn tenets is not to be taken lightly. Now, I perceive you to be a sensible girl. You are not a wanton trollop."

At these words Myra bowed her head.

"You were probably promised marriage, but somehow the odious brute put you off with some story. He might string you on with some excuse outlining why you would have to postpone your nuptials because he observed that you were naive. I say this not to excuse you, for it must be understood that I can never excuse what you did, but rather to illustrate that I understand that we're dealing with people and not merely abstract principles. There can always be human factors which mitigate the strict judgment of society. Myra, I believe that you are deserving of such consideration."

Through this harangue, Myra sat motionless as before, but lifted her head when he paused. She wasn't quite certain just what was transpiring, but since his tone was softer, she believed that he was preparing to be kind. Consequently, she looked up at Mr. Beauchay with hopeful eyes.

"It took a prudent heart to give up your baby and place him where he might receive the kinds of advantages that you could never provide. I think this is to be considered highly in your favor. You have impressed me as well as having been penitent. For this reason I ask you merely to leave Bella County and find employment elsewhere. This may seem rather harsh to you, but you are a symbol, and I, as head of this plantation, must keep general order. But, I am also a merciful man and feel for the agony that you must be in about your son's future. It is for that reason that I consent to bring up your son in my own household."

"Thank you, Mr. Beauchay, sir. I only hopes that you'll hear goods of me from now on."

"Yes, yes, you can take a week to gather your things."
Myra did not seem upset in the least over Beauchay's judgment. She almost seemed as if she had gained something—something of which even Mr. Beauchay was ignorant.

Chapter 8

"A Short Chapter on a Short Subject"

THERE WAS A GREAT OUTCRY on the estate against Beauchay's treatment of Myra Dow. Some thought he was too light on her. Others thought he was too strict. However, both camps thought it odd that he should agree to keep the foundling and raise it. Why would he agree to do such a thing?

Almost as quickly as this debate had begun, it ended again. This was because of the ensuing tragedy which occurred. Mr. Beauchay had assembled two very able and experienced midwives as well as the best doctor in the county to attend his wife, as she was nearing the time of delivery. But to everyone's surprise and grief, the baby was late and complications arose in the delivery of the eleven pound infant, which led to the eventual death of Mary Lou Beauchay one week later. Mr. Beauchay was shocked and tears ran down his cheeks when he heard that there were problems developing. He stayed by his wife's bedside constantly until the end. When that time came, his grief was so overwhelming that his sister decided that they ought to take a trip to Texas. Now, Beauchay was a man who normally liked to stay at home, but he was in no condition to argue. His grief had made him passive and completely languid.

After the funeral and two long months of mourning, the two packed their bags and went to Corpus Christi by boat. They left the two babies in Maria's charge and Jefferson took over the farm.

During this time, Jefferson was saddled with many cares. It had been left up to him to make all the funeral plans, arrange the burial, and caucus with Jessy on how the household should be set-up—at least in the short term. Though Jefferson had been handling most of the business of running the farm, he was now responsible for social structure, too. All this would be temporary until Samuel could recover himself. Where these added responsibilities would have been welcomed when he was a younger man, Jefferson now only became tired. Still, he did his job and carried it out to perfection. Jefferson had been silently in favor of Samuel's decision to keep the foundling Dow (not to be confused with the name 'Doe'), who was given the Christian name John after Jefferson's own middle name.

"John Dow," Jefferson said proudly as he looked at the baby. It would be important, he knew, that the child feel completely at home and be given attention equal to Beauchay's child, Jason. Without a real mother, the presence of the two children would be mutually beneficial, thought Jefferson. Growing up alone was always harder and less desirable than having someone who could act as a brother. So Jefferson was determined that they should be raised as brothers and treated as such.

Chapter 9

"Samuel's Excursion to the West"

NOW TO SOME, it might have seemed rather strange for a southern gentleman like Samuel Beauchay to suddenly pack for a trip and leave total charge of his estate to a black servant. To those who would have made this inquiry to Samuel Beauchay, it must be stressed that the relationship between Jefferson John Brown and Samuel Louis Beauchay was quite familiar since they had been children. In Samuel Beauchay's memory during the early Reconstruction, things on the Beauchay Plantation were in a shamble. The grand mansion was badly damaged. The workers were scattered. The land was reverting back to its natural condition. It was within this context that Jacques Beauchay returned from the War and started rebuilding. Within three years he married Laura Vanderkamp, whose father had died during the War. Laura was the only one of the Vanderkamps who had managed to hold onto some of their once immense family wealth. Wielding this wealth and their strength, the Beauchays started the slow task of rebuilding the ruins of their former grandeur.

The first stop was to get a force of workers who would work cheaply, because Jacques Beauchay, by himself, could only work a small portion of land. Many of the other estates (notably the Stuart's and Rutherford's) were taking on black families and letting them farm their land for a certain percentage of the crop which each family produced. The "rent" thus extracted was what those once grand families lived upon. But there were problems with such a system. First, it was extremely inefficient since each family was only working a small plot of land. Many farming methods which could be more quickly executed when working on a larger scale couldn't be employed on the small plots. This produced much waste and a generally smaller crop. The result was that the money exacted was not very much and the style of living among the 'first' families was greatly reduced. Besides, since the land did not belong to the sharecroppers, they did not have a stake in caring for it. Capital improvements on the hovels they lived in were supposed to have been made by the land owners. But they also were poor (that is, compared to their former wealth—compared to the share croppers, they were still rich). This method did have one advantage, however: it offered an income to families which had land, but no money.

Jacques Beauchay didn't take this very popular route, saying that he'd rather let the whole thing go than alter the concept of a single family working a farm. He wanted centralized control. It was about this time when the situation was the hardest for the Beauchays. Their income did not meet their expenses. Then Franklin Brown and his wife, Mary, along with their little boy, Jefferson, came to the farm asking for work. Jacques said that he wasn't letting his land, but if Franklin were interested in helping him with planting his (Jacques') crop, that he (Jacques) would pay him a fair wage.

Franklin, who was a huge man with massive shoulders and biceps, accepted and worked so hard that they planted nearly three times the crop that Jacques had planted himself the year before. Seeing that this new crop was so large, Jacques Beauchay offered to let Franklin stay permanently.

This was the beginning of a successful friendship. Mr. Brown had a tremendous capacity for work and got on well with Jacques. They would work hard until dusk and then would drink a quantity of home brewed whiskey while they joked and swapped stories. The tension that was raging in much of the South at this time, with the disenfranchised whites forming bands against the newly empowered blacks, did not exist between these two. They were like a major and his field commander. They listened to each other— though Jacques made the final decisions. (However, Franklin was not without influence, for the power of suggestion often dictates that an advisor can have more power than the commander.)

It was Franklin's idea that the Beauchays and the Vanderkamps gather a common labor force and establish a store, school, and church (though the school wasn't established for many years later). It was also Franklin who discovered the quickest ways to market their cotton and other crops so that they could reach the refineries and mills more directly and thus eliminate two middlemen. In only ten years, the estate was showing signs of becoming prosperous.

Then Jacques Beauchay died. Franklin took his death very hard. Since his own wife's death six years before, he had depended upon Jacques for manly comradery. Jacques had treated Franklin with great fairness respecting personal intercourse and access to goods of the estate. It was almost as if Brown were not a black---so close was the tie between the two men. Jacques was criticized severely for his intimacy with Franklin, but being a loner by nature, Jacques ignored the ugly remarks of his neighbors.

Beauchay left most of his money to his wife and two children to be executed by his brother, Marcel. Franklin was left a house and a permanent place on the estate and one thousand dollars for "Helping me build back part of a great farm."

Marcel and Franklin did not get along. In fact, they were struggling and fighting constantly, but Franklin did not wish to leave the place where he had spent so many years. And Marcel, because of the will, could not force Franklin out.

Finally, after six years, Franklin died. He left his money (about $2,200) to his son, Jefferson. But Marcel stole the money and kept Jefferson a virtual prisoner until Jefferson escaped and ran away. Samuel Beauchay, who was also fourteen, hated Uncle Marcel and his harsh manner and so acquired a tender feeling for his "black brother." The more racial hatred Marcel showed the Browns, the more Samuel felt a liking for them. So when Jefferson left, he secretly cursed his uncle and vowed to someday make restitution for his uncle's cruelty.

Though Marcel was an odious wretch in Samuel's eyes, the farm blossomed as Marcel made use of many of Franklin's principles (changing them slightly and calling them his own). He also meted out some of his harsh nature in the form of severe discipline, which created an order in the entire management—from field boss to lowest hand. And so the farm prospered in its martial peace, which contrasted in most respects from most of the other owners in the county.

When Samuel Beauchay took over the farm, he was nineteen and the estate was making money and operating efficiently. Still, Samuel never forgot Jefferson. And some years later, when he saw him in Baltimore, he offered him a job as foreman of his entire estate. At the time Jefferson refused, but in an unexpected turnabout one year later, Jefferson accepted.

Chapter 10

"Squire Vanderkamp Pays a Visit"

AS WAS MENTIONED EARLIER, public opinion was very sympathetic to Mr. Beauchay after the death of his wife. But soon after he left for his trip, people began to talk again about how he was leaving his child to be brought up with this John Dow (whom many mispronounced as 'Doe'). Dow was of questionable origin for not only was his legitimacy in doubt, but so was his color. His assumed mother, Myra Dow, was a mixed breed: part black, part white, and part Indian. This meant her offspring could not be considered white (even though he might have more "white blood" than black or Indian.) Such arithmetical problems captivated the minds of the good people of Bella County. More talk began about why the seemingly level-headed Beauchay was taking in a foundling. This seemed like a strange act, particularly when the child was part black. They all remembered (either directly or by reputation) Marcel Beauchay and his proper segregationist/white supremacy attitudes. How could Samuel act in such a vulgar manner coming from such a refined environment?

No one spoke openly about Jacques Beauchay and his pedigree (either out of ignorance or design), consequently; there was no opposition to this opinion. The only possible explanation, some said, was that Samuel and not the shopkeeper (who had never been questioned about the affair) was the real father of John Dow. If this were the case, it would be understandable why he might, out of a misguided sense of honor, care for the child. One could half-admire such an honorable intention even if one didn't think it was right for a black and a white to be raised together in the same quarters as equals.

One day when Charles Luther Vanderkamp III came for a visit, he stepped inside to find to his surprise that only Maria Dodd was in the house. Everyone else was working and Jefferson was in town. Walking over to the cribs where the babies slept, he smiled and said to Maria, "They're lovely children."

"Yes sir," said Maria in reply.

Then, as his fancy was taken by John's fat little arms he was prompted to say, "That must be Mary Lou's child; he looks like a Vanderkamp."

Maria didn't want to offend Mr. Vanderkamp, but she did have a passion for honesty and the statutes of truth which forced her to correct the gentleman. "That baby is the orphan."

"That's John Doe?"

"Yes sir, *Dow* sir; that's John Dow."

"Well, I'll say he certainly is a well formed little bastard, isn't he?" Vanderkamp laughed at the unintentional pun he made. But this must have completely escaped Maria for she failed to laugh. She looked down at John and covered him up where his blanket had slid down.

"Well, mention that I came . . ." mumbled Vanderkamp as he left Maria to care for the children.

Chapter 11

"A Georgia Rose in Texas"

PROBABLY THE LEAST EXPECTED EVENT of their four month trip to Texas for Samuel Beauchay was his sister's marriage. They had arrived well enough and checked into a fine hotel, but Samuel was quite despondent. He was completely distracted over the loss of his beloved Mary Lou. It was all he could do just to be company to his sister (even if it could be termed 'companionship by default'). But Dorthay, with her usual resourcefulness, got him out several times to some fine restaurants and floor shows, though it was to little avail since Samuel would sit in dejection and grieve his spouse with his entire energy.

Soon Dorthay gave up trying to make her brother go out and instead went out by herself. Now, though Dorthay wasn't a pretty girl in the bud of her youth, she did have something attractive about her: a good disposition and a surprisingly youthful figure. She was not forward, but neither was she bashful as girls so often are during their age of innocence. In other words, she was a pleasant woman who knew what she was about. This was the probable reason that she had six gentlemen ask her to dance at the party she attended.

One of the gentlemen, Farvil Corntiff, captured her fancy sufficiently so that she accepted an invitation to dinner for the following week. All seemed perfectly delightful as Dorthay was receiving more attention than she ever had in the accumulation of almost all her previous existence. True, Farvil was fifty, a mature gentleman, but this seemed to add to his perfect charm and *savoir faire*. However, enchanted as she was with Mr. Corntiff, another man caught her eye the following week after she had just spent a divine evening full of European culinary delights. This man was a common sort and he worked in the bank. His name was George Dodson. George was very different from Farvil. George was rough and had few manners. This sometimes made him rather crude in his speech. He was young and physically strong, which contrasted with Corntiff in every way down to the former's ruddy complexion, which certainly differed from Farvil's white, delicate, perfumed skin. Dodson even had difficulty remembering how to pronounce Dorthay's name. He kept calling her 'Dorothy'.

"Ain't heard no name 'Dorthay' before," he would grumble. It was clear that Dodson was Corntiff's inferior in every way, yet in the end it was he and not Farvil who won the heart of Dorthay.

Now Samuel Beauchay began to get uneasy about his sister seeing all of these men. He was slightly shocked when she went to the party by herself, but was more than flabbergasted when she announced that she was seeing a suitor on a regular basis. Beauchay began to be drawn from his isolation, deciding that his sister needed an escort. The decision to break his seclusion was entirely based upon what he considered propriety (even though his sister was thirty four years old). And so Samuel, of his own accord, began to accompany his sister everywhere she went during the evening. Immediately he formed a dislike for Dodson.

Samuel thought that his sister would be safe during the daylight hours, but she had been slipping out behind his back with Dodson to coo and cuddle as lovers are often known to do.

George Dodson was a lusty man. He ate and drank in great quantities so that it was no wonder that during their daytime intervals, he would press himself upon Dorthay with *great energy*. But Dorthay was no fool. She knew just how to establish a defense, which she might allow to crumble as she saw fit. In short, after four months, they were married and all three decided that it would be time to return to Georgia.

Chapter 12

"A Short Account of the Character and Particulars of one George Dodson"

IN HIS DEFENSE, it should be noted that George Dodson was a hardworking man who had started from nothing and had supported his birth family at an early age. His younger brother, Rodney, was ever an admirer of his brother and tried to emulate his brother's success. Rodney was such a good imitator that soon he surpassed his brother in wealth as he engaged in the import-export business (which through some strange and extraordinary sense of business acumen enabled him to undersell all of his competitors substantially). In fact, his prices were barely above the tariff. It was almost as if he didn't have to pay the same taxes as other importers, so cheaply did he sell his wares.

But George, who was going to live for a time with Samuel Beauchay on the family estate, had plans already of borrowing from his brother-in-law and getting an estate of his own which he could develop.

The trio took the overland route back, and Beauchay found it nearly unbearable even though he could get up whenever he chose and walk away to the club car for a slow drink and a cigar. Such recreations were necessary to maintain one's temper around George. Dodson never seemed to be able to speak for five minutes without getting excited or pawing Samuel's sister, with whom he frequently excused himself as the two retired to their compartment.

The whole thing was so crudely carried off that it made Samuel shudder. There were intangible things as well that made

Beauchay dislike Dodson. But still Samuel tried. He told himself that he was supposed to be tolerant of all kinds of people (especially of people in one's family). George Dodson was a person (once it took an entire cigar to confirm this fact to himself). Therefore, George Dodson should be tolerated. It all made logical sense.

But then why was it so hard to do it? Each effort by Beauchay was met with the common, selfish, twisting worm (or so Beauchay saw Dodson) displaying his true nature. Samuel's last effort was in the first-class diner. Dodson had made it very clear that he wanted his meat cooked *well done*. When the waiter brought Dodson his food, Beauchay smiled to himself at how very well done it had been cooked. But Dodson cut into the meat and yelled at the waiter across the car that the steak was raw.

"Please lower your voice," said Beauchay.

"I'll talk any way I goddamn want to," replied Dodson, who repeated his chiding of the black waiter. "Boy, get over here and get me another steak. C'mon and move that fat ass of yours."

The waiter, somewhat embarrassed, turned and started for the table. Everyone in the car was staring at Dodson and his rude manners. Beauchay looked at his sister, who was petrified with humiliation, and then began to remonstrate to Dodson again. It was at this moment that Dodson picked up his steak and threw it at the waiter. Dorthay and Samuel got up and left as George continued to hurl his abuses. Samuel wanted to ask his sister why on earth she had attached herself to such an ill-mannered lout who didn't know what it meant to be either polite or kind. But consideration for his sister and the pity that he felt over her humiliation prevented his uttering anything except, "Would you like to sit in my cabin for a while?"

"No thank you, Samuel," replied Dorthay, not because she didn't want some solace and comfort which her brother could give her, but because she knew that if she did accept the offer after walking away from her husband that George would throw her around. How different a man could be after one is married! The being that could be controlled suddenly becomes bent upon dominion. She had anticipated that after the ceremony there would be a power struggle of sorts, but what she didn't foresee was that Dodson would win so quickly. There was something about the man which was naturally drawn to power and domination. Perhaps this was what had drawn her to him (along with other primitive aspects of his nature)?

"I think it would be best if I waited for my husband within *my*--I mean *his* room."

With that, Samuel Beauchay left his sister to the fate which she had chosen for herself.

Book Three

Concerning Critical Opinions

In further reflection on the audience, I am always careful to discriminate those viewers who consider themselves either critics or those who venture upon critical opinions. This is not meant to include the viewer who comes to the drama and falls asleep or finds the performance such that several stiff drinks are required to make viewing tolerable. These reactions of the physical kind cannot and should not be commented upon except to say that he who is unhappy during a drama and continues in such a state through successive acts (and projecting through successive plays over the years) is an unfortunate personage, but is also the backbone of the Stage's financial support. I had the unfortunate experience of being in such a state recently at a play by some Swedish author, whose name I forget at the moment. At the conclusion of the first act, I said to the chap next to me that I didn't enjoy it at all because the actors spoke in such peculiar ways that I couldn't get the meaning of what they were saying. The man next to me replied that the play was being done in Swedish and that I must learn the language if I were to understand what was going on. Naturally, I did not have the time to learn another language, what with my sewing and all, but my escort that night did take up Swedish and now she's going to all the plays in Swedish by the same author and is enjoying them (with some bloke named Olaf, I believe). It just goes to show you that sometimes one must either abstain from a form or work extra hard if one is to enjoy certain dramas.

      To those who go to plays and profess to understand what is going on, and to be sufficiently sure of themselves that they might offer sneers or suggestions, my following remarks are directed. It has always seemed to me that the best critics of my clothes and costumes are those who themselves make clothes in a similar manner. They know what goes into each piece and the problems connected with a particular fashion. Because of this they are better able to comment on how I have handled the material to form a pleasing or appropriate product. I have found that playwrights seem to agree with my estimation of the best qualified critic. However, most critics do not fall into this category, nor is it requisite to be a participant to understand what problems are involved. I know several directors who cannot act and yet they tell their players how they should deliver their lines (and often for the best). What must be necessary is not direct participation in the action itself, but merely a sensitivity of it. This acts like a simulation of the action. This simulation is a vicarious placing of one's self into that activity as if he were actually doing it. Such simulation, if carried out with care, can serve as a substitute for the actual experience.

Now artificial things are neither good nor bad in themselves, but only become so in relation to some standard. I once asked a director how he liked a particular waistcoat that I had designed and he said that it was fine for a waistcoat. (The implication was that it would make a poor piece of scenery.) Things are good in respect to standards which are determined through some conception of their proper function. Now, it seems that here is where all the trouble occurs: what is the *proper* standard and what is the *proper* function? One is deduced from the other. For example, say an author writes a touching sentimental drama and some critic thinks that this genre (sentimental drama) is odious; then no matter how skillfully the play is written, the piece will be received very badly. The critic here is saying that sentimental drama is not a valid genre of drama. Therefore, no sentimental drama can meet the proper standard of drama and perform that function correctly. What is unfortunate about this is that many good dramas can become dependent upon powerful critics, and this influence is felt by the producers who back dramas in the first place. These critics may thus promote a single conception of what good drama is and how it should be written. In the case of the producer, this often equates to what brings in the most money, but this question is not within the critic's realm (except as there is a relation between a critic's reaction and the public's). The critic can influence the public who rely upon his reviews. It is therefore incumbent upon him to make the most honest and fair judgment that he can. A critic must realize that if he has a preconception of what good art is, and if this preconception is different from the artist's, then the critic can never offer a fair review unless the critic acknowledges the *données* of the artist and, at least for the moment, agrees to suspend his disbelief. For example, the artist may think that the purest drama is one in which the only things said are various arrangements of the numbers one through five. One character declares, "One, two, four." The other replies, "Five, five, one." Now the critic may believe that a drama based upon such a principle is ridiculous, but if he is to be fair, he must temporarily accept this premise and determine whether the play is successful by its own standards.

One part of the critic's judgment about the play must include this meta-evaluation. Of course after this duty is discharged, the critic is perfectly within his rights (and yea, his responsibility) to decry the genre which dictates such absurdities. This latter attack must, of course, illustrate the *why*. Why is this form contrary to the highest principles of drama? This requires the critic to enunciate the function (or one function) of drama as he sees it and how the play in question (or rather, the genre in which the play was written) falls short of this.

All this may seem perfectly agreeable, but the real practical problem is that many good dramas which are not in the current mode of taste are never produced. This is true no matter how skillfully they are constructed. The reason is that current taste is formed from the momentum of what has immediately preceded it. Changes or variations are rare.

When there is a drama contrary to current trends or fashions, the general public longs for (or requires) instruction in how they ought to appreciate it. This instruction should come from the critics (who ideally are the most flexible for change, but in practice they are often the reason why novelty is so sporadic). In order to judge a new and different work, one must look to the past. Not the recent past of the current fashion, but to all periods of history and literary practice. If there is a justification for some new mode, it must come from here. New structures are built on the bones of the most skillful authors and thinkers of our heritage. It is from these that a rationale for "novel' *données* arises. Even as this heritage illustrates a plurality of artistic and intellectual modes, so it also quickens our souls to multiple possibilities open to the artist.

Exhibits:

Come and hear about my marvelous dream,
Which came upon me in the middle of the night
While the rest of humankind were asleep in their beds.
It was as if I beheld a wondrous tree
Towering high into the sky shimmering with light
And the brightest beam was a beacon
Covered with gold.

> *The Dream of the Rood* from the *Vercelli Book*, ed.
> W.F. Bolton. my tr.

So much has knowledge fallen away in England that there were very few this side of the Thames that could understand a thing (their services) in English, or further (could) translate a letter from Latin into English, and I think that not many beyond the Thames (Mercia and Northumbria) could either.

> Alfred: "Preface to the Pastoral
> Care" Mss. *Bodleian Hatton* 20.
> my tr.

Battle had also claimed all but a few of Finn's retainers
In that place of assembly; he was unable therefore
To bring to a finish the fight with Hengest,
Force out and crush the few survivors
Of Hnaef's troop . . . .

Finn then swore
Strong unexceptional oaths to Hengest
To hold in honour, as advised by his counsellors,
The battle-survivors; similarly no man
By word or deed to undo the pact,
As by mischievous cunning to make complaint of it,
Despite that they were serving the slayer of their prince,
Since their lordless state so constrained them to do;
But that if any Frisian should fetch the feud to mind
And by taunting words awaken the bad blood,
It should be for the sword's edge to settle it then.

> "The Tale of the Finn" from *Beowulf* tr. Michael
> Alexander

. . . when students learn economics they are presented with views of human nature that are opinion *as if they were* facts: people are only rational machines (as opposed to those who blend reason with emotion—especially love), who are selfish egoists (because that is the only way to solve the assumed zero-sum characterization of nature), who only believe in negative duties, and create explanatory models of explanation that are reverse engineered to create boundary conditions that guarantee success. These devices are not those of dispassionate seekers of truth but those of individuals seeking disciples. Disciple-creation is the function of religion and not of academic discourse.

> Michael Boylan, "Learning Economics: A Cautionary Tale" *Sociological Forum* 30.1 (2015): 380-388.

I. Where the organization is structurally modified as in idiocy and insanity, or organically weak as in many diseases, the heredity is the preponderating factor in determining the career; but it is, even then capable of marked modification . . . . by the character of the environment
2. Where the conduct depends on the knowledge of moral obligation (excluding insanity and idiocy), the environment has more influence than heredity . . . .
3. The tendency of heredity is to produce an environment which perpetuates that heredity: thus, the licentious parent makes an example which greatly aids in fixing habits of debauchery in the child. The correction is change of environment.
> Richard Dugdale, *The Jukes: A Study in Crime, Pauperism, and Heredity,* 1877.

The moral 'ought' implies 'can.' If we say that A morally ought to have done X, we imply that in our opinion, he could have done X. But we assign moral blame to a man only for failing to do what we think he morally ought to have done.
> C.A. Campbell, "Is 'Freewill' a Pseudo-Problem'?" *Mind* 60.240 (October, 1951): 446-465

But the individual nevertheless remains merely a state in a process which began long before he came into existence and will long outlast him. He has no ultimate responsibility for a species trait or a cultural practice even though it was he who underwent the mutation or introduced the practice which became part of the species or culture.

B.F. Skinner, *Beyond Freedom and Dignity*, (1971): 200.

The first prerequisite for rational control of an instinctive behavior pattern is the knowledge of the stimulus situation which releases it.

Konrad Lorenz, *On Aggression* (1963): 263.

Hundreds of experiments have been made that demonstrate a universal inborn ability in all sorts of animals to select a beneficial diet if enough alternatives are presented from among which they are permitted free choice. We have available a startling experiment which is pregnant with implications for value theory. Chickens allowed to choose their own diet vary widely in their ability to choose what is good for them. The good chooser becomes stronger, larger and more dominant than the poor choosers, which means that they get the best of everything. If then the diet chosen by the good choosers is forced upon the poor choosers, it is found that *they* now get stronger, bigger healthier and more dominant, although never reaching the level of the good choosers. That is, good choosers can choose better than bad choosers what is better for the bad choosers themselves. If similar experimental findings are made in human beings, as I think they will be (supporting clinical data are available aplenty), we are in for a good deal of reconstruction of all sorts of theories. Only the choices and tastes and judgments of healthy human beings will tell us much about what is good for the human species in the long run. The choices of neurotic people can tell us mostly what is good for keeping a neurosis stabilized, just as the choices of a brain injured man are good for preventing a catastrophic breakdown, or as the choices of an adrenal atomized animal may keep him from dying but would kill a normal animal.

Abraham H. Maslow, *Toward a Psychology of Being*, (1962), 150-151.

"Give me three babies from any family and let me control the environment   and
I will produce a great poet, philosopher and Nobel-prize winning scientist."

Anonymous psychologist at the end of a cocktail party, December 31, 1969

Blue eye color in humans may be caused by a perfectly associated founder mutation in a regulatory element located within the HERC2 gene inhibiting OCA2 expression. This can occur within any racial group in the world.

Hans Eiberg, Jesper Troelsen, Mette Nielsen, Annemette Mikkelsen, Jonas Mengel-From, Klaus W. Kjaer, Lars Hansen, *Human Genetics*, 123.2 (2008): 177 DOI: 10.1007/s00439-007-0460-x

My life had its beginning in the midst of the most miserable, desolate, and discouraging surroundings. This was so, however, not because my owners were especially cruel, for they were not, as compared with many others. I was born in a typical log cabin, about fourteen by sixteen feet square. In this cabin I lived with my mother and brother and sister till after the Civil War, when were all declared free.

Of my ancestry I know almost nothing. In the slave quarters, and even later, I heard whispered conversations among the coloured people of the tortures which the slaves, including, no doubt, my ancestors on my mother's side, suffered in the middle passage of the slave ship while being conveyed from Africa to America. I have been unsuccessful in securing any information that would throw any accurate light upon the history of my family beyond my mother.

Booker T. Washington, *Up From Slavery* (1901): chapter 1.

Well chilern, what dar is so much racket dar must be something out o' kilter. I think dat 'twixt de niggers of de Souf and the women at der Norf all a talkin' bout rights, de white men wil be in a fix pretty soon. But what's all dis her talkin' 'bout? Dat man ober dar say dat women needs to be helped into carriages, and lifted ober ditches, and to have de best place every whar. Nobody eber help me into carriages, or ober mud puddles, or gives me any best place [and raising herself to her full height and her voice to a pitch like rolling thunder, she asked], and ar'n't I a woman?

Sojourner Truth, *The Narrative of Sojourner Truth,* (1878).

He [Martin Luther King, Jr.] began to empty the refrigerator and heavily packed food cabinets, placing everything on the table and the kitchen counter and, when those were filled, on the flower-printed linoleum floor; taking things out slowly at first, his eyes squinted, scrutinizing each item like an old woman on a fixed budget at the bargain table in a grocery store. Then he worked quickly, bewitched, chuckling to himself as he tore apart his wife's tide, well-scrubbed Christian kitchen. He removed all the beryline olives from a thick, glass jar and held each one up to the light, as if perhaps he's never really *seen* an olive before, or seen one so clearly. Of one thing he was sure: no two olives were the same. Within fifteen minutes, Martin stood surrounded by a galaxy of food.

Charles Johnson, "Dr. King's Refrigerator" from *Dr. King's Refrigerator and Other Bedtime Stories* (2005).

Gemini

Fixation

Chapter 1

"Two Boys"

THE TWO BOYS GREW UP TOGETHER under the watchful eye of Jefferson, and though they were raised under the same roof in identical conditions, they were quite different in their interests and dispositions. For example, little John loved to play with animals. Because of this interest, he was given (via Jefferson's intercession) a dog and a calf which John was allowed to raise entirely by himself. John loved both animals and spent hours feeding and playing with his "friends," for they were friends to little John. The lad would animate the creatures with voices and personalities of their own, in the way that many children often do. John liked to pretend that they (the calf and the puppy) were his children and that he was protecting them from the Yankees during the War. For this bit of historical background, both boys owed a debt to Samuel Beauchay. Mr. Beauchay would go on for hours, reciting stories which had been told to him as a boy. In each of them, the Northerners were painted as savages who tore down a mighty civilization much as the Goths did to the Roman Empire. During some of these ghastly stories, Johnny would become extremely frightened and would hide in shivering expectation of a possible visit by that butcher General Sherman, who in Dow's fertile imagination, might at any moment appear.

Jason, on the other hand, liked playing jokes on people. He was a very clever boy and could manipulate events in a manner far beyond his years. Because Jefferson was generally busy, and the other servants were too slow to appreciate his little games, Jason would most often make John the subject of his little pranks.

One day when John was feeding his calf, Maybel, and his dog, General Lee, Jason called Dow to help him in the shed. John went into the shed, but found no one. However, after John was safely inside, Jason shut the door, trapping John inside as Jason dropped the latch bar down and hid behind the shed to hear what reactions John might have to his predicament. Immediately John became nervous because he hated to be within enclosed places. He cried out, "Jason, Jason, let me out of here!"

Jason did not answer, but merely smiled at how he had duped John again.

"Jason, I don't like it in here, please let me out."

Jason stood up and started to walk away. Then he stopped and threw a rock at the back wall.

"I hear you Jason. Enough is enough; now let me out of here right now!" But Jason, who didn't like to be ordered about, walked back to the house for some lunch. As he was eating, Jefferson came in and asked where John was. "I don't know; I haven't seen him," replied Jason.

"Well, you know that you two are supposed to eat together."

"Perhaps he's out with those stupid animals of his again," replied Jason as he ate his soup.

"That boy just never knows when to stop," said Jefferson. Dow was known to become so involved in playing with his animals that he would lose all track of time.

Then Samuel Beauchay stormed in the door. "Where's John?" he said in a voice showing a restraint for an anger which might at any moment be unleashed.

"He hasn't come in yet," replied Jefferson, "he's probably still out with his animals."

"His animals—those confounded beasts! They've gotten loose and the calf (who by now was getting medium sized) was causing havoc in the upper field by trampling crops. Where is the little rascal? I'll teach him some responsibility."

Jefferson, who had all along assumed that John was with his animals, became anxious that some accident might have befallen the boy, for he was never careless when it came to his pets, whom he loved so dearly.

"I think I'll go and look for him," said Jefferson.

"I'll help you," piped Jason, who realized that things might get a little sticky if John should relate the entire story.

"Sit down and finish your lunch, Master Jason," said Jessy, who didn't like the idea of people hopping up and down from the table.

"She's right, son. Let Jefferson go; he'll bring Johnny back here."

"If Johnny is in trouble, I want to help him," said Jason.

Samuel Beauchay was touched by the loyalty and concern of his son for John. Such a sentiment should be encouraged, not stifled. Therefore, he allowed Jason to go with Jefferson. Outside, Jason asked if he could search the cattle yard as he was familiar with that area and knew it better than any other. Jefferson quickly agreed and so the two were off searching for the lost boy.

Meanwhile, John had gotten onto the rafters of the shed and managed to pry loose a board in the roof and was at that moment climbing out when Jason saw his playmate ascending the sharply slanted roof. Instantly he ran to the shed. John turned his head at the noise of Jason running, at which point he lost his grip and tumbled down the roof and into an open bin of chicken seed.

Jason started screaming for Jefferson, who came running at once.

"Are you all right?" Jason asked Johnny, but he got no answer as the latter lay motionless.

"Johnny. Johnny," yelled Jason frantically. He was now shaking Dow. Then Jefferson arrived and picked up the little boy in his arms and brought him back to the house.

Fortunately, there were no broken bones. John was simply suffering from the shock of the fall. When he came to, he could respond to Mr. Beauchay's questions.

"You know, John, that it is dangerous climbing around on roofs. They're not designed for young lads to go prancing about on them."

"Yes sir," said Johnny almost inaudibly.

"It's a wonder that you weren't very seriously injured. Why, that fall must have been fifteen feet off the edge of that roof. And if that seed hadn't been there. . . What I'm trying to tell you, young man, is that one must exercise more caution in the things he undertakes. When you act wildly, you can get hurt."

"I might add that as a result of your little escapade, your pets did some damage in the upper field. As punishment for your failing to take care of your animals, I am taking them away from you for two weeks."

Dow was so upset that he couldn't speak and his eyes (which were red from crying in the shed) again welled up with water.

Jefferson, who listened to Mr. Beauchay's speech, wanted to question Johnny himself. Something about the episode did not seem quite right to him. But he decided to stay quiet and leave the boys to their play.

Chapter 2

"An Instance of Mr. Newton's Third Law of Motion"

FOR A LONG WHILE THAT AFTERNOON, John would not do anything; he simply sat on the back steps, picking up handfuls of dirt and letting the particles sift through his fingers. He had wanted to talk and reveal that he was not really to blame for what had happened, but two things stopped him: first, his reticence to admit that he had been fooled so easily by Jason and second, to avoid the charge that he was merely acting to foist the blame upon someone else. Mr. Beauchay always put such great emphasis on accepting blame that the lad decided it would somehow be cowardly not to bear the burden with manly courage. Though in his sorrow he felt in no way like a man, but like a little boy who wanted his beloved animals. Suppose they should forget me, he wondered. Suppose they should think that I've abandoned them!

Now Jason was somewhat distressed at how far his innocent scheme had gone. How was he to know that Johnny would try and escape? Each time he passed by the house that afternoon, he saw that dejected figure playing in the dirt. He finally decided to make some restitution if he could, so that Johnny's depression might not become so acute as to drive him to reveal what had actually transpired that morning.

It just so happened that shortly after this resolution, a grey and brown striped cat wandered near to where young Jason was building a tree fort. At first Jason was very annoyed at the intruder, who climbed up the tree and made a number of disturbing sounds while Jason was trying to concentrate, so that the boy took a handful of nails and hurtled them at the cat who simply leaped up upon a higher branch and continued his teasing of Jason.

Then it occurred to Jason that perhaps the little cat could be useful to him in a way he hadn't grasped at first. So the boy called to the cat, but the cat (understandably) was suspicious of this human who had, just moments before, threatened him with the nails, so the cat stayed exactly where it was.

Jason saw that perhaps he should employ a different approach. He took a cookie that he had in his shirt pocket and broke off a piece and offered it to the animal, but again there was no response. Perhaps, he thought, it's afraid that my cookie is poisoned or something. So Jason took a bite out of the cookie and again offered it to the cat, but as before, the reply was a stubborn and resounding rejoinder in the negative.

Finally, Jason lost all patience and lunged for the cat, who being much quicker, went to another branch and then to another until the cat and boy were near the top of the tree. Jason had the cat far out on a limb and it could go nowhere from its present position, but as the limb was too thin to support the weight of the boy, he could not reach his quarry directly. So he decided to bend the branch back and so capture the cat. The plan was working when suddenly the branch snapped and down tumbled cat and branch.

Luckily, cats right themselves in the air and the agile animal was able to land on another branch not too far below. Almost simultaneously, Jason lumped down to the branch (nearly falling himself) and snatched the cat, who, disconcerted from the fall, was in the midst of giving itself a bath. Jason caught the cat and wrapped it up in his shirt so that he wouldn't get scratched and carried the bundle to the house where he presented it to Johnny, who was still sitting on the back step, alone.

"A cat, where did you find it?" asked Dow, his face illumined over the feline visitor.

"He strayed near my tree fort. I thought that you might like something to make up for the animals you lost today."

"You think I can keep him?"

"I don't see why not. He just strayed onto our property, and anyway, if he does belong to someone they'll come and claim him. What's the harm?"

Johnny was easily convinced by these arguments as he was preoccupied with talking softly and petting this lost traveler.

Having fulfilled his mission, Jason returned to his tree fort where he intended to stay until it was time for supper. All the rest of the afternoon, Dow played with the cat. They became close friends at once and seemed to enjoy each other's company.

However, when Samuel Beauchay came in from the fields, he became furious. Storming up to the lad he yelled, "What are you doing, young man?"

"Playing with a kitty-cat," said Dow at once.

This answer served to infuriate Mr. Beauchay as being impertinent. "I can see very well what you are doing, young man. What I want to know is why you are deliberately disobeying my orders about not playing with any animals for two weeks?"

"I'm sorry, sir, but--" started Johnny, when he stopped as he became confused at just what to say next. He wanted somehow to tell Mr. Beauchay the whole story, but when he was put on the spot and charged point-blank for a crime he didn't feel guilty of committing, it was more than he could do to muster any kind of defense.

Fortunately for the child, Jessy, the cook, had witnessed the scene of Master Jason's gift and believed that it was time for her weighty intervention, "'Scuse me, sah," she began opening the back screen door. "Buts I couldn't help but overhearin' you admonishin' of Masta Johnny when ails he did was ta 'cep this kitten as a gift from Masta Jason who gaves it to him. And nots only that, but Masta Johnny here first didn't wants the cat fo fear he weren't doin' right." This long speech was quite unusual for Jessy, who rarely indulged in oratory as she preferred deeds to words. But this occasion demanded that she speak up.

The words deeply affected Samuel Beauchay, who was left speechless to such an extent that all he could say was, "Bring Jason here immediately."

When Jason arrived, his father confronted him. "Well, Jason, young Johnny here almost took the blame for something that you did."

Instantly, Jason was taken aback. He imagined that Dow had informed his father of the entire incident concerning the shed. His mind scurried frantically to prepare a tight defense of his own actions so that he might not be left with the entire brunt of the blame.

"Yes sir, I'm sorry sir," said Jason penitently, yet sufficiently ambiguous so he wouldn't incriminate himself more than he had to.

For Jason preferred forming his own defense only after appraising the force of the attack.

"You know that I forbade him to play with animals, yet you brought him a kitten."

At this point it became clear to Jason that all he was being reprimanded for was this simple breech.

"I'm sorry to disturb you, sir, but I assure you I did not mean to disobey you. When I heard your sentence at lunch I took it to mean that Johnny was only forbidden to play with the calf and the dog for two weeks. And so when I saw him here alone and I came upon this cat, I thought that my dear friend might be cheered by another animal to play with. So I persuaded the cat, with no little effort, to come with me so that I could present it to Johnny."

Mr. Beauchay was touched by this simple and sincere speech. He felt warmth for his son and an admiration of his Christian concern and compassionate heart. Yet he felt a responsibility to lightly rebuke the boy for not coming to him first. The conclusion of this tirade was that both boys were promised a trip to Varner's Junction for ice cream sodas.

Chapter 3

"Further Episodes in the Life of George Dodson"

WHEN GEORGE AND DORTHAY first came to live in the house, Beauchay gave them the farthest rooms away from his own (most likely because he wanted to give the newlyweds the privacy that he knew they wanted). In fact, Beauchay and the Dodsons saw very little of each other for quite some time as George spent most of his hours in Varner's Junction getting to know the people there and having a few drinks while playing cards in the saloon. George was a man who liked to gamble and was generally successful--though not overly so.

Oftentimes during one of the card games George would drawl, "You know, ah like poker quite a bit, but you know in Texas they used to have large gaming establishments and my, were those places fine--yes sir, real fine."

As he pronounced "establishments," he would elongate the 'e' and shorten the 'a' while putting the primary accent upon the last syllable and a secondary accent on the antepenultimate so that it came out, "eee-ste blish-ments"."

"What do you mean gaming establishments?" someone would often ask during the game. Then George would launch into a description of what was a gaming establishment. He would go into vivid detail about roulette and various games of dice, like craps. There were also card games like pharaohs and Texas Wildcat in which contestants played from a wooden box, drawing cards in duels against each other and ultimately against the bank (a term which signified the available house money).

"Why, I've seen men win or lose thousands on a single hand from that wooden box," declared George to an enraptured audience. "The game's really so simple that even durn fool easterners could catch on (by easterners, George meant northeasterners). Them easterners think that they could whump some old Texas hayseed, who they thought must be pretty dumb." Whenever George would relate the mistaken impression that Northerners had for rural Southerners, the men at his table would laugh and slap each other on the back. "The risk in the game is its simplicity. What it take is a man who can bluff the pants off another gent. You just sit there with one card up and one down, which is dealt to you by a feller a keepin' the box, and then you gotta figure out whether you or him is closer to three or nine, with three being better an' nine. You can ask for another card, but you always play against one other man, and one of you looks at his cards and puts up a wager, which if the other accepts starts the action."

"Never seen anything like that, George.

"Yep, sounds like quite a game."

"We could play it around here 'cept that there ain't any high rollers 'round here yet, but someday maybe, if Varner's Junctions gets to be a big city."

It was a strange coincidence that during his stories, George seemed to have unusually good luck, which might be accounted for as a type of normal precipitate from his grand tales of fortune, or perhaps his audience's minds weren't on the game during the story. There certainly couldn't be any other reason.

"Did you ever play?" asked a man at the table in a credulous voice.

"Certainly I did, but I've only played the Big Game when I had a stake, because a gent can lose his shirt in a game such as Texas Wildcat."

"I've never heard of these gambling places. Where did you say they were?"

"*Gaming*, friend, not *gambling*—it's true that gambling goes on, but gambling has such a goddamn awful sound to it; like it's a cutthroat business or something, when really it's not like that at all. There's no cheating and everyone's very comfortable in a fancy setting--you play with your own skill against the cards and the odds and it's that simple. If you win, you get a little of the green stuff for your efforts. If you lose, then hell, you've at least had a damn good go of it, eh?" George boomed loudly, laughing and lightly slapping the back of the man sitting next to him. This man would laugh too and so each would down their drinks in one swallow, which they did in a single motion (though not always without any coughing or gagging).

They would play to all hours until two of the five players folded, and then they would have a final round of drinks and call it a night with the winner buying.

After one such night, George rode up to the house, half-singing out of one side of his mouth and smoking a cigar out of the other (it was quite a feat, one that George had practiced to achieve). Then George heard a sharp crack. He stopped his horse and felt himself suddenly jolted and bound tightly around so that his arms were secured to his side. His mind was not attuned to what was happening—here he had been riding so peacefully, smoking and allowing his mind to lull gently, and his breast was full of song when everything changed. His head jerked so that he had to concentrate upon who he was and what was actually happening: a hard yanking motion, then drawn backwards, hauled head over heels, falling to a jarring impact: *inebriated, giddy, reeling of sodden consciousness/ his obfuscated sensations and judgments were pierced by a* dull *aching of muscles, a stinging vibration as the annoying disquiet of a thousand natural sounds all amplified to ear splitting levels of harassing persecution so* that *the contrast between the remembrance of what just had been and what was now happening seemed completely incongruous/ without transition as if he had been suddenly yanked from one conscious state into another directly with no contiguity between the too.*

George was lying on the ground. Wrapped around him was a leather strip which was attached to something behind--a whip. He turned around and saw a figure standing so far into the shadows that only the arm that held the whip was visible.

"Your wife is in labor and she is having a hard time," the voice said. George couldn't make out who it was. As he was still groggy and shocked, his senses weren't as sharp as they might have been. Then he grabbed the leather strip with his hands in an attempt to free himself when he felt another jerk. He was lifted up by the same force momentarily and then dropped as the leather unlashed itself in spite of his hands and left him standing (though his momentum carried him back to the ground).

The mysterious hand and the whip vanished.

Scrambling to his feet, he raced into the shadows but he couldn't see or hear anyone. All was quiet. In his mind, Dodson tried to recall the voice exactly as he had heard it. But the task proved too difficult. He was not even sure whether it had been a black or a white man who had been talking to him; the voice sounded like both.

His annoyance and desire to fight were somewhat abrogated by his aching muscles and the burning welts on his hands left by the whip when it spun him into freedom as he had futilely tried to grasp it. Suddenly he realized that he was immensely tired and decided to head home to go to bed. All the events of the past minutes seemed as if they must have been a dream. He belched aloud as his head gradually relaxed and he felt the radiating ease of the bibulous evening in all its initial completeness.

When he scaled the stairs on the east side of the house, he noticed some noise and commotion. Wondering what it was all about, he asked one of the servants what was happening.

"Yo wife's havin a baby, Mista Dodson."

"Goddamn," replied Dodson as he was suddenly struck by the events preceding. They had not been a dream. But what was all the fuss? Certainly his wife had been pregnant. But that was her concern. Why was his comfort being infringed upon?

"Where the hell is she?" yelled Dodson. "Why didn't someone tell me why the goddamn baby—my goddamn wife and her goddamn--oh hell—shit," babbled Dodson as he pushed his way to his bedroom door where Samuel Beauchay restrained him from going inside.

"Where have you been?" started Beauchay. He held Dodson by the shoulders to restrain the latter from entering.

"Let me go!" screamed Dodson.

"You shouldn't go inside. The doctor's in there and he can't do his job with all of us interfering," said Beauchay, trying to be calm with his brother-in-law.

"Get out of my way," yelled Dodson again.

"Listen George--"

"Get out of my way, goddamnit, it's my friggin' wife in there and I have the goddamn right to see her---"

"She's my sister, too--"

"Let go of me you asshole, I want to see my wife, and you can't stop me."

"Look Dodson, you can't go in there. I won't let you. The Doctor has got to be alone to help her."

"Help her! Goddamn, like he helped *your* wife? Now--"

"I understand how you must feel, but believe me, it's better that--"

"You let go of me because I won't let you stop me!"

"It's her only chance, you thick-headed, stupid gutter snipe."

Dodson swung wildly at Beauchay, who ducked and easily subdued the frantic, drunken Dodson. The latter was placed in a large overstuffed chair. Dodson sat still for a few moments and then he bolted out the door, but before he could get to the landing, he became sick, retching over the balcony that stood above the oldest and most treasured of the Beauchay Family's furniture.

Chapter 4

"Receiving Lessons in Those Essential Subjects"

JOHN AND JASON were officially tutored by a fellow named Alfred Russel. Unofficially, the boys were given various assorted lessons by Jefferson. Jason preferred Mr. Russel to Jefferson as Mr. Russel was more akin to what he believed to be his own propensities and inclinations. For example, Alfred taught that economics was the most important discipline for a lad, followed by reading and numbers. This was because economics was what made society function. All other disciplines could be subsumed under economics. Politics, most certainly, was economically based. A wise politician knows that when the general populace is relatively affluent, they are less likely to want a change in government. However, if they become too wealthy, then they take heed of items which are far away from the needs of life: i.e., social needs. It is best to keep the electorate just affluent enough to insure their jobs, but not rich enough to foment social unrest.

Science and technology, naturally, in Russel's theory, account for the ways to increase production and therefore raise the aggregate flow of goods and services through the economy. They are tools of economic growth which must be regulated lest they stimulate too-high rates of investment and risk the fluency of liquid capital. Literature and art are also useful tools as they turn people's thoughts away from their monetary insecurities which, left alone, would cause a disorderly scramble for more and more. And finally, theology and philosophy serve to shackle the most engaging minds with unanswerable problems. Without this exercise of seducing these superior minds, they otherwise might be leading insurgencies against the economic and political fabric. "Man lives," Russel would often say, "at the most basic level, in the realm of economics. For first of all we are economic animals who have to provide for some of our unlimited desires with the necessarily scarce resources that are available."

Jason believed this to be most perceptive and, as he grew up, came to believe in the profoundness of this dictum more and more. John, on the other hand, being the naughty uncontrollable child that he was, rather inclined towards Jefferson and the books he would offer the boys about adventure and mystery. John much preferred reading tales of King Arthur or chilly thrillers of Edgar Allen Poe to the dull pedantic drivel of business and economics. Jefferson used to tell John that, though these subjects had their importance, they were not intended for young boys, but would be acquired, much like shaving, when one grew older.

Mr. Alfred Russel also found that Jason was a much more prudent child than John and so took a greater fancy to him. (The fact that he knew that Jason was really Mr. Beauchay's child, and that John was not, therefore indicating that Jason, potentially, was the heir to the Beauchay estate, had nothing to do with the favoritism he felt, for truly Russel was a clear thinking and practical individual.)

One day, Mr. Russel took the boys into town to show them the bank. After they had toured the big vault and listened to the vice-president tell them about how a bank makes money and is a friend to the community, they had some free time before they were due back so John and Jason went to look at the shops. When they got back to the carriage, Mr. Russel noticed that John's pockets were bulging and that he had something in his mouth.

"What have you got there, young man?" Russel demanded sternly.

"Candy, sir," replied John.

"Candy?"

"Yes sir, peppermints; Jason and I each had some."

This answer surprised Russel somewhat. He knew how expensive candy was in Varner's Junction and he didn't believe that Jason, being a prudent boy with his money, would actually spend it--waste it on some overpriced candy from town, especially when the meals at the estate were always complete with sweet desserts like cakes and pies. "How much did you two boys spend?"

"I didn't spend anything," said Jason.

"What?" began Russel, as Jason's statement had a note of larceny to it.

"John bought the peppermints for both of us," replied Jason proudly. So Jason got the candy and didn't have to pay, chuckled Russel to himself. What a clever boy he is. His enthusiasm over Jason burst forth as he said, "You mean that you convinced Johnny (who he knew didn't have much spending money) to buy you candy?"

"He didn't convince me," said Dow immediately. "I bought it for him because I wanted to; it's nicer to share."

"Yes, of course," put Russel awkwardly, "but--didn't it take most of your money?"

"It took all of it," John added directly and simply.

"All of your money?" said Russel in a lightly reproaching tone.

"We both like candy; do you want a piece?" asked John.

To this, Russel only smiled and nodded his head while winking at Jason who took a piece of peppermint candy and proceeded to chew it rather than suck on it.

Another day, Russel stormed into the house to talk with Mr. Beauchay. "That boy, Dow, hasn't been to classes for three days. I thought I should tell you."

"Three days! Why that's very strange because he isn't sick," replied Beauchay. "I'll go and send Jackson out to find him." But no sooner did he utter these words than they heard someone whistling Dixie, slightly off-key. They recognized him immediately as Dow. Dow was the only one in the house who whistled at all. (Others tried to dissuade him from his music making, particularly since it was done off-key, but still John continued in his unrestrained and naughty manner to whistle in the breeze with his head held high so that the wind would make his curly black hair fly into a tangle.)

Beauchay called outside to John, asking him to come inside. When the little truant arrived, he was carrying a fish on a string.

"I caught it for you, sir," said Dow, presenting the five-inch crappie to Mr. Beauchay. "It took me three days to get it, but I finally got one."

Mr. Beauchay was touched by the child's gift, but nevertheless, when he lifted his eyes and felt the stare of the angry tutor, he remembered his original task, though feeling less certainty in the resolve than he had before. "Johnny," Mr. Beauchay started harshly. But before he could add another word, John cut in and said, "Take him, sir. He's all yours." Whereupon John lay the fish on Mr. Beauchay's desk directly in front of him.

"Don't put it on the desk!" shouted Beauchay. "It'll ruin the shine." Johnny quickly took the fish back.

"I'm sorry to have shouted, but you must never put a wet object upon a piece of fine furniture because the water will hurt the wood. Now, you take that fish down to Jessy and we'll have it for supper some night," said Beauchay, getting up and walking about while he straightened his hair with both hands. After a moment he added, "Thank you, it is really a very nice fish."

Dow started to go when Beauchay said, "After you do that come back up, I want to talk with you again." And with that, Beauchay faced the tutor. "I'll speak to the boy, though I rather think it would be better for me to do it alone. You may devise some sort of punishment for him, if you like--extra reading or something; whatever you think is best."

"Yes sir," replied the tutor as he made his way to the door before stopping and adding, "the boy acts without thinking."

"Yes," agreed Beauchay. "Yes he does. We'll do what we can."

Chapter 5

"A Visit by George Dodson"

THE FACT THAT GEORGE DODSON did not volunteer for the War in Europe was almost the last straw as far as Samuel Beauchay was concerned in his relations with his brother-in-law. Even though the war had now been over for a year and a half, Beauchay still held it against Dodson.

After the birth of their first child, Dodson had successfully appealed to Beauchay for a small loan to buy a very modest place in the eastern part of the county (the old Rutherford place). Samuel Beauchay had so wanted to get rid of the parasite that he would have agreed to almost anything. But even with Dodson away from the immediate area, his presence was still strongly felt. For example, when he came to make installments on his loan, he would arrive in his ugly green shirt and brown cotton pants which he wore everywhere. This was topped with a yellow wide-brimmed straw hat with a bright red and blue striped band. He was usually puffing away on a long, thin cigar that covered the stink of alcohol on his breath. Beauchay knew that the money Dodson was paying him with was won at gambling in the saloon and not from the very small part-time job George had at the general store in Varner's Junction.

Dodson had a reputation for having a way with cards, though Samuel Beauchay wondered how much it had to do with simple luck as opposed to a skillful and dexterous hand. In all, there was little that Samuel would put past the man who had taken his sister. So it was always with great relief that he watched that cocky fellow turn around and close the door after his 'business visits.'

Since seeing the low born gutter rat, as Beauchay used to nick-name Dodson, was such a distasteful experience, Samuel Beauchay rarely got an opportunity to visit his sister. An accidental meeting with George would be more than Samuel could take.

Though there were rumors of Dodson having a little bit of money saved in the bank, nevertheless, he kept his family living quite frugally, as if they were quite poor. His children, Theodore, Woodrow, William, Howard, and Grace were always seen going about in the same clothes. Dodson maintained control of his wife who he still called 'Dorothy.' Samuel thought that this control was maintained by the fact that his sister was constantly pregnant. The few times he did see her convinced him that she was a changed woman. He's changed her name and changed her soul, Samuel would say.

These thoughts twisted about like wisps in Beauchay's cranium as he watched the figure dismount, lift the flap of his olive shirt for a cigar and stride towards the house in his casual, insolent manner. George Dodson had come to make the last payment.

"Hello there Sam, old boy," began Dodson.

"Very good, thank you," replied Beauchay tersely as he gritted his teeth at the detestable contraction of his name.

"How are ya?" queried Dodson, and then without hardly a moment's pause, "I've got the money, Sam old boy."

"Fine, shall we walk to the study? I'll make out—" began Beauchay, but he didn't finish his sentence as he saw Dodson pick-up an expensive vase. "If you please, Dodson, that's an expensive heirloom. I'd rather you not handle it."

"It's just a vase. A nice vase, I'll admit, but just the same, only a piece of clay pottery. No need to get--"

"On the contrary, there's every need. But I don't care to explain it to you as I'm afraid the explanation would be wasted."
Dodson began scratching his ear and making clucking noises with his tongue. "All right, old man, it's your house--Sammy."

And with that, Dodson followed Beauchay to the study.

"This is the last payment according to my record," said Samuel Beauchay upon reaching his desk.

"Yes, the last," responded Dodson as he handed the money over to Beauchay.

"How's my sister?"

"Fat again."

"Again?"

"Yes, it'll be the sixth."

"You do go in for large broods, don't you?" said Samuel wryly.

"It's kind of a family tradition where I come from. Sort of shows whether you can get 'em and *keep* 'em as well, pretty hard sometimes when you--"

"Yes?"

"Get older," replied George pointedly.

"Well," started Beauchay, feeling the jibe about his wife's death in childbirth, "What will you name it? You're running out of presidents." Beauchay was referring to the fact that all the Dodson male children were named for presidents of the United States.

"Don't know. Maybe I should name him after you."

"What if it's a girl?"

"I'll name it the same."

"Thank you, but I think I'll decline the honor."

"Suit yourself, but now I'll have to try and think up a good name."

Beauchay clenched his fist but checked himself. He began filling out the loan satisfaction papers as quickly as he could while Dodson clucked away.

"Here. I think all is ready to sign," said Beauchay.

"Fine," said Dodson, getting up. "You know, I'll be glad to get this out of the way."

"You could have taken care of it long ago," replied Beauchay.

Dodson began laughing. "You mean by taking advantage of the post-war bonus and veteran's benefits. Yes, as you've pointed out before, I could have made some money out of being a soldier." Then Dodson laughed quite hard.

But just as suddenly as the noise had begun, it stopped with a single cluck of the tongue. Samuel Beauchay was somewhat put off by this, but was determined to conclude the nasty affair in a most expeditious manner.

"Sign right here, please," said Beauchay to Dodson, who was now scratching his ear. Somehow it seemed to Beauchay that Dodson's cigar smelled worse than it usually did. He probably buys those cheap Virginia Stogies, thought Samuel.

Dodson quickly glanced over the paper and affixed his signature, but before putting down the pen he said, "You know, next week, they're going to be electing the officers of the bank."

Beauchay was silent as he was afraid of what he suspected was coming next. "Well, anyway, I didn't think I'd have to talk to you about it, but well, it seems there is a deadlock for the post of vice-president, if you come and cast your vote in the probable manner." George tapped his ash onto red oak floor and ground it in with his shoe.

"What are you trying to say?' returned Beauchay.

"As you know, Colonel Rutherford, bless his eighty-year-old heart, will most certainly be retained as president, but there is a vacancy for the position of vice-president and out of the six trustees, three are backing me for the post. Now, I'm not asking you to support your brother-in-law—why, people might talk of favoritism or something such as that; all I want is for you to disqualify yourself on the vote--abstain--because a relative of yours is running for the post. It's only fair, don't you agree?"

"And insure your election as if I voted for you because you'd then have a plurality?" snapped Beauchay.

"Not at all. You would be abstaining from a vote of which you are, by blood, not a disinterested party."

"Not by blood, *by marriage*. You're no blood of mine. And I do believe that it does not hamper my ability to make decisions."

"Maybe not in your eyes, but what would others think?"

"Hang the others," cried Beauchay, wishing that his visitor, having completed the transaction, would now depart.

"Maybe you don't care what others think, but I'm certain that some people might talk if there was a connection shown to your vote and that loan that is being processed for you at the moment."

"How did you know about that?"

"As I've said, I do get around a bit," said Dodson, clucking his tongue once again.

"There's nothing irregular about that loan. I have to improve the houses on the west field. It simply takes a large outlay of money—anyway, I applied for that loan weeks ago."

"This election was known months ago."

"I will not stand for your insinuations. You've signed the paper, given me my money, now kindly leave my house."

"But of course," said Dodson as he got up and strolled back towards the door. "It's not myself who is making any accusations against anyone, I'm merely telling you what will be said."

"The deuce with what will be said," responded Beauchay as he handed Dodson a receipt, which Dodson shuffled back to receive.

"Think about it," Dodson said as he was in the doorway.

"I will not," replied Beauchay flatly as he followed the other downstairs.

With that Dodson left. Samuel watched him go and then turned around to walk back to his study when his coat brushed against the vase, which Dodson had replaced far away from its customary abode. Fortunately, Beauchay was able to catch it and thus prevent it from shattering on the floor.

Chapter 6

"A Short Account of Some Tactics Necessary in Small Towns"

IT WAS DIFFICULT for Mr. Beauchay to understand *why* George Dodson wanted to be vice president of the bank. Perhaps, thought Samuel, he wants to begin doing some honest work, or maybe he's trying to make enough money so that he can expand his property. All this was slightly unclear to Beauchay, but one thing was for certain: he had to stop Dodson with every available resource in his power.

So he mounted his horse and went around to the other members of the board of trustees to attempt to influence them against the crucial, possibly disastrous election of George Dodson.

He found that the first two men he called on were out, and so Beauchay left his card. When he arrived at Major Wheelwright's in Varner's Junction, he was a little disheartened, but not despairing.

"Your man's been here already, Samuel," greeted Major Wheelwright.

"That's just my point, he's not my man."

"Well, he's your kin."

"A butterfly is kin of sorts to the boll weevil, but just because they're both insects doesn't mean that they're similar."

"What have you got on your mind?"

"I don't think we should elect George Dodson to be vice-president of the bank."

"Well, I'll agree with that. I never did like the fellow, but I'm afraid we'll have a hard time stopping him. Up till today I thought I was the only one who opposed him. But now I see there's two."

"Is there no one else?"

"I'm afraid not, unless you want to count Victor Stuart. He hasn't been strongly *for* something in years."

"Dodson needs a majority to be elected. If I can work on Stuart--" began Beauchay.

"--Promise him a break with some of your machinery. That could bring him some more money at harvest."

"My machinery is pretty busy at harvest; anyway, I hate to make an appeal like that—why that's bribery. I'd throw out anyone who suggested such a thing to me."

"So would Victor, twenty years ago, but things are changing. Times are hard for them. Right now, I venture, they don't have enough money to be able to afford such scruples."

"I'll talk to Victor," said Beauchay after a long pause, "but I don't think I can bring myself to make him such an offer. It doesn't seem quite right to me."

"It's not right to let that Dodson, a common gambler, become vice-president of our bank, is it? And remember that Colonel Rutherford is getting on in years. He could pass away suddenly and then Dodson would be in a perfect position to gain control of the bank."

"Yes, Major, it's a hard decision."

"I know you're an honest man, Samuel, and it's against every instinct in your body to even consider trading machinery for a vote, but also consider that we're up against a dangerous man, one who can change the whole complexion of this county if we give him the chance." Then Major Wheelwright paused and knocked out the pipe he had been smoking. He took apart the stem to clean it when he stopped and looked again at Beauchay. "Sometimes, Samuel, you have to fight the rascals on their own ground, under their rules, if you're going to win."

Then Major Wheelwright took out his cleaning stem and rag and started swabbing out his pipe. "You know, down South here, we gentlemen cannot seem to learn that simple fact--in order to beat the dogs, you have to become a dog. If we'd followed that sixty years ago, you and I would be a lot happier today. We've got to profit from history, Samuel. The Yankees did it to us, once, are we going to let the same thing happen again?"

As he talked, Samuel became disturbed. There was a certain amount of truth in what the Major was saying. *Perhaps we did lose the War because we refused to sink to the low level of our enemy, who plundered and scorched the earth, killing women and children by the thousands in their march to the sea. But how much could we have respected the Confederacy if we, too, acted on the bestial level in an attempt to win the War? Wasn't it better to be honorable and lose, than to be dishonorable and win? But then, on the other hand, wasn't what they were fighting for honorable? Wasn't it more honorable than the alternative? And if it were more honorable, then why shouldn't the attainment of that more honorable outcome make the methods of attaining it honorable as well? Perhaps there were only the results to consider and the struggle to achieve or instigate certain end products was not in itself something to be judged at all. Perhaps it was only a struggle (taken literally) to be defined in terms of what it was; in other words, a contest in which the participants do what they can to bring about certain changes. In such a contest the only rule that exists is the simple fact or reality of that struggle.*

However, this also caused problems, for if one accepted the struggle for itself, and that was the point in question, then if one lost the struggle, then the losing party would be guilty of bringing about an evil end and so would be just as morally reprehensible as its wicked opponent. If the South had followed the same barbarous tactics as the North and had lost anyway, then the Southerners would be guilty for not only the evil of re-instigating the rule from Washington, but also for all the actions in the struggle that would become evident (as by-products) once the struggle had ceased. Thus, they would be guiltier on a Moral Scale than if they had lost and yet didn't assign all value to the outcome. In other words, if they had assigned all value to the result, then if they were defeated, all was lost since everything depended solely upon the outcome. If, on the other hand, they distributed the value between the methods of deriving the outcome and the result, itself, then even if the outcome were negative, the justifiable means which were employed in the vain quest would enable them to retain at least part (or maybe all) of their original moral justification and thus circumvent, completely or in part, any and all of the responsibility of the adverse moral actions that might result from the victor's reign.

In the case of Dodson, though, Beauchay wasn't as sure whether the absolution from moral responsibility was enough. For if, indeed, Dodson did, as Major Wheelwright suggested, change the complexion of the town, and as a result, it wasn't a fit place for his son or his son's children to live, then what solace would there be in knowing that he, Samuel Beauchay, didn't bear the theoretical moral responsibility for the result?

Samuel Beauchay's mind was still confused on this subject when he rode up to the Stuart's place. It was once such a grand plantation in the eastern part of the county, where Marshall Stuart had artists, musicians, and painters overflowing on the grounds, bringing culture to their little county. Samuel remembered hearing stories of how every Thursday night the Stuarts would have a concert for any of the fine families in the area, either in their grand ballroom or out in their once exquisite gardens designed by a Spanish artist. There would be poets who would read their verse, and once a month there was grand ball with an elegantly catered feast.

Amidst all these thoughts of splendor, Samuel Beauchay rode up to the now crumbling remains of that once-grand palace of beauty, which had been greatly destroyed by the War and, in the years since, had been partially, though inadequately, restored. Gone were the carefully manicured grounds and the splendor of flowing colors which were replaced by a small lawn and three of the original seven fields--the rest having been sold to a firm that constructed a golf course. Victor Stuart was a small, restless man who was always moving his fingers about, stroking his thumbs softly in rapid succession, which produced a sound something like someone snapping his fingers.

Victor was at home and saw Beauchay coming and went to greet him, "Samuel Beauchay, I declare, it is good to see you."
"Hello, Victor," replied Samuel Beauchay tersely as he vaulted off his horse gracefully.

"I was just telling Sally Lou that I thought that was you approaching as you have a most distinguished equestrian style. If my son, Victor, Jr. had been about I would have had him study you carefully as he takes quite an interest in horses, you know."

"Yes, quite. Thank you, Victor, but me--" Beauchay began, but Victor cut in immediately.

"--Would you like to come in and have a drink or something?"

"No thank you, I really can't stay long, but we could walk about a while and I'll tell you what's on my mind."

So the men tied Beauchay's horse, but Samuel didn't say anything about the election.

"Lovely land here on the eastern side," said Beauchay.

"Yes, I wish we had more left."

"Oh, how is that golf course? Does it bother you any--the noise, visitors or anything?"

"No, all that is quite fine, really. I suppose the real problem is just having it there. But you know," said Victor in a nervous voice, strumming his fingers loudly, "One does what one can."

"Yes, I suppose so," replied Beauchay as he sense that there was more behind Victor's words than the mere denotative meanings. Some fomenting anguish was there, an aching over what could have been, if only. . .

It was a fleeing away from a past which hides one in its shadow: a darkness of failure and shame from which nothing can lift the woeful discontent. For Victor bore the guilt of being the one who has presided over the decomposition of a once splendid whole.

"It's hard working these fields around harvest I suspect, with no machines," said Beauchay almost absently.

"These blackies are awful; can't tell them anything," replied Stuart.

"Yes, I'd reckon that you'd get a better harvest if you had a machine to help you."

"Don't know nothing. I tell you *they* keep their homes like animals. Why, you should see how filthy they are," sneered Victor.

"One problem with not having any machines is that you never know if you can get your crop in on time—lots of waste. You know, that's just it: waste."

"Waste. It's almost a complete waste having those blackie share croppers around— keeping their own little plots and running down my land because they don't care at all about keeping anything up." Victor lifted his lips into a menacing grimace.

"Yes, that's just what I was saying. What you need are machines," returned Beauchay.

Stuart stopped a moment and turned his head, staring at Beauchay. "Pardon me, but I was just trying to see if you were a little hot from the sun today."

Beauchay smiled, not knowing what response to make to this statement.

"Where would I get the money to buy or rent a machine? And even if I did, those darkies don't know down from up. All they understand is how to swing around from African trees like monkeys." Victor chuckled to himself and strummed his fingers very rapidly. Then he looked at Beauchay and let out a terrifically loud roar of laughter that lasted for only the briefest of moments before he became serious again. "No, thoughts like that only make me extremely aware of how dismal the future of this place actually is within the present system. What I need is capital and lots of it if I'm to turn this thing into a success. What it takes is just one big break."

They walked together silently for a time with Samuel Beauchay afraid to mention his offer after such a response on Stuart's part.

Finally Victor broke the silence again, "Oh, I know we've had chances, like when father sold these fields, but the problem was that he sold them one at a time to someone else who made a tidy profit by selling them in a lump sum to a fellow who wanted to build a golf course. If I had only seen how much was to be made by selling the plots together, I could have advised him--but then I guess none of us ever really does see. We don't ever really understand the true value of things until it's too late and then we regret our indecision." Victor stopped moving his hands and looked up over the tangle of shacks which spotted his fields.

"You know," Victor started again, "maybe I'll have a chance to get something back once your brother-in-law--what's his name?"

"Dodson," said Samuel weakly.

"Yes, that's his name. Whenever that Dodson fellow becomes vice-president of the bank. He promised to have my application for a loan reviewed and to personally recommend that it be accepted. You know, I could certainly use that money now."

"But you're on the board of trustees," said Beauchay. "Can't you get a loan on the strength of that?" The moment Samuel uttered these words, he knew he had said the wrong thing. He wanted to make Victor see that he mustn't depend upon Dodson. That there were other avenues of possibility to be explored. He needn't put his hopes on a Texas scorpion. But his response hadn't had this effect, rather it had the effect of highlighting the real impotence of Victor's compromised position which only served to demonstrate the hopelessness of Stuart's future. This reinforced Victor's anxious fixation upon the large bank loan which he was convinced was his only hope.

So Beauchay added as quickly as possible, "What I mean is that you certainly don't need people like Dodson. Remember, you're a Stuart and they were the first fine family in these parts. I know you'll pull through all right, Victor." It was difficult for Samuel, for no matter what he said, it only served to illustrate to Victor his own helplessness.

"Thank you, of course, but I can't feel hopeful anymore in simply affirming my heritage. True, my ancestors were quite successful, but I have long since given up any ambition of repeating their success. The times are just too difficult . . . Oh yes, and to Dodson, yes he's a little *common*, but they've been growing in power for some time--the common folk, I mean. What seems to count these days is how well one can adapt to the new conditions and people like Dodson adapt very well. That's why they thrive."

"And you'll thrive too, Victor. We've already passed the hardest times. There's always a good market after the sluggishness that immediately follows a war. The market will make it worth our while to plant maximums—just wait and see. The old ways will never die, Victor, and we shan't give up to the Dodsons of the world yet."

"It's getting late," said Victor, after a pause in which he started strumming his fingers again.

Beauchay wanted to tell Victor not to despair, for the South didn't become what it was as a result of people like George Dodson, but Samuel felt that his last speech had probably conveyed the message strongly enough. He put his hand on Victor's shoulder before walking back to his horse.

Chapter 7

"An Incident where Jason shows the Virtue of Being Able to Plan Ahead"

JASON BEAUCHAY owned a beautiful fishing rod that his father had once given him. However, he never used it and so it sat in a closet acquiring age, but not wear. One day Jason proclaimed to John in the middle of a conversation on another topic that he hated fishing and that he was going to throw his rod away. But John tried to persuade Jason that such a fine rod should not be destroyed and that one day he, Jason, might take a fancy to fishing and then wish that he had his rod. But the other was not to be dissuaded, saying that when one was sixteen, he should know his own mind well enough and so was determined that he would never enjoy the sport of catching fish.

Jason turned to go, but John stopped him and put to him finally that since he, John, liked fishing immensely, that perhaps Jason would loan the rod to him instead of throwing it away.

"John, if I thought you fancied my rod, I'd have given it to you long ago. By all means, take it and some of the tied flies that were given to me and enjoy yourself." Jason said these words in a tone of high rectitude while grasping John by the arm in a sincere manner.

John was greatly affected by this show of kindness and felt tears coming, but as he was still in the company of another male, he held back his watery secretions until a moment of solitude.

So elated was John over both the gift itself and the spirit in which it was given, that Dow instantly declared, "Jason, I like this gift so much that I'm going to take it out at once to try it."

"You mean in the pond?" asked Jason.

"The pond, nothing--this rod is for stream fishing. I'm going to take a horse up in the hills and catch some game fish."

Jason seemed completely caught up in John's enthusiasm, for he smiled and laughed with John as he helped the latter get ready for his trip.

***

John Dow loved fishing and camping. The quiet of being alone in a natural setting allowed him to slow down from the quick rhythms of the everyday world. Riding in the hills, he heard the sound of quickly moving water, indicating that he was near some rapids. Dow slowed his horse, hoping to find a large pool in which to fish. To his good fortune, he found that the river bent below the rapids, forming a very large pool where that evening he would surely catch some fish.

He tied his horse and took off his gear along with his saddle and blanket. Then he walked to the river to get some water and get a closer look at his choices before returning to groom his horse. His camp was only thirty yards away from the wide waters. The sounds of the liquid flowing smoothly under the louder crashing of the shallow rapids about the protruding erratic stones helped lull Dow into a kind of hypnotic state as he went through the routine of bunching the corners of the canvas around small stones in order to tie the mushroom-shaped objects at the stem with his thin rope and thus secure a structure for his lean-to.

Next, he dug a small circular trench where he placed rocks from the stream: this would be his fire with which he would keep out the cold of the spring night. But by the time he had accumulated sufficient fire wood and piled it according to size, the sun was setting just over the trees and the fish, John knew, would be biting. He got out several flies, two of which he had tied himself, and attached them to some strong leader and then the leader to his line. After this, he fastened a very small piece of split shot to the knot where the line joined the leader so that upon hitting the water the sound of the small piece of lead might attract some fish as well as effect a balance between the fly and the lead, which would cause the fly to hop once after hitting the water. The fish were attracted to this "dancing fly."

John fished till after dark and then started a fire and enjoyed some of his catch. At home, Jason was preparing for his father's birthday which was the next day. He was getting his father a new horse. Perhaps this description of the gift is not entirely accurate. Jason counted on his father giving him his (father's) old horse (which was a magnificent animal indeed) upon the receipt of Jason's gift, which is why Jason sold his present horse as a down payment on this new one. The balance of payments upon which, were, as yet not decided upon. Perhaps they would come from his allowance, or perhaps Jason would ask his father for the money directly since, at any rate, what really counted was the thought behind the gift and not whether someone could actually pay for it.

Jason planned to ride the horse from town at lunch time the following day to surprise his father, who would not be the least bit aware of his plan and who probably had forgotten that it was his birthday.

The next day, Samuel Beauchay got up early to see the sunrise. He thought it was a sight of power to see that fiery ball lift itself once again to its lofty heights in the heavens. It was another year and he was rapidly approaching sixty, a number which had always seemed so terrifyingly old to him. He had already outlived his father in age by seventeen years and his uncle by eleven. But their memories seemed hurried beneath decades of past glimmerings. Somehow it seemed that when he got older, he didn't want to allow himself the luxury of thoughts about the past or the future. It was an inescapable fact that one's natal day once occurred. Indeed, it seemed frightening to him that he was incapable anymore of really feeling with his whole person just what a birthday meant to him. All that was left were the whisperings of when once upon a time each anniversary was enjoyed to its full measure. This meant one year more powerful and one year closer to his goal of restoring the Beauchay Estate to its former glory and the State of Georgia to its lawful sovereignty. But such words now seemed like the strutting upon an empty stage: the nonsense of childhood and signifying nothing.

All that was left for him was to finish what he had started. The plantation was slightly better off than when he took it over. Certainly the family wealth had increased, but all was so insecure. So much money had to be paid in the spring against the expected returns at harvest. But the reality was that several bad years could bring ruin. Despite his prosperity, he understood that he could do nothing else but continue. It was all he knew.

Samuel Beauchay dressed and walked out into the fields with Jefferson that morning to decide what they should do about several urgent matters. When he returned to lunch, he was slightly disappointed that neither John nor Jason were around to wish him well. Somehow it seemed quite important that someone tell him how happy he should be feeling—even if he didn't.

This need was pressing if only to offer him an avenue of escape from his morose thoughts. When Samuel was almost finished with his meal, he saw a figure approaching on a horse that he'd never seen before. It had fine lines and galloped without any horizontal sway. Soon he saw that it was Jason, and so he got up to meet him.

"Well, where have you been, young man?" asked Beauchay.

"In town," replied a breathless Jason.

"And where have you gotten this strange horse? I call it strange because in all my years of riding and owning horses, I've never seen anything like it."

"It's not mine," said Jason with a glimmer of a smile.

"Wicked boy. You didn't, I mean you couldn't have--" started Beauchay, unable to find the exact words to say what he wanted to say in a polite, non-accusative manner.

"No father, I didn't steal it," Jason burst out smiling. "I bought it, but it's not mine. It's yours. Happy birthday!"

Samuel Beauchay was so struck by these words that all he could do was to run up and shake his son's hand vigorously and then inspect his new animal.

"What are these spots on the beast's posterior?" asked Beauchay. "Are they marks of a cross-breed?"

"No father, this is a full blooded Appaloosa. It's a horse from the West. The Indians raised them for speed over distances."

"An Appaloosa, my, what a handsome animal," said Beauchay, turning his face towards his son. "You have made me a very happy father indeed. Thank you very much for this gracious and lavish sign of your affection for your old father. And now, let's have something to eat!"

Even though Samuel Beauchay had almost eaten one entire lunch already, he gladly consumed another with a keen appetite that seemed to have been renewed with the arrival of his son.

The next morning, John rode home smelling a bit of home-made whiskey (which he had consumed in a considerable quantity the night before) and with a saddle bag full of salted and smoked fish. He was greeted by Jefferson, who saw him approaching.

"Where have you been?" asked Jefferson gruffly.

"Out fishing with--" started Dow when he was interrupted.

"Fishing. Didn't you remember that it was your benefactor's birthday?"

"What?" said Dow, who never had a good memory for dates and had, in the excitement over the new rod, forgotten completely about Mr. Beauchay's birthday.

"Yes. Yesterday Mr. Beauchay celebrated his birthday and you weren't even around, but out fishing!"

Jefferson didn't have to say one word more. Dow was crushed. He loved Mr. Beauchay and was grateful to him for all that he had done and the kindness he had shown him. John was terribly angry at himself at having forgotten such an important date. Instantly he leaped off his horse and started for the house.

"He's out in the north field," said Jefferson.

Dow turned and raced with his catch of fish to the north field where he found Mr. Beauchay.

"Sir?" began Dow apprehensively.

"Yes, what do you want?" answered Beauchay.

Dow could tell by the look on Mr. Beauchay's face that he was angry at him. With such an intensity, this irritation radiated over Beauchay's whole person. This might mean my expulsion from the estate, thought John. But most of all, Dow was conscious of the terrible pain that he must have caused in his thoughtless impulsiveness over the rod.

"I'm sorry I wasn't here yesterday on your birthday. In all honesty, I was out on a fishing trip with a new pole and I forgot it completely, but I wish that you would accept my catch, which I've already smoked and prepared, as my tardy gift to you."

"I'm not a selfish man, John, at least I don't think of myself as one, do you?"

"No sir, why, you are the most generous man I've ever known."

"Well, it's good to hear you say that, and that also must indicate to you that I don't exaggerate the impact of events affecting myself or certain slights to my person, real or implied." Beauchay paused, but Dow didn't say anything. "Now, I would be lying if I said that I did not look for you on my birthday and was somewhat surprised that no one knew where you were. Today, I am also caught by your declaration that you forgot the date completely because you bought a new fishing pole and wanted to try it out.

"These things shock me slightly and, if I might be candid, also *wound* me. For I had always understood that you thought of me as if I were your own father. But I am not angry at you, because it takes a vain man to become angry at someone for simply forgetting a courtesy. No, I'm not angry, but I am taken aback slightly. They say you can always tell what a person feels by his actions as opposed to his words. Well, my boy, that's very true. Your actions spoke very clearly about where your priorities lay." Then Beauchay was silent for an interval at which time John Dow merely bowed his head in shame over his thoughtlessness.

"As for the fish," began Mr. Beauchay again, "I will accept them to show you that I don't hold a grudge against you, but have only the warmest hopes that this incident will soon be forgotten."

Dow thanked Mr. Beauchay and returned to the house where Jefferson helped him unpack.

"You did the best thing under the circumstances," said Jefferson after John had recounted to him the episode in the field. "It's always best to admit, fully and openly, your mistakes. Then you have nothing to hide and cannot be shown to be a liar, which would mean no one could trust you." Then John showed Jefferson the fishing rod which Jefferson instantly recognized as the rod that Mr. Beauchay had given Jason several years ago. "Why, you didn't buy that rod," said Jefferson.

"I never said I did buy it; Jason gave it to me."

"He's been giving a lot of gifts this weekend," said Jefferson, frowning.

"What do you mean?" asked John.

Jefferson, who never cared for Jason, became especially furious when he thought that the whole weekend had been planned by the young fellow for achieving the maximum theatrical effect in the presentation of his gift. First, he got rid of John so that he might not have any competition, and then he entered with his gift, just when Samuel Beauchay thought that everyone had forgotten his natal day. Very clever, and for that reason very reprehensible in Jefferson's eyes (though it is true that the whole operation would not have worked if John had not been the reckless, impulsive boy that he was). But still, that didn't alter the fact that Jason had been manipulating people again as if they were pawns in his special game. It wasn't just the cleverness that bothered Jefferson, but the cleverness at manipulating people to one's own advantage that bothered Jefferson (especially when shades of mendacity were calculated into the picture). All these were arranged, Jefferson was convinced, to create an illusion which was only partially true: namely that Dow forgot Mr. Beauchay's birthday, while Jason not only remembered it, but gave a splendid gift as well.

However, Jefferson knew quite well that these were only suppositions on his part. They couldn't be proven. And so his hands were prevented from pointing the accusing finger at Jason. Possibly for this reason and possibly because he wanted to spare Dow the non-innocent view of ugly deceit as long as possible, Jefferson kept still and merely replied, "Yes, young Jason gave his father an Appaloosa horse for a gift."

"A horse!" exclaimed John. "He must have had to save a long time to buy a horse."

"Yes, I suppose so," replied Jefferson softly, though he was convinced that there was probably a scheme behind that too.

Chapter 8

"To Keep the Reader Informed of Some Strange News from Town"

THE ENTIRE COUNTY WAS SHAKEN when Sally-Lou Stuart returned to town and two days later killed Lucius Smith, and tried to kill George Dodson except that he wasn't in his office at the bank when she burst in. He was across the street when he saw a woman carrying what he thought was a rifle into the bank. Because of this, George had called the sheriff who then accompanied George to his office where she tried to fire a shot at Dodson (and probably would have succeeded had not the sheriff's hands been quicker). The gun discharged and sent a bullet wildly into the street.

"I tell you, I never seen a woman so much like a wild cat," drawled George over his cards. The local saloon had gone out of business when Prohibition was enacted and lay dormant for some time until a firm had purchased the place cheaply and turned it into a gambling house. No one knew the identity of the owners or where exactly they were located, but they had hired Lucius Smith to be the proprietor. He, in turn, had hired several black men from Richmond to run the games, which were mostly poker and assorted card games, with dice and other recreations supervised by dealers every night between eight and twelve o'clock.

"Why should she want to shoot at you, George?" asked one of his poker companions.

"I don't know, it's all very mysterious to me."

"You mean she just goes in and busts into your office to shoot you?"

"Yup. Daftest thing, isn't it?"

"What I'd like to know," said another, "is why she killed Lucius."

"Who knows," said a third, "I always thought she was a little daft when she left old Victor a few years back."

"Daft my ass," said the second again. "Why, she was just a little bayou bitch, that's all. Why, she ran away with one of those traveling actors, remember?"

"If I had been Victor, I'd have run after them with a gun," put forth the third as he took a drink from a private flask.

"Let's not be too hard on Mr. Stuart, boys," drawled Dodson slowly as he blew out a puff of cigar smoke. "He's had his problems too, you know."

"That's for sure," echoed the second.

"He's been trying to build up that place of his, and that's quite a task," said Dodson again.

"That old letch, Rudolph, really ran down the place," added the third.

"He's had a lot to do since his old man passed away," said the second again soberly.

"Or passed out, you mean--for good," said a fourth, laughing loudly as he took a swig from the private flask which was being passed around.

"Well, one thing's for certain," said a fifth in a steady, unwavering voice, "what with old Colonel Rutherford and now Lucius Smith, the undertaker will have a good week of it."

"That's for sure," laughed the fourth again spasmodically. The others faintly picked up his laughter. They all tried to join in except for Dodson and the fifth man who leaned back out of the glare of the overhead light.

The arraignment of Sally-Lou (Thompson) Stuart was visited by a large part of the town. The local paper was covering the story in a special edition as everyone seemed as if they couldn't get enough of this sensational tale. All through the courtroom there were rumors about an alleged affair between Lucius Smith and Kathy (Vanderkamp) Thompson, Sally-Lou's mother.

--I heard that Lucius Smith was Sally-Lou's lover--no you've got that wrong, he was her father, remember she was married when she was sixteen--yes, I remember, the little trollop--always hot for anything in pants, she was--did you say she was married when she was fourteen?—how could Lucius have been her son, he was thirty

eight years older than she was—well, you know that Lucius was illegitimate—really? didn't know that--sure, it was common knowledge, he used to get money, they say from old Colonel Rutherford—please, have a little respect for the dead--you can't hide the truth—well, there's a difference between hiding the truth and idle stories--

The judge entered. "Mary-Lou, will you approach the bench."

--Kathryn Thompson was a virtuous woman--virtuous woman, my foot, why she married her first cousin--so what? There's a lot of people done that. Don't be such a prude--I heard that she didn't marry her first cousin--

"Mary-Lou Stuart, you have been charged in the crime--

--what do you mean, of course she married Harold, --no, that's not what I mean, I heard that Joanna (Thompson) Vanderkamp was not her mother--why, heard such a story?

"in connection with the killing of one Lucius Smith last week--

--I heard that her father was Rudolph Stuart--I heard it was Richard Vanderkamp, he had quite a few, you know--no, that's ridiculous, all this talk is absurd, please stop it--

"--and the state sees fit to charge you with murder in the first degree--

--I heard that Victor Stuart was really the offspring of Richard Vanderkamp—no, that's wrong, I heard that it was Kathryn Vanderkamp and Rudolph Stuart--this is getting grotesque, that would make Victor and Sally-Lou brother and sister—Margaret Rutherford I understand was Kathryn Vanderkamp's real mother--wasn't Sally-Lou the one who used to run around naked as a child?--no, that was--

"How do you plead?"

"Guilty, your Honor, and proud of it."

--did you hear that--you mean about Rudolf Stuart and Julia Rutherford-- no, what Mary-Lou just said--you mean she admitted being illegitimate?--be quiet and listen, she said she was guilty-- well the whole town knows that--yes, it's common knowledge

***

In the old store where George Dodson used to work part-time before becoming associated with the bank, there was an ancient barrel filled with soda crackers. Around the barrel, a few old men would sit and pass the time of day while playing an occasional game of checkers or listening to the new radio that Ike Jacobson, the store owner, had recently purchased from a mail order house in Atlanta.

"Think Dodson will be the new president of the bank, Ike?" said one old timer who was engrossed in a losing game of checkers.

"Don't rightly know, Jake, 'cept I 'spose that seems the most likely occurrence, don't it?"

"I don't like that young feller, he's too uppity for my blood," said Jake as his opponent, on the attack, jumped one of his black checkers.

"Don't know about that, Jake," said Ed. "Seems right neighborly to me, my son plays cards with him in the old saloon and tells me Dodson's a fair man."

"Sure he's fair, 'cause he don't never lost; that's why. If I never lost any dem burn money a playing poker, I would be sweet as roses maself," said Jake as he motioned his friend to move his checker.

"Ain't really fair; he loses sometimes," replied the other.

"Only sose thats he can win again, real big. He's a settin' the suckers up like they does at the state fair: ya win five bucks once and then you lose fifteen. Then you win ten and you lose twenty. You can't win at those kinda rates--your move."

"Don't know 'bout that. My son says that he's a right neighborly feller. Says he's a fair man, and ah--what do you think, Ike?" said Ed as he moved his red queen to take another black piece.

"If you ask me," starts Ike, who had a big chaw of tobacco in his mouth that was getting quite juicy, "that Dobson has an interest in that saloon."

"Gaming establishment, Ike," put Jake as he watched Ed get a third red queen.

"Gaming, saloon, I don't care what's you want a call it, all I know is that Dobson feller is gettin' mighty big 'round these parts, mighty big."

"Yep, that's right, Ike, mighty big, but when they gets real big then they don't never stop tryin' to get bigger and bigger until they makes some mistake somewhere."

"I don't think Dodson's going to make too many mistakes," said Ed as he jumped another black piece.

"I wouldn't be none too sure' bout that, Ed," said Jake as he quadrupled jumped all four of Ed's queens and thus ended the game. "Sometimes it happens to the best of 'em."

Ike just shook his head and skillfully chimed the brass receptacle on the floor in front of the side counter.

***

The entire town was animated in the sensational statement of Sally-Lou's pleading guilty. However, she changed her plea when the judge explained to her that she wouldn't have a trial unless she pleaded innocent.

"What did she mean?" And "Why had she been placed under such a heavy guard at the jail?" These were the questions being tossed about. It seemed to most people that she was keeping some terrible overwhelming secret that no one really wanted to hear.

"Who do you think the new owner will be of this place?" asked one of the players as George dealt the poker hand.

"Lucius wasn't the owner of this place; he was just the manager. I hear there's some big group of businessmen from Atlanta that own a string of old saloons around the state."

"You know, George, what this town needs is a good bootlegger."

"I suspect they'll get a new manager for this place soon. It can't run itself, you know," said Dodson as he threw in his cards.

"Things happened so fast last week and now, all of a sudden, it's real quiet. It kind of makes you uneasy."

"Yes, it'll take a while for this town to fully quiet down again. But I suspect that when the trial begins, tomorrow, things will start normalizing themselves again," said Dodson reassuringly.

"You going to have to testify, George?"

"They talked to me about it and, of course, I said I'd be happy to do anything they wanted me to do in the cause of Justice. But I suspect they have enough evidence without my two bits."

The news of the next day was still hot when Rod Dodson came to town accompanied by a pug nosed man named Oscar Whren. They checked into the hotel and stayed only a few days before leaving as strangely as they had come.

"You know, Ike, I think it's very peculiar 'bout the way Dodson dresses," said Jake.

"How's that, Jake?"

"Well, he's always got on that straw hat of his and that same old shirt with a starched Arrow Collar and one of them durn Texas string ties."

"Nothin' wrong with string ties, Jake. Used to wear one yourself when you was younger," replied Ed.

"I don't know. Maybe I did, but then I was no aspirin' president of no bank, neither."

"Have a sody, Jake? They're on me," said Ike as they all sat back to listen to the ball game.

--have you heard--yes, I've heard she was strangled--someone told me her eyes were gouged out of her head and hung on strings--you got it all wrong, it was a bullet through the heart--paper says they don't know what killed her--and with all them policemen too, how could anyone have gotten through--

SALLY-LOU STUART DEAD

--and they say that his name is Bill Marsh—what does he look like—he's six feet tall and has a German moustache—he's an Italian and speaks broken English--you've got it backwards, he's a nigger who broke out of jail in Mississippi for killing a white man--who is this man, the killer?--no, he's the new manager of the saloon--

EARLY THIS MORNING, THE BODY OF SALLY-LOU STUART WAS FOUND

--is he married--no one knows, except-- what--except he's going to change the name of the place or something--I hear that he ran a hot house in Memphis before coming here—nonsense, he was a hero in the European War-- was he a pilot—he received every decoration the Frenchies could pin on him and he's frightfully handsome--

"The cause of death is, as yet, undetermined and will be forthcoming as soon as"

--someone told me that they're buying the barbershop next to the saloon--what for--you say he's handsome? Is he married?—who knows--what did they buy it for?—you know it never made any money--

"The unexpected death came on the eve of what promised to be the climax of the two week trial, the testimony of Mrs. Stuart, herself, as she was scheduled to take the stand—"

--I swear, everything just seems to happen so quickly—he's in the hotel with another fellow, a Canadian—I think—did you know that they're going to close down the hotel--why, how did you hear that?--Sam told me that he just isn't getting the business now that they've got that new stretch of track east of here; we'll be by-passed by most of the trains--did you get the name of this other

man-- then he's not married?--Does he have a beard—which one do you mean?

"Doctor Murdock says he'll have to go through some tests to determine the cause of death—"

--does that other come from--you know hardly anybody showed up to old Colonel Rutherford's funeral, it was disgraceful--what kin did this Lucius Smith have?-- I'll bet she had some secret and was murdered to be silenced--he served this town for so many years and he was a good man, too-I always said she was crazy and that she'd cause Mr. Stuart a lot of heartache, she was a slut—first his rotten father and now his wife—poor man, he deserved so much more--

"Citizens are advised not to panic and to let the authorities do their jobs."

"You know, Ed, you don't get as much sody for your money as you used to."

"That's a fact, Jake; that's a fact."

Chapter 9

"A Trip to the Woods"

ON THE QUIET BEAUCHAY FARM, Samuel Beauchay was mercifully away on a trip to meet with some of the other large planters in Atlanta about cotton prices, which were dropping in comparison to the high prices that had been prevalent during the European War.

Jefferson was alone in charge of the farm. The boys were just coming back from a short nature trip with their tutor, who was explaining to the boys the ecological intricacies of their district. This subject interested John, though he had considerable practical knowledge on the subject already, but did not interest Jason. The latter could care less about bugs and grasses. Perhaps the boredom of the trip made Jason antsy, but soon, upon his strong and frequent complaints, the company was returning to the house with a jar full of insects which they had collected.

It might seem odd that Mr. Russel would suggest such a trip at all, considering his economic and political inclinations, but Samuel Beauchay, upon the suggestion of Jefferson, had encouraged Mr. Russel in the strongest terms that it would be well advised from his (Mr. Russel's) point of view, as well as that of the boys, to diversify the education of the children. And so Russel decided that a nature trip might be just the thing to broaden the young men's experience. He presented the idea with great enthusiasm, even though he was somewhat unprepared to act as a qualified guide on such an excursion since his own formal training in this subject area was nonexistent. He had only the library to aid him in his effort to familiarize himself sufficiently for the excursion.

"Now boys, that is a bracken fern: it can be identified because it is composed of a compound leaf and it is edible." As he talked, John listened some and looked about on his own while Jason occasionally took notes (though it must be admitted that an inordinate amount of his time was engaged in the artistic pursuit of adorning the margins of his pages with likenesses of automobiles and fancy clothes, which he would have liked to own if he suddenly inherited his father's money).

"Excuse me sir, but how does one eat a bracken fern?" asked Dow, who had known someone who had tried eating the leaves of the fern and had gotten sick from the experience. This seemed to contradict some of what Russel was asserting (though John didn't consider that other parts of the plant besides the leaves might be edible).

"And over here," continued Russel, in an arrogant tone, showing that he didn't care to answer Dow's silly questions, "is a clump of sedges which are like grasses except--"

"Sir?" interrupted Dow again.

"Not now, John," said Russel impatiently, as he wanted to finish his speech without bother. "The sedges are flat and not round like grasses."

"Those bracken ferns--" started Dow again.

"Young man, I'm not finished yet."

"But we're walking away from my question."

"Ask any questions when I'm done, and not before."

"But what if there aren't any more bracken ferns when you-"

"That will be quite enough," said Russel sharply. "Now you can always remember the difference between sedges and grasses by the jingle--" There was a loud crack as Jason's pencil broke. Russel glared at Jason.

"Can I have a knife, sir?" asked Jason. "My pencil broke and if I am to take notes on what you are saying, I need to have a pencil lead with which to write."

"Take John's; he's not using it," quipped Russel, as in fact Dow wasn't taking any notes but simply looking about.

"Sedges have edges!" blurted Russel as John handed Jason his pencil. The force of this statement made both boys turn and caused Jason to believe that the remark was directed towards him.

"Pardon, sir?" responded Jason, unable to quite understand what exactly was going on.

"The jingle: sedges have edges. It's how you tell grasses from sedges," said Russel in exasperation. "Sedges are flat and hence have edges; grasses are round. It's that simple."

"Are sedges edible too?" asked John.

"What?" said Russel, who was so elated over getting out all that he had to say that he was hardly prepared for this question. Then Jason sneezed so loudly and violently that he dropped his notebook in the mud and splattered the liquid earth all over his tutor.

"Damnation, Jason, what's gotten into you?"

"Oh shaw, sir," said Jason, emitting several sounds before sneezing again--this time as he was bending over to recover his book from the mud. As he bent, his handkerchief slipped out from his pocket and proceeded to make a most untimely and awkward floating descent through the air towards its murky destination. Jason, who was most fond of his handkerchief, and badly needed it to make amends for his previous misfortune at the humble mud puddle, most desperately tried to divert with several vain lunges the probable destination of the silk hanky. But Jason's flailing hands failed to snare the elusive linen. Finally, with one last effort, he swung both arms but with the same futile results, except that in his attempt (or because of the sincerity of his attempt) dear Jason lost his balance and soon followed his hanky--face down--into the cold murky pool.

Now, if the notebook splashing a little dirty water on Mr. Russel had caused him no little distress, then it can be understood what when, while clearing his spectacles (victims of the first accident), he saw the vague shape of a figure falling in his direction (for he was on the opposite side of the mud hole from Jason) he, Alfred Russel, might become somewhat excited.

This is exactly what happened as he instantly decided that the most economical course open to him of the several available to him was to vacate said position before said body caused said mud to cover his person. With this immediate resolve, he decided to scurry away from the vicinity when his feet, which were subject to the same conditions as on the opposite side of the mud hole, failed to perform their function of offering sufficient friction against the earth which would enable a person to execute a proper escape route. So though his feet continued with the same speed that prompted him originally to attempt his flight from the scene of the impending disaster, the slippery surface belied his intent. Thus, having no friction to allow the resultant force vector of the body to move forward, his feet merely continued in their direction as if the ground wasn't there and slipped over the mud until they were propelled upwards in the air due to a sudden shift in the subject's center of gravity, which caused the resultant force vector to alter the body's normal position.

In short: Russel fell on his seat in the mud hole while his glasses flew straight up in the air and landed only a few feet from him.

The sight of Jason, face down, and Russel, seated, in the mud hole was indeed a comical one. Though out of respect for the feelings of his two companions John restrained himself from laughter as much as he could, nature being as it is, his stoic effort served merely to slightly muffle a gentle roar of amusement.

After helping his comrades out of their difficulty and offering his shirt to help them clean their faces and hair (their own muddy clothes were useless for this task), they proceeded with even greater vigor towards their homeward destination. Now, as their trip had been somewhat protracted, and since neither Jason nor Russel were in a sociable mood, and since John didn't feel simply like vegetating around the house, he decided to ride to the Vanderkamps.

Dow felt like an ancient warrior atop his steed, similar to the types he had read about in the books that Jefferson had given to him. John wanted to be proud Achilles, killing all the Trojans, or mighty Hector in all his honor. The lad did make a pleasing sight on his horse, bare chested (as he had not replaced his shirt, which he had loaned to his friends) with his smooth young skin bronzed from the sun. Atop his head his curly black hair was striking as it leaned over in the wind. He was a finely built young man with chest muscles that were developed beyond what was normal for his years, a true indication of his great strength developed from his outings in the fields and the woods.

His mind was intent upon an imaginary battle in which he, John, was the great hero saving his comrades and bringing glory to his Country and to Almighty God. As he was concluding the battle, he brought his horse to a canter as the sound of the hoofs on the gravel made him feel all the more noble and victorious, when he was shaken from his dreaming by the sound of a motor car coming behind him. Sensible that horses hated the sound of loud engines, he steered his animal to the far left side of the road--off on the shoulder.

But the car apparently wanted the entire road and steered towards the animal to scare him. The horse reared back just as the car was passing and caused the driver to run into the ditch.

John was upset. The driver of the car had intentionally tried to frighten his horse and could have caused it to slide into the ditch or slip and break a leg—not to mention the possibility of John falling off and sustaining an injury.

The driver got out and turned, cursing John. It was Victor Stuart II. "Why can't you keep that damned animal off the road?" yelled Victor.

"The road's as much for horses as it is for those jalopies," returned Dow, who had never been particularly fond of young Stuart, who was four years his senior.

"Not when you can't control that horse, it isn't."

"It wasn't my fault. If you hadn't buzzed me--"

"I didn't buzz you, damn it, I was on my side of the road driving peacefully along--" John didn't know about all the trouble that had concerned the Stuarts in town, especially Victor's mother and the allegations about sundry, unnatural liaisons, or surely John wouldn't have allowed himself to become angry with young Stuart. But as the farm was often an isolated station away from the mad goings on of the town, he was, in truth, completely ignorant of what had transpired.

"Your side of the road, my foot! You deliberately drove towards my horse, which was on the opposite side--"

"Bull crap!" returned Stuart.

"The opposite side of the--"

"Bull crap--"

"--road where you were supposed to--"

"--You've got it all wrong—"

"-be with your automobile--"

"--you little nigger bastard."

Suddenly Dow was silent. He knew that he had been born of unknown parents. He had heard the term bastard used in connection with himself before, but he had never been accused of being a *nigger*. "What did you say?"

"You heard me you son-of-a-bitch nigger. Get your nigger hair and nigger body away from me, you ugly black thing."

Why was Victor saying this? John suddenly recalled how Jason had always remarked that his hair was *kinky, black,* and ugly. John looked at the new automobile. It was shiny, sleek and black. John knew that he could smash that sickly arrogant face. Victor, he could understand. Yet *Jason,* why? How beautiful Victor's blood would look if John punched him hard in the nose. What if he broke his nose? Would that make Victor ugly?

Dow jerked the head of his horse around and he managed to aim at his retreat under tight control as he said in disgust, "You make me sick."

"That's it. Run away nigger--*you* are sick--you goddamn--"

But Dow was out of hearing range so Victor got back into his Stanley Steamer and began the process of freeing his car from the ditch.

Chapter 10

"The Art of Checkers and Civilization"

"WHY D'YA 'SPECT she did it, Ed?"

"Don't know, Jake. 'Spect she was tired of all the fuss."

"But she done caused all da fuss herself with that murderin' in the first place. I don't know why she came back to town at all."

"That's jist how women are, I guess. Never know when they'll light-off with some fancy dan."

"Still," said Ed, "seems kinda funny that she should poison herself."

"I don't know; what did she have to live fer?" said Jake.

"Maybe she didn't do it?"

"What you talkin' bout, Ike? Course she done it. You think she's still alive or somethin'? Why there's lots of people who went to her funeral," responded Jake, tilting back in his chair.

"Just fer excitement, I reckon," added Ed.

"I think she's dead all right, what I don't git is why she'd go to all the fuss 'bout creatin' a commotion and then all of a sudden-like go and kill herself. Don't make no sense to me."

"You sayin' someone poisoned her, Ike?"

"I don't know nothing 'bout no murderin' or anything like that," Ike paused as a lady came in to buy some cloth. When the lady left Ike picked up where he had left off. "All's I know is that there was two people she wanted dead and she only got one of 'em."

All three shook their heads slowly as Jake got out the checker board.

***

"Deal me a hand there, Billy," said George Dodson as he entered the gaming establishment.

"Yes sir, George, or shall I say, Mr. President?" Dodson smiled at this retort and pulled out a chair with one hand while with the other he reached for a cigar.

"How does it feel to be a big shot, George?" asked one of the players as the rest smiled or chuckled at this question.

"I don't know; do you think I'll lose my money any faster?" Everyone laughed at this response as George added, "I'll expect you boys to start depositin' your winnings in my bank for safe keepin'."

"We'll do that, George."

"Cause that way I won't lose none. If I win, I put your money in there. If I lose, you return my money there. All the same: it's under one roof."

"Someone said that you're building a new vault, George, so that no one can break in and steal our money."

"Yup, that's right. I'm sending all the way to Canton, Ohio for a company who will do it. They're going to put in a new vault and re-model the old one, which we'll use for legal paper."

"But why do we need a new bank vault, George? No one's ever tried to hold this one up."

"You never can tell. There's been a lot of violence going around these days. Gangs are springing up everywhere. Besides, we're going to expand."

"Expand!"

"Yes, it's time for growth and we can all make a lot of money, if we play our cards correctly," said George as he looked at his hand, which was an inside straight.

***

At the Beauchay estate, Samuel was just returning from his three week conference when he heard the news from Charles Vanderkamp that George Dodson had been elected president of the bank.

"Why didn't someone tell me?" said Beauchay in a voice that was straining to control a raging anger.

"I would have, Samuel, except there wouldn't have been anything you could do. With Major Wheelwright gone, well, you're the only one on the board whom Dodson doesn't control."

"I could have done something."

"I'm afraid not, Samuel. Why don't you have a drink?"

"Where did you get that? You're own stock?" asked Beauchay about the illegal alcohol.

"No, this is brand-name merchandise. There's a new place in town that's selling a little of it; a drug store or something. I guess the guy had a few cases that he was trying to get rid of and so I sent in one of my boys to get me some."

"So you're sending hands into town to buy from some bootlegger? Charles, don't you know that if you and I, the big and important people in the area, don't abide by the law, then nobody will?"

"Oh, c'mon Samuel, nobody thinks the law is a good one. They're trying to repeal it in Congress right at this very minute. It's a Yankee law. Anyway, we all like a drop now and then. I know for a fact that you aren't averse to the taste of a good drink, eh?"

"Yes, I like a drink as well as anyone else, but the law says--"

"Law, law--what kind of law is it? A Yankee law, that's what. They passed it because in the North there aren't any civilized people so that when they start drinking they can't stop until they get stoned. The northern cities are full of lushes and winos. It's their primitive, animal-like tendencies showing through."

Both men laughed at this, though Charles Vanderkamp III thought it more humorous than his counterpart.

"Still, it's the law, Charles."

"Law, why is it the law? When did they enact such a law in our state capitol? The people of Georgia don't want any such law and by gosh, if we don't want any law from those Yankee Senators, then we don't have to follow it."

"That's anarchy," said Beauchay, though it must be admitted that he was somewhat moved by his neighbor's persuasive argument.

"It's only state's rights, Samuel."

"Well, whether you're correct or not, I don't like the looks of a national brand whiskey being sold."

"It's better than local stuff."

"That's not what I mean and you know it. That booze had to come from somewhere and you can assure yourself that it didn't simply originate from some local drugstore."

"I told you where I--"

"--New drug store, nothing, Charles, it takes connections to get brand name whiskey like that and I don't think that you or I want to let outsiders into our community."

"And turn Varner's Junction into a Chicago, I suppose?" laughed Charles Vanderkamp. "Listen, Samuel, I respect your point of view and I'm sympathetic to what you have to say, but believe me, I think you're making something out of nothing."

"Charles, it's like being out in the swamp and you see something that looks like a 'gator, but you're not quite sure so you keep going until you know for sure. In other words, when you can see that gator staring at you a few feet away, then you know what you're up against. But if you wait until you are that sure, then there is nothing you can do to stop the gator from devouring you. A boat's no match for a gator at close range. Sometimes a person can pay quite a price for certainty, Charles. Afternoon," said Beauchay as he picked up his hat and exited.

---Maybel, there hasn't been this amount of new faces in such a long time-- they say some's bought the hotel and is going to keep it running--and Barbara Ann had twins, declare, so many new faces--I've always adored that hotel with its dining room--I told Barbara Ann, now you just watch how much horseradish you eat or you'll have twins and sure enough she did--did you know that the glass for that chandelier came all the way from Venice, Italy—a person has to watch themselves when she gets big, why anything can happen--I do hope they put in some new carpeting; the old is just worn clean through. Why, I remember when I was big, why my husband, rest his soul, wanted a boy so badly that he had me lay outside under the full moon and expose my belly, I told him that nothing about the moon could make me have a boy, but then he told me about the tides and all. Well, you never can tell what will happen when you get big--it's not that we wouldn't have put him up at our place, but it's so small, you know, and anyway, Jeremy said his brother wouldn't mind at all--

The tall man seemed pensive when Samuel Beauchay returned home. The latter noticed Jefferson's reserve and suggested that they go and inspect the fields together.

"He's taking over the town, Jefferson."

"You know young Johnny's been having a hard time lately."

"My own sister's husband, and I've got to stop him."

"There was a rather bad incident last week."

"Of course, I don't know whether he's brought in the bootleggers, but they couldn't have gotten in at the very least without his implicit, if nothing else, approval and a juicy payoff somewhere."

The breeze blew about the two men but they paid no attention to the dust or to the bugs. I've got to get to town, Samuel thought, and see just what has happened since I've been gone. There is a distinct possibility that it's already too late. I should have done more when I had the chance. What did I do? If only I had acted, I could have averted the cancer which has grown. If only Dorthay had had more sense than to mix with such a vagabond villain as that Dodson. He's going to change this town and destroy our way of life if I don't do something. . . . Just look at Charles Vanderkamp, a man who I thought had more sense than that--buying and thereby supporting outside criminal elements in Varner's Junction.

His eyes, I can't get the vision of those eyes from my mind. Jefferson was full of thoughts about John. The aging man ambled with his hands in his pocket, eyes staring blankly at the ground. He didn't have to tell me, really. *When he looked at me like that, I knew. . . It had to happen someday and yet I didn't do anything to prevent it. I should have given him the talk. You can't hide something like that. I should have prepared him in some way or other.* His mind was obsessed with the boy.

--*Johnny, what's troubling you, boy.--Nothing.--Well, that's just about the worst kind, that nothing, because when nothing causes a long face, like you have right now, then I know that either you are an idiot, because idiots can become happy or sad with a snap of the finger over nothing, literally nothing at all, or you're really bothered about something and you don't want to talk about it. Now I know you aren't an idiot, so it must be the second alternative. --I hate myself; I want to die. --Now you are talking like an idiot. Maybe I ruled that first alternative out too quickly. --Jefferson, I got blue eyes, don't I? --What's gotten into you, of course you have blue eyes. --And you have brown eyes, right? --Yes, it doesn't take much to observe that. We've several other differences as well, for instance I'm taller than you. --Stop and tell me-- Then the boy started crying, like he did when he was little: uncontrollably. In all my stupidity, I still didn't see what had happened, what was bothering him.*

Samuel Beauchay brushed the hair out of his eyes without a notice. His thoughts were in Atlanta, amidst the other large growers who had gathered.

--*what you're proposing, Beauchay, is too radical, it'd never work. --Yes, it can, all we have to do is form a state-wide organization and encourage other states to do the same. We'd get our price back up very quickly if we controlled supply. --Sounds like unionism to me and you know, Beauchay, that's something we don't care much for, you know. --Call it whatever you want; it's just a group of farmers. --We are not just a group of farmers, Beauchay. --Yes, of course, but if you're worried about image, perhaps farmers would sound better for public relations.--The word farmer is never better! Sir, I am a plantation owner, a planter perhaps, but not a farmer. --That's beside the point. --On the contrary, sir, I think it is precisely the point. You seem to think of us as a group of common farmers. Well, sir, we are gentlemen. Yes, sir, that's exactly what we are. --I suppose you know yourselves best. --I don't like your tone, Beauchay.--What we need is some way to offset the demands of northern industry. For years I've been convinced that the only way to get a steady, reasonable price for our goods would be to organize and pool our common goods and sell it in large lots. --Sounds like Communism to me. This isn't Russia, Beauchay. --If we operate on a large scale, then we will be in a position to control the price. --We already have an organization. What do we need with another one? --I'm not suggesting another organization, we could use the existing one, but at present we are doing nothing that is useful. --I beg your pardon, sir-- I mean nothing that will counter those Yankee industrialists from cheating Southerners out of the profit that is their due. --Let's not appeal to patriotism to sell your proposal, Beauchay, --The buyers are a cartel. --No, they're not, the* fat cats were busted by *Roosevelt, don't you remember? --What was reported to have happened and what actually did happen are two different states of affairs. --Are you insinuating--I'm not insinuating anything, but simply stating that if the buyers are collected, then we ought to be also, as suppliers. --Mr. Beauchay, you* talk *like a Wobblie. --I assure you, sir, I am not. --This sounds like some half-crazed idea born in the bottom of an empty whiskey bottle. --I assure you, this is not some incoherent idea, but one that has been well-conceived and carefully plotted for quite some time.--It will never work. -- Why not? --It's crazy, that's why. --Give it a chance. --We're making more than we did before the War, why should we risk it in a cooperative. --Gentlemen, we were losing money before the European War and we'll be losing money again if we're not careful. --And the sky might fall, but we can't prepare for that eventuality because if we did, all our time would be devoted to ghost hunting and we would become paralyzed with sickly fear and* unnaturally *feminine trepidation.--Gentlemen, I hope that the night has freshened your minds to my proposal.--We've discussed this enough.--I move to table Mr. Beauchay's proposal* until *he can supply us with some hard facts. --Yes, the details; when is this to be carried out? Can it actually be done? Is there a realistic future in this scheme?*

--Who were my parents? ---No one knows, John. --I've heard that Mr. Beauchay was my father and some hired woman was my mother. --You can't tell about these things, John. It's a topic that most people like to keep confidential. That's why it's difficult to know sometimes just what happens that way between people. . . Why didn't I become candid with the boy? Here he was asking for my help and I simply talk around the subject, letting him believe whatever his gravest fears might be. *--You can't scare me with your talk. --Shut-up nigger, we don't like uppity types like you in Baltimore. You can clear out. –But my mother, was she some woman from the fields? --It doesn't matter who a person's parents are, John, it doesn't make you any better or any worse. --Yes, I know all that. but I want to know more about her, was she, I mean ah . . . But still I couldn't understand what was bothering him or why. --Do blacks, I mean Negroes have blue eyes? --I don't know. I have never seen any with blue eyes, but that isn't to say that it is genetically impossible, or any such thing. I don't know enough biology to determine whether they're any prohibiting factors. Possibly some may. Why do you want to know? What difference does it make?*

This was all the boy could bear, at which he cried out to me-- *I'm not a nigg--, a Negro, I'm not, I'm not, I'm not.* He screamed in a frenzy as the previous moments of conversation were finally making sense. *--Did someone say that you were black, son? --They called me a nigger, a bastard nigger. But I'm not; I've got blue eyes. I'm not, I'm not--am I?*

Then I remembered the first time that expression had been used to designate myself, and the empty hollowness I felt-- especially at college where I wanted to be a person. I became a category which somehow made me different from the very beginning. Anything that I did could be prefaced by: "that's pretty good, for a nigger." Or, "it's surprising how well he did, considering . . ."

I was not Jefferson John Brown, but a nigger: a six letter word that is cognate of the Latin word for black. I would automatically possess those universal characteristics attributed to being black. For without any effort, I could assume an identity and a role prepared by those who designated me as a genre. It was a swap: my new body for their old archetype. I could be something already programmed; complete with child-like flaws, which are acceptable since they had been placed there.

--I'm going to the meeting. --Don't Jefferson, I'm afraid. -- Listen, darling, these meetings are important if we are ever going to make any progress for our race. We can't expect anyone to do it for us. --But maybe if you wired the N.A.A.C.P. for some help. -- Honey, if you're scared about being here in the house unprotected, I can call Nathan over. --It's not me that I'm worried about. -- Look, I'm going to call Nathan over here anyway. I won't have you in jeopardy.

Thoughts of the many threats that he had received went through Jefferson's head as he walked to his neighbor's house. -- Say, Nathan, will you watch my wife for me while I'm gone. I have an uneasy feeling. At Jefferson's feet was John, the cat, who wanted to follow Jefferson. --C'mon girl, you've got to stay here and guard the house. The cat jumped in Jefferson's arms. He held and stroked the cat, noticing that the medallion that hung around its neck was broken. He took it off and put the strange shaped cross in his pocket, promising himself that he'd fix it at the first opportunity.

Then there was trouble. Fighting, disorder--everything destroyed; just as before. There was nowhere--no never nothing like the clashed edges of idealism and reality opposing.
"It can be done, blast it, oh, why would they listen?" said Beauchay.
The purpose of his life spread out before him in cold nothingness. First Peabody's murder and now--
"If only they would listen," said Samuel turning back to the house.
Jefferson was all alone. If he kept it up he would be next. That didn't bother him, but what did was the utter futility of--
Beauchay stopped and put his hand on Jefferson's shoulder, turning him around. Together they trudged back to the house.

***

"Now George, you must see that it is to our collective interest to force this thing out in the open." Beauchay stood before the aging sheriff who was sitting in his rocking chair in front of the police station.

"Don't say I blame you, Mister Beauchay," answered the sheriff.

"Well, you know what you were elected to do."

"Yep."

"Well, why don't you do it then?"

"Maybe I will."

"Maybe, George, the law is being broken over there in that drug store, and it's your job to stop it."

"You've been gone for a while, Mr. Beauchay, a lot has happened in the past couple of weeks."

"Yes, I know that; I've heard. But that doesn't mean that you're going to sit back and do nothing!?"

"Folks like it quiet, Mr. Beauchay. Being a big important land owner, you should appreciate that."

"Yes, the quiet is mighty fine. I love quietude so long as it's the peace of nothing happening, but when it's the peace of ignoring problems that need taking care of, then there is no peace, George, and we're dreaming if we imagine that there is."

The old sheriff scratched the back of his head slowly and sighed as if he wanted to be rid of all this commotion.

"Well, when I find some evidence that the law's been broken--" began the sheriff in his slow drawl.

"—Evidence, what do you think I'm giving you, George, the morning weather report?"

"I need hard evidence, Mr. Beauchay, you know that. To convict a man in a court of law, you need more than just accusations."

"Well, you won't get any evidence just lulling around here like a bump on a log."

"These things take time, Mr. Beauchay, lots of time."

"Yes, I know: life should be leisurely and calm, but when your town is being subverted more and more each day, then a man must move quickly."

The old law man got up and straightened himself so that he could shuffle back to the door, a sign to Beauchay that the interview was over.

"Got to make my rounds now," said George, who Samuel Beauchay saw as an archaic relic of an age gone by; an age when there was little need for a sheriff except to break up an occasional fight in the bar and to tip his hat to the ladies as they walked down the street. And though George Edwards was only four years older than Beauchay, himself, it seemed to Samuel that in actuality, Edwards was decades older. He was a fixture from the days when Old Colonel Rutherford used to be the only man in town who still wore stiff white collars and imported silk ties from Paris; when there were town holidays and everyone came to the estates for feasts and games. Yes, Samuel Beauchay could fondly remember several grand picnics that they had held at their place and how there would be dancing and games. The old men bet on the horse race and the young men would play croquet and pitch horseshoes. They didn't have much, really, in comparison to before--nothing like the lavish balls that he used to remember his uncle describing. But still, it was an exciting time--when everyone would get together and forget his suffering and hard times for one afternoon as white people of almost any station came to share in their sense of Southern Pride and community.

But now, no one seemed to care about those picnics. Ever since the European War, when the change in atmosphere caused a temporary halt which threatened to become permanent, nobody seemed to want to take the time. All that was left of the festivities of many weekends was the annual county fair and even that was just a fossil of the old festivities. Perhaps that was why everyone in town and thereabouts took the annual fair so seriously. Why, there were people entered in the horse race and the shooting contest from all around the state.

But a fair was different. It was bigger. It was less personal. No one could say anymore that he knew most of the people in Bella County. The loss of the picnics did a lot to cause that. There were scores and scores of faces that Samuel Beauchay knew he had never seen. These faces might have become familiar some sunny afternoon over a glass of something cool as the people made merry and he could vicariously enjoy a gaiety and freedom that he had never known as a youth growing up upon the ashes of a defeated Georgia.

How wonderful it seemed to Samuel that young people could gather and lose themselves in the unrestricted realm of playful pastimes with no care about the decisions and tensions. And then there were church meals. Families brought dishes, potluck, and so shared food as well as conversation. It was during these moments that the old men would spin yarns and talk about other times and so instruct the young in what it meant to be a Southerner with a magnificent heritage to maintain.

As George shuffled away, it seemed to Beauchay that he could almost hear the sheriff's old bones rattling, his hip rubbing the old, rusty Colt forty-five revolver, which he had probably purchased on a trip to Atlanta for two dollars. The last thing Samuel Beauchay wanted to do was force this man-monument of forgotten summers to risk his personal safety by poking his nose where it might get injured. Still, Beauchay saw the town and the imminent threat that ambuscaded behind the store front of the drug store. This outside influence could destroy everything in a way that the War Between the States never did or could: that is, destroy the fiber of the people. The town could survive a razing of property, but not the desolation of moral spirit which was being threatened by that festering bacteria of degeneracy at whose vanguard stood his brother-in-law.

"I hate to cause you so much bother, George," Beauchay said to the sheriff's back. "But we have to do something, or else we'll be as guilty as they are."

"Yes, Mr. Beauchay, yes, I'll see what I can do," said the other as he stopped once more to stretch in the late afternoon sun. Samuel Beauchay decided to check out the drug store for himself. So he headed over and walked in and sat at the counter.

"What'll you have?" asked a boy of about sixteen.

"Vanilla ice cream will be fine," responded Beauchay.

As the lad set about preparing the dish, Samuel Beauchay asked offhandedly, "This place is quite new, isn't it?"

"Yes sir," said the boy.

"Kind of strange how they could get this equipment and everything here so quickly since the last owners didn't leave very long ago."

"These fountains came all the way from Memphis."

"Almost sounds like they've planned on coming in for some time, doesn't it?"

"Yes sir, they sure got it in quickly."

Then the boy handed Beauchay his ice cream and Samuel dropped a nickel on the counter.

"What's your name, boy?"

"Lucas Reed, sir."

"Lucas Reed, oh--are you Peter Reed's son?"

"Yes sir," answered the boy, who was busily engaged in the project of washing the already clean counter top.

"Have you worked here long, Lucas?"

"No sir, just four days."

"How'd you get the job?"

"My pa got it for me."

"Do you like the job?"

"Yes sir, I ain't got no complaints."

"Do you have a nice boss?"

The boy started cleaning a part of the counter that he had just finished cleaning. "Yes sir, I ain't complaining."

The boy was now furiously polishing the same circular area of counter over and over, but Beauchay wanted to get closer to the kind of information that he needed. "I don't think I remember the owner of this store, your boss I mean. What did you say his name was?"

"Ah, Mister Marsh."

"Marsh, Marsh--that doesn't sound like a name from around these parts."

"It's not," came a voice from behind as the storeroom door swung open, revealing a small man wearing an apron. "I'm not from these parts," finished the man. "My name is Marsh, Bill Marsh. I'm the owner of this drug store, and may I have the pleasure of knowin' to whom I am addressin'?"

"Certainly, Mr. Marsh, My name is Samuel Beauchay."

"I heard you asking the boy here some questions," said Marsh, who waved the boy into the other room with a gesture to which the lad quickly responded.

"Do you want to know anything in particular, or were you just passing the time of day?" he said bluntly.

Beauchay tried to size Marsh by his physical appearance, but this task was exceedingly difficult—All Marsh's features were unexceptional. This made physiognomy impossible.

"Yes, I heard you had some special commodities that you are selling."

Marsh hesitated momentarily as if (it seemed to Beauchay) he were deciding about whether Beauchay was a good risk. Samuel wondered whether Marsh would ask him to go into the back room or ask the boy to take some time off, for Beauchay was certain that the boy had nothing to do with any illegal alcohol.

"Well, what did you have in mind? As you can see, we have a number of very special items on the counters here," said Marsh, motioning about the store. So he's going to play it that way, is he, thought Beauchay. Well, at least he's not some rube who accidently came into a small stack somewhere as Vanderkamp deluded himself into believing. This fellow knows his racket or else he's an extremely trained employee of someone who does.

"I heard that sometimes you carry extra merchandise which you don't keep on your shelves," said Beauchay.

"Well sir, to tell you the truth, we've just opened and there's quite a few items which we will have, but don't as yet carry. Perhaps if you would like to make a special order I could fill it for you in a couple of weeks." Marsh got out his pen and poised himself to copy the necessary information on a slip of paper.

Beauchay rubbed his nose and smiled. "No, that won't be necessary for the moment. But I would like to have a look around, if you don't mind. You see, I'm curious at how you've set it up," said Beauchay as he started to make his way towards the storage room when his path was blocked by Marsh, who managed to interpose himself between Beauchay and the door.

"I'm afraid you can't go in there, Mister Beauchay."

"Why not?" asked Beauchay innocently.

"It's not the policy to let customers into the back room, what with there being prescription drugs and the like back there."

"Oh, you're going to be a pharmacy too?"

"Yes, if we can get a pharmacist."

"Don't you know? It seems rather strange that an owner of a drug store doesn't even know whether he's going to have a pharmacist or not."

"A pharmacist was planned for this store, but when he's coming has not been arranged. He might stay in one of our other stores."

"Your other stores? You mean this is part of a chain?"

"Yes, ah, didn't you know that?" asked Marsh, angrily as if he was upset at having given Beauchay that piece of information.

"Oh, then, you're just the manager of this store and not the owner."

"Do you have any more business, Mister Beauchay? Perhaps you'd like some more ice cream?" said Marsh in a controlled tone as he quickly recovered his composure.

"No thank you, I've had enough for this afternoon," said Beauchay as he left now in complete certainty that Mr. William Marsh was indeed a bootlegger, who was being controlled by someone else. But the element that surprised Beauchay was how Marsh was tipped off that he, Beauchay, would be a person that couldn't be trusted. Either Bill Marsh was naturally cautious or he had some information about whom to trust.

As Beauchay passed the old saloon, a familiar old odor was mixed with the normal cigarette and cigar smoke. It didn't occur to Samuel Beauchay until he was riding back to his farm that the smell was alcohol. Perhaps they were buying their booze somewhere else, or maybe there were several distributors. Maybe the drugstore wasn't the central distribution point at all. Possibly several establishments were buying from a common source. But who or what was this common source? These things Samuel Beauchay resolved to discover; however, the next day he became preoccupied with a small fire that burned a share cropper's house and part of the field. Beauchay's attention, for the time, was again diverted towards his fledging estate.

Chapter 11

"Containing an Account of some Sore Subjects"

"YOU DON'T REALLY KNOW what race you are, John," Jefferson began, "but whatever race or mixture you are, you are certainly not a *nigger*. What I mean, son, is that nobody is a nigger because that denotes a class of associated pejorative traits which the declarer feigns not possessing. If there is anything to be said about man's love of condemnation of his fellow man and the persecution of his differences it is, 'let he who is without fault cast the first stone. . . and judge not lest you be judged.'"

Dow simply stared at the ground, his hands folded, biting his lip.

"Do you understand what I am saying, son?"

John still didn't raise his head. All that he understood at that moment was that anyone could have been his parents--even Jefferson himself. Why was his skin always so brown when often other children would get burned in the heat of the sun and become red? It was because, he told himself, that his skin was of a Negro. This meant that he really wasn't like Jason at all. Jason was white and he, John, was black. And yet, he said to himself, I have blue eyes which would mean that I am white (which he now felt he wasn't). It was all very confusing.

The question that teased him the most, however, was the identity of his parents. He became obsessed with it.

"Who were my parents?" he blurted suddenly.

"I don't know."

"Who do people say they were?"

"You can't go by what people say, John."

"I know that argument; you've used it before with me. What I want to know is who do people say my parents are."

"Whoever they were, they've probably long since gone," said Jefferson, who in all honesty didn't believe that John should know that most people firmly believed Mr. Beauchay and Myra Dow were John's parents. He, Jefferson, also believed this to be true, but he wasn't certain, so he didn't feel right in telling John about it. Certainly, John just minutes before had mentioned Samuel Beauchay as a possible parent. Jefferson had been able to fend off this inquiry. But Jefferson did not know if John's statement originated from ignorance (a wild guess) or from some information that he, Jefferson, didn't know Dow possessed. Somehow, it seemed to Jefferson that no good could come out of his revealing to John his own opinions about who Dow's parents were, because first there would be no real way of checking without directly questioning Beauchay, which would be a project that Jefferson didn't feel willing to undertake. And second, there might be entire reserves of unspoken resentment that might pour forth against Mr. Beauchay from the young boy, who was understandably troubled by this entire situation and the state of unknowing. Though this fear was largely seminal and not explicated within Jefferson's mind, he nevertheless felt an overwhelming inhibition against discussing with Dow any further the possible candidates responsible for his genetic origination.

"You know if you don't tell me, I will find out from someone else."

"Why do you want to know?"

"Because I have to know."

"But what does it matter?"

"It matters."

"No, it doesn't, for whoever they were, whoever they are not, if they are even still alive, you are still *yourself*. Nothing can alter that. You are what you are, independent of your parentage. Examine the possibilities: if they were scoundrels, then are you a scoundrel? Will the knowledge of their personage make you a scoundrel? How can there be any logical relation between how and what they were and what you are not? How can you really benefit from finding out—even if that were possible? For how can you ever find out about something that happened sixteen years ago? Do you suppose that even if you did stumble upon the right woman, that she would admit to being your mother? She may have since married and have had other children—all of whom would be hurt by such an admission. No, son, there's little likelihood of finding out for certain even if you did find the woman, a task in itself that is fraught with so many obstacles that you could scarcely be confident of attaining your goal. Because who's to say that men are correct? One might become ensnared in lies that people have traded back and forth in their gossip and have come to believe simply from the longevity of the tale as opposed to any real evidence that would, in any fashion, substantiate it." Jefferson paused. His tirade was more for himself than for Dow. The manner in which he phrased it lost Dow quickly, who was still deeply troubled and not able to devote his concentration to Jefferson's arguments.

"In conclusion, John, you'll never be able to ascertain from any source the certainty of your parentage. Therefore, it is foolish to spend any more time in this line of inquiry."

Dow, now perceiving that Jefferson had finished, felt a strong surging within his chest, such that he couldn't respond in any way but with tears as he put his head against Jefferson's shoulder and hugged his friend while he cried.

Chapter 12

"A Reflective Chapter on Ambitions and Executions"

DORTHAY DODSON CAREFULLY took a freshly baked chocolate cake out of the oven. She found that she spent most of her time in the kitchen even though they could now afford a cook. It was something to occupy her time and center her thoughts. Her little ten year old daughter, Grace, had said she'd help her, but Grace was out playing with little Georgie Jr. instead.

Then in popped young Howard from playing.

"Can I help you mommy?"

"Yes, dear, just wash your hands first," reminded his mother, who was very happy that she had company--not only company, but the company of her eleven year old Howard. Somehow, Howard seemed different to her from the others. Whereas each of his siblings had some of the commonness of her husband, only Howard seemed immune to his vulgarity, and for this she loved him above the rest.

"What are you making, mommy?" asked Howard as he washed his hands in the sink.

"A chocolate cake for everyone."

"Good, I like chocolate cake."

"I'm glad, dear," she responded, when really her thoughts were on the tone of young Howard's voice and how it reminded her of her own brother's voice when they were small. What a dashing figure he was to her as he always talked boldly of recovering the *old life* that Colonel Rutherford had described to them once as youngsters. How Samuel had filled his sister's heart with dreams of a future that would never be actualized. How she had longed to find a man of her brother's stature and vigor, but the War had taken care of the best breeding stock. This depleted the suitable young men for belles like Dorthay who longed for something elegant.

Instead, those who returned were cowards and un-masculine runts that produced deformed litters. Most of the true men had died, for only a few of the front line personnel, which included only the cream of the junior officers, were not buried before the surrender. The men, by and large, who returned were mostly the ones who couldn't make the front line assignments or were too cowardly to accept them. But even the brave men who returned were different from when they had left. They seemed like they were sleepwalking through life and they drank too much.

Uncle Marcel, she thought, was an exception to the rule. There was nothing in the War that made him effeminate. There was no hint of weakness in his virile personality which subdued all and everything that stood in his way. He never married because (she was convinced) he knew that the breeding stock was too depleted for him to have children. Those weak-willed females didn't recognize a real man when they saw one. It would be to waste his seed. Yet, he was wrong. The only hope for the South was (and is) for the few strong men left to assert themselves to rebuild the fallen empire. It would take men who knew the value of courage and exercising raw power. Men like this would become giants and form a new ruling class in Georgia. They would create a power structure and social hierarchy so magnificent that a millennium could not topple its mighty bulwarks.

At times she believed that George would be such a man. Certainly he was strong enough and had a great will, but there was that incessant crudity about him that always bothered her. True, there had been something sexually alluring about being involved with a man so common and crude. Perhaps this was the irrational part of her that had first attracted her to George. But in other moods her breeding won out. When she was alone, she knew she couldn't repudiate the heritage of Philip Beauchay. And George Dodson, for all his strength and power, would never be anything except common.

But men like Philip Beauchay were no more. Philip had been one of the more powerful men in Georgia. He was appointed Colonel in the Confederate Army before being killed at the "young" age of sixty-three (for he was still a vigorous man at the end). They said that it took nine Yankee bullets to finally kill him. Three quarters of a dozen pieces of lead finally felled that magnificent figure from his horse. Philip had chosen his rank over a general's post because he wanted to fight and lead his loyal Southerners to the glorious victory he knew they could achieve. Perhaps it was a kindness that he should die before the tide turned against the South. Though perhaps had he lived, he might have made the difference in key battles like Gettysburg and Shiloh. How could the brave Confederates win when their best officers were dead? Didn't the Chancellorsville victory come at the price of Stonewall Jackson? Why did the War take so many of the best men? There were many stories of the valor of Dorthay's grandfather that used to thrill her as a little girl. But perhaps the most poignant to her was one that Colonel Rutherford told her about the first battle of Bull Run. They had been weak on their flank. A vital rail link was being threatened, so Colonel Philip Beauchay was ordered to reinforce. When he rode up with his men, he witnessed a relatively even fight, though events were starting to go poorly for the Confederates. Many Southern boys were becoming afraid and fleeing from the scene of the fighting so that soon it would be impossible for those Southerners who were staying to be able to hold back the superior numbers of the Yankees. Philip Beauchay, instantly assessing the situation with his keen senses, rode forward. He pointed his saber over his head and led his men with a fierce battle cry that froze those boys who were running away and instilled new bravery into their hearts. The sight of one man on a thoroughbred horse galloping headlong into gunfire brought his men fiercely running behind. All the Confederates were inspired by his courage and bravery so much that they fought like fresh troops and turned back the superior Yankee forces, and so were instrumental in the Confederate victory on that battle field.

Of his sons, her father and uncle, it was her uncle who most distinguished himself, fighting in General Lee's army with distinction.

Her own father was a man who detested war with a passion, though he did fight in the west during the early part before sustaining a wound from which it took him a year and a half to recover. For many reasons, her father was a quite disagreeable figure to her because he represented appeasement rather than vigorous and all-consuming zeal. All this she heard from her uncle

Marcel, for her first-hand recollections of her father had long since vanished as she was only three years old when he died.

Marcel was a rough man who controlled the blacks on his plantation. For this she greatly admired him. He built his financial situation from a position of almost bankruptcy (a position which her father left to him when he died) to a very sizeable figure (or so she had been told).

However, Marcel hated social gatherings that had a formal nature like balls and parties (though he did offer his land to be used in the annual horse race which later was incorporated into the county fair). This aspect of him was different than either Samuel's or Dorthay's taste. Samuel used to talk about how he would make their plantation the social center of the county when he finally got control of it. They would spend days and days making plans for imaginary events which would, in their dreams, occur when Samuel became owner of the estate.

It was during this time that Dorthay liked her brother most. His strength and grace made him a more exemplary man than Uncle Marcel, who didn't share Samuel's enthusiasm for formal delicacies, though it should not be implied that Marcel was in any way impolite or common. He was simply cast from a rough mold. His was a simple life. He sought to improve his power by extending the boundaries and increasing the revenues of his land.

Dorthay enjoyed the thought of finery like she read about in books. She cherished her regal and aristocratic dreams. Then Marcel died. Suddenly the whole lot fell to her brother. She had such high expectations for her future and the complexion of the estate. But instead, their style of living was cut back some without explanation. Her brother became moody and sometimes wouldn't talk to her. She thought that perhaps something happened to southern gentlemen when they passed from the stage of aspiring heir to actual owner that turned them into a new species. The metamorphosis had lasted for almost a year when he announced that they were going to travel in Europe for a vacation. Again, her dreams were kindled as she spent long hours in preparation for what seemed to her a most glorious opportunity to realize a longing that she had envisioned: to return to the land of their ancestors where "knowing how to do" was the highest compliment a French gentleman could receive.

During the trip, her brother became slightly more intimate, but was still not his old self. A change had transpired. If the real test of a man is how he handles himself in positions of power, then her brother was not faring as well as she had imagined he would. Yet there were flashes of the Samuel Beauchay with whom she had climbed into the hayloft and hid while the darkies were working in the yard. Here they discussed any number of topics and tomorrow's fragile realm of 'maybes'.

These flashes, as well as the inherent charm of the places they saw, buoyed her spirts for years even as her brother was drawing further away into his own world; a place which didn't include her.

Dorthay became convinced that the man on the farm was neither keeping a sturdy hand on things nor infusing the environment with culture. There would be moments when she would be sure that he was going to turn things around as he would act brilliantly during some particular crisis. At these times he was the brother of old.

But in most other times, he would be indecisive and inactive. He locked himself into his study or took day-long rides on his horse away from everyone. In short: he wasn't the same man day-after-day, but vacillated between a normal queerness and a visionary of grandeur.

It was for these brief moments of magnificence that Dorthay lived. She hoped that they would last or that the next moment would arrive soon. All the while she felt that the fortunes of the estate were slowly dwindling from her vision of how Marcel had left them.

Then Samuel married. His wife brought him further down because she was a weak woman. Mary Lou Vanderkamp had always seemed to Dorthay, even when they were growing up, to be one of the poorest examples of the marriageable stock in the county. And I was right, Dorthay congratulated herself: she died after her first child-- while I've had seven--that is, six of my own. Named after the Presidents: Theodore, William, Woodrow, Howard and then Grace and George Jr.

Samuel still maintained his delicacy and love of the fine arts, and at intervals became passionate about them, though he soon resigned himself to talk about how the cities were becoming cultural centers and the people in the county had best content themselves with what they could see upon sorties to the cities.

This was much different from the man of her dreams. She was pleased that he kept his book shelf stocked with blue leather editions of classic English novels and bought countless folios of piano music, which he used to play with his sister (that is, whenever the noise did not give Samuel's fragile wife a headache). But somehow she felt he had less of that electric magic about him now that he was married--even in his best moments. There was no restless urge to make his estate the grandest. He seemed satisfied with simply running it at the levels that it had always been operated since falling into his control.

With the entire state in the depressed condition it was at the turn of the century, it was ripe for someone with power to enter and to organize. But Samuel didn't have it in him--no that's wrong, she said to herself, he did have it in him, for all the hours spent in endless discussion showed a mind grand enough to dream, a mind capable of greatness. Yes, it was a mind that could dare--yes, dare to imagine new ideas and to organize them into plans. Samuel could have been the man to save the southern way of life, but his wife and something else foiled the execution. Dorthay was certain that his wife was principally responsible for bringing him down so that he could never realize his destiny.

Dorthay started melting the chocolate and asked Howard to measure out some sugar for the frosting. The kitchen was chilly because it was on the east side of the house and it was late afternoon. The wind was gusting over their newly acquired, unplanted fields (formerly owned by the Stuarts) so that some dust was being blown about. The wind sprayed the grit against the window screen, causing a scraping noise that made the kitchen, Dorthay thought, seem very hollow, like the inside of a block of wood, being devoured slowly from the outside by microscopic invaders.

Theirs was the old Rutherford place. Dorthay asked Howard to get her sweater as she huddled over the hot stove thinking about a day such as this in 1864 when Cybil Rutherford and her four children were butchered in cold blood by hulking Yankee animals, who dismembered Cybil so severely that all her limbs could not be reconstructed for the burial.

Outside, the wind was wailing. Often she wondered why she had been so drawn to George. His very baseness was magnetic. At other times though (particularly when she was alone) that common streak in her husband made her revolt inside. It was so foreign to her Beauchay blood.

As the frosting began to thicken, she set to beating it furiously with her wooden spoon to enrichen the texture of the sweet, full-bodied icing.

Book Four

The Man Behind the Work

I'm often asked if I know the author of a particular piece that is presented upon stage, and if I'd make an introduction in the green room. I confess that I regularly get the opportunity to talk to the writer when the play is in rehearsal, because he generally has much to inquire about how the director has asked for certain specifications and such. But I'm always impressed about how much interest some authors show in their work, down to the last detail, while others merely leave it to the production crew and spend their advances. Why is it that people like to talk to the author? Part of it must be the special appeal of a famous personage, though often an author is quite unknown to most of the public when they play our modest establishment. Perhaps the public feels that they can better understand the work if they speak with the man or woman who constructed it. I must confess that there is something attractive about this arrangement. Who knows more about what's in a play than the author? I held this view for many years, until I heard a producer and a writer arguing over whether this fellow was going to direct his own show. The writer made the argument that I just presented to you, while the producer said that a writer doesn't have the distance and objectivity to really see what's in the script and what might make it good theater or bad. This intrigued me, for it had always seemed to me that only the writer could truly know what his or her own play meant.

      This question got me thinking, and I went about talking to people about this very topic. Some people would say to me that once the play was down on the page, the author understood no more about what it was than any other critic who knew the text well. A writer under this theory might create something and not have the foggiest notion of what it was really about. The writer who has had one big success which he never repeats might be an example of this. He wrote something, and got lucky, not really being in control of what he was doing. The writer could not repeat his success. However, it seems that what a writer is thinking about must have *something* to do with what it means, even if it is out of her hands at some point and the property of the critics-at-large. The critic who is also a creator must have an advantaged position in the understanding of the artifact, for only she knows what prompted her to write such-and-such line in a particular way and not like something else.

In defense of this last idea, I must recall an incident that happened to me when I was first being introduced to the ways of the theatre by a gentleman named Robert Herbertson. Mr. Herbertson knew the theater from London to Bristol, but now was in a little building in Coventry. On the front of the proscenium that faced the audience were the initials W.S. with a little devil's head on each side. I had always assumed that the initials stood for William Shakespeare, the patron of English theatre. I had paid little attention to the little devils. One day I was sitting with one of the workers in props and told her the story (which I invented) of the origin of the initials and how they came from Stratford-on-Avon and had been removed from there when a theatre burned down during the Glorious revolution of 1686 and brought to Coventry. It was a marvelous story, but unknown to me Mr. Herbertson was listening, or rather was in a position where my little fancy could be heard. Backstage he told me, "That bloody 'W.S.' stands for Walter Skelton, son of the man who built this theater in the last part of the nineteenth century. It seems that the father hated his son and so he put him in the most comical place he could, considering that his son had taken clerical orders and was a most disgraceful wretch who believed that the Theatre was the Devil's workshop."

The point of this long digression is to illustrate that something can, objectively speaking, have a coherent meaning that is completely different from the meaning that was intended. Now, this would indicate that *to say* something and *to mean* something are really different enterprises. In more skillful writers, perhaps, what they say is what they mean to say. The mistaken advertising bulletin which said, "Being theater goers, we at Temple theatre have a lot to offer you this year," could not have been intended to be read as it does read. The Temple theatre organization was just that, an organization, and not the theatre goers. The poor construction of the sentence seems to indicate a reversal of roles. This is an extreme example of the objective product, saying something entirely different from what was intended.

It seems that, with an artful author, there is a control of intention and meaning so that the former is infused into the latter and a reader conversant with the rules of grammar and vocabulary will be able to get the "sense" from the passage. This does not preclude other meanings that may be in the work that the author did not intend, but in clear writing it seems that such interpretations must not be contradictory to the author's intended meaning, or else the writing was ambiguous from the beginning. Other readings must conform to the general thrust of the author's intention if he has done his job properly. For the task of setting words and stage directions on the page is one in which a focus is being attempted, either about thoughts or feelings. When this focus is sharp, anything outside of this purview cannot (by a good reader) be mistaken for that which is inside. Consequently, any interpretation of the meaning of the focused thought or feeling must conform to what has been selected by the author, i.e., to fall within that focus. Thus, a well-focused piece of writing will elicit interpretations (by good critics) that are not in essential contradiction, though there may be endless incidental disputes. Any ambiguity must be intentional and contribute to the story in a self-conscious fashion. But it cannot be accidental or it will cause problems that indicate that the author, himself, was confused (unless, of course, this is itself an issue).

The conclusions one may draw from this are that an author is important to her work because she is the seat of the intention. Also, though an author may not understand all of the meanings that are within her particular work, she should have controlled her medium sufficiently so that the range of interpretations falls within the parameters of her own focused intention, or follows directly as corollaries.

Thus, whenever one of my friends or acquaintances asks to see an author, I say, "Of course," and I take him to see the fellow and stand conveniently within hearing so that I might also learn more about the man behind the work. And though I do not believe that the work is less important than the man or the imagination which produced the work, I won't go to the other extreme either but rather like to think of my own designing of costumes, which reflect a process. The process is important, and can be understood only through its concrete entities: the author and his text.

Exhibits:

"Francis is going to be married."
"Who's the lucky man?"
"I am. She rejected me."
                    Talk outside a Las Vegas, wedding parlor.

"Marcia, I could *die* for your sake."
"You are always saying that, but you never do it."
                    Chatter among two West End costume designers

The events which have just been related mark a turnabout in the old enmity between Latin and Celt. The Gauls will never again march upon Rome with a light heart. For now once the battle will be upon Gallic soil and the Gauls will be the invaded and not the invaders. The founding of Ariminum in 268 B.C. just below the Rubicon is a permanent sign of this change in fortunes.
                    De Bello Gallico, Caesar. my tr.

Worshippe ye that lover is bene this May,
For of your blisse the kalendis are begonne,
And sing with us. Away, Winter away!
Cum, Somer, cum, the suete season and sonne!
Awake for shame! that have your hevynnis wonne,
And amorously lift up you hedis all,
Thank lufe that list you to his merci call!
                    "Spring song of Birds" John Lydgate

This is o word for al; this Troilus
Was nevere ful to speke of this matere,
And for to preisen unto Pandarus
The bounte of his righte lady deere,
And Pandarus to thanke and maken cheere.
This tale was ay span-newe to bygynne,

Till that nyght departed hem atwynne.

Soon after this, for that Fortune it wolde,
Icomen was the blisful tyme swete
That Troilus was warned that he sholde,
There he was erst, Criseyde his lady mete;
For which he felte his heart in joie flete,
And feithfully gan alle the goddes herie;
And lat se now if that he kan be merie!

And holden was the forme and al the wise
Of hire commyng, and eek of his also,
As it was erst, which nedeth nought devyse.
But pleynly to th'effect right for to go,
In joie and suerte Pandarus hem two
Abedde brought, whan that hem bathe leste,
And thus they ben in quyete and in reste.

> *Troilus and Criseyde* III. 11. 1660-80
> Geoffrey Chaucer

She came to the curtain and cast her eye
On Sir Gawain, who at once gave her gracious welcome
And she answered him eagerly, with ardent words
Sat at his side softly, and with a spurt of laughter
And a loving look, delivered these words:
"It seems to me strange, if, sir, you are Gawain,
A person so powerfully disposed to good,
Yet nevertheless know nothing of noble conventions,
And when made aware of them, wave them away!
Quickly you have cast off what I schooled you in yesterday
By the truest of all tokens of talk I know of."
"What?" said the wondering knight, "I am not aware of one.
But if it be true what you tell, I am entirely to blame."
"I counselled you then about kissing," the comely one said;
"When a favour is conferred, it must be forthwith accepted:
That is becoming for a courtly knight who keeps the rules."
"Sweet one, unsay that speech," said the brave man,
"For I dared not do that lest I be denied.
If I were forward and were refused, the fault would be mine."
"But none," said the noblewoman, "could deny you, by my faith!
You are strong enough to constrain with your strength if you wish,

If any were so ill-bred as to offer you resistance."
"Yes, good guidance you give me, by God," replied Gawain,
"But threateners are ill thought of and do not thrive in my country,
Nor do gifts thrive when given without good will.
I am here at your behest, to offer a kiss to when you like;
You may do it whenever you deem fit, or desist,
In this place." The beautiful lady bent
And fairly kissed his face;
Much speech the two then spent
On love, its grief and grace.

Sir Gawain and the Green Knight st. LIX

Troilus spoke to her in a similar
Manner as they formed a tender embrace.
Speaking in playful words
As lovers do to express such delights
While kissing one another's mouths,
Eyes, and breasts, expressing
Greetings which their letters

Had left unexpressed.
Troilus felt gay contentment and song
No other lady of beauty or attraction
Held he in esteem as long
As he could have his Cressida with him.
He believed that all the throngs
Of men lived in sad distraction

In comparison with his good fortune
So pleasing was life's continuation

"il Filostrato" Boccacio, III, st. 69, 72, tr. mine

The one, Alethes, of vile lineage sprung, Who in obscurest shade his
    course began,
Rose, be smooth flatt'ries and a fluent tongue, To the first honors of
    the grave Divan;
A supple, crafty, various-witted man-- Promo at deceit, perfidious in
    his phrase, He with a smile of sweetness could trepan;
And wove his webs in such ingenious ways,
That each caluminous charge had all the air of praise.

"Jerusalem Delivered," Tasso, Canto II. st. LVIII, tr. J.H. Wiffen

When all treasures are tried, Truth is the best.
Learn it to these lewd men, for lettered men it know:
That Truth is treasure, and the triest on the earth.
"Yet have I no kind of knowledge," said I;
"yet must you knew me better,
By what craft in my corpse it commences, and where."
"You dotard daff," said she, "dull are your wits;
Too much Latin you learned, lad, in your youth:
Heu michi, quia sterilem duxi vitam iuvenilem!"

Notes: lewd= simple; triest=best; daff=dullard; Latin= Oh, what a useless life I led when I was a youth.
The Vision of Piers Plowman, Passus I, 11. 133-139

So then, have as much love as you like,
Go to gatherings and parties,
But in the end, it will be no better life
You'll only break your skull.

Jenin L'Avenu
Go get a bath
And when you get there

Jenin L'Avenu
Don't wash till you're bare
And use the tub that's there

Jenin L'Avenu
Go get a bath
François Villon, stanza one of a double Ballade; "Rondeau, #7" tr. mine.

Three years had passed since the death of the virtuous Zelia. For a time, Alfred was in extreme torment; by day, he seemed to see a vengeful hand descending toward his head; he trembled at night because the darkness brought him hideous, frightful dreams. Soon, however, he banished from his thoughts both the painful memory of the martyr and the terrible threat Georges has made; he married and became a father . . . . Oh! How gratified he felt, when he was told that his prayers were answered, he who had humbly kissed the church floor each even, beseeching the Virgin of Sorrows to grant him a son.

Victor Séjour, *The Mulatto,* (1837) tr. Philip Barnard.

You bid me hold my peace
    And dry my fruitless tears.
Forgetting that I bear
    A pain beyond my years.

You say that I should smile
    And drive the gloom away
I would, but sun and smiles
    Have left my life's dark day.

All time seems cold and void.
    And naught but tears remain;
Life's music beats for me
    A melancholy strain.

I used at first to hope,
    But hope is past and gone;
And now without a ray
    My cheerless life drags on.

Like to an ash-stained hearth
    When all its fires are spent;
Like to an autumn wood
    By storm winds rudely shent—

So sadly goes my heart,
    Unclothed of hope and peace;
It asks not joy again
    But only seeks release.

Note: "shent" means "damaged"
    Paul Laurence Dunbar, (1913) "Worn Out"

Cancer

Solution

Chapter 1

"Introducing the Heroine of this History"

THOUGH IT IS NOT A LAW of logical necessity that neighbors, people who live in close proximity, need as a result to be amiable; in fact, it is often the case that such proximity causes enmity instead. However true this may or may not be in regards to society at large, it was not true between the Vanderkamps and Beauchay's, who were the closest of friends. Both Samuel and Dorthay even played with Charles and Mary Lou when they were children (owing partly to the close proximity and also to the good relations between Charles Vanderkamp II and both Marcel and Jacques Beauchay). So it was not at all surprising that Jason and John made frequent visits to the Vanderkamp estate to play with young Rodney and his sister.

Young Rodney was a boy who loved sports, almost, as the popular expression goes, from that time at which he could ambulate without the structural assistance of another's hands or any other artificial aid. This owed partly to his naturally athletic constitution and partly to his father's notion that a good athlete in the family would show to other families what a fine blood line was indigenous to the proud Vanderkamp tradition. Indeed, this parental encouragement went as far as prompting the gift of a baseball to Master Rodney on his fifth birthday, a gift which he could not, due to his young years, fully appreciate at the moment, but which his father was convinced would prove to be one that he (Rodney) would long cherish and hold dear as one of the most apt gifts that he ever received. And though as a lad Rodney was quite short for his age, his father was also convinced that this was to be no true indication of his son's final stature, of which the father believed would be considerable indeed.

Rodney's sister, Julia, was entirely different from her brother. Like all Vanderkamp women, she was endowed with soft features and an extremely pleasing appearance. So much so that many of the young lads used to come over to the Vanderkamps on the pretext of seeing Rodney, when really they wanted to see fair Julia (for so young people are often bashful about making any direct demonstrations of certain feelings). It has been said that a woman of real beauty cannot be adequately described by herself, but only through what others think of her. And so it is also of little girls, for Julia charmed all the young men that came to visit Rodney. Now it is often true, also, that such women who men (boys) find attractive, many times make enemies of other women in direct proportion to their own appeal to the opposite sex. However, this was not the case with Julia, for she was loved by almost everyone who spoke to her, for her real beauty was in her kind heart (though this did not take away from her outer beauty or compete with it as it does in many women, who feel that a beautiful exterior requires one to create an opposite interior to balance the effects of one against the other; rather in Julia, one acted to reinforce the other so that the total effect was devastating).

One day, as often happened in the spring and summer months, John and Jason were visiting the Vanderkamps. Jason preferred Rodney over Julia, though he was not a match, athletically, for Rodney, who used to defeat his neighbor regularly in wrestling matches and various ball games that the latter devised so as to be operable with only two players. This was partly due to Rodney's natural propensities, and also to the fact that Jason was slightly chubby as a boy and was a slow runner.

Julia, though two years younger than her brother Rodney, often liked to watch her brother play with his friends when there were no little girls for her to play with. However, when John and Jason would come over, John, who liked Julia's quiet nature, which he felt was much like his own, would sit and talk with her under the shade of a tree while Jason and Rodney would play some game or other in front of them.

John's behavior used to amaze Jason, who knew John to be a very fast runner and who could probably apply himself very ably to Rodney's feats of skill--for some odd reason, John would often (really most of the time) prefer playing quieter games with Julia, instead. This is not to imply that John in any was a feminine sort of boy. On the contrary, he loved the woods and all forms of personal adventure within. But he also loved playing with animals and games that were centered around make-believe. Julia was the only friend of his who shared such an interest. So John would often engage in pastimes of 'estate owners' which was a game where John would pretend that he was an estate owner and Julia was his wife. Together they would go through all the strenuous duties that estate owners and their wives had to go through during a normal day's activities. It was on one such day when John and Jason came to visit--John went to play with Julia and Jason went with Rodney--that John made Julia a present of the cat which was the same cat that Jason had presented to him after the incident of the shed. The cat had been in John's possession for over a month when Mr. Beauchay declared that it was John's cat; that it had probably strayed from its mother and was lost. Since it had not been claimed, for often owners are happy rather than sad upon the scattering of a cat's litter, John felt fully justified in calling the cat his own. However, John had long contemplated giving Julia a gift of some sort as he knew that she loved animals too, and she did not have any pets of her own (her father had said that large farm animals were not proper pets for a young lady). So John, despite his deep attachment towards the little cat, knew instantly once the cat was officially proclaimed his by Mr. Beauchay that he wanted to give the cat as a present to Julia.

Julia, much to John's pleasure, was delighted over receiving the gift and instantly named it Lady Sophia, after a fairy tale character. She cuddled and talked to the cat softly, and Lady Sophia seemed enraptured by it all as she walked back and forth between John and Julia, rubbing herself against their legs and making low guttural noises.

Over a week passed before the next visit of John and Jason to the Vanderkamp's. During this time, Julia had gotten an innumerable collection of toys which she had either found or had made for the amusement of her little kitten.

Now, the Vanderkamps had a small pond nearby their house which was fed by the same waters that ran to the river. The pond was shallow for about three feet but then dropped off quickly to a depth of twenty feet or so. The lake was mostly ornamental, for due to a weedy bottom it was good for neither swimming (as one could get his feet entangled in the stringy vines) nor fishing (as the line would easily become caught in the same way, causing the loss of bait and hook). Despite its uselessness, or perhaps because of it, the pond was very beautiful with trees around it and a tiny island in the center which the boys were always scheming to paddle out to, if they only had a boat.

It was at this lagoon that John and Jason found Julia and Rodney on their next visit. Julia was singing to her cat and playing with Lady Sophia and her new toys. Rodney was trying to stand on his head (a feat which he could only accomplish for the shortest of intervals).

Jason didn't like the idea of trying to test his acrobatic skills as he was afraid of breaking his neck with such crazy antics, but John was intrigued with the challenge as he had never seen anyone trying to stand on his head before. And so, while Rodney was showing John the rudimentary postures for the performance of said feats of daring, Jason talked with Julia.

"Why do you just sit and play such silly games with that old cat?" asked Jason to Julia.

"Lady Sophia isn't old," said Julia lightly, "she's just a little kitty."

"Your little kitty has pretty sharp claws," said Jason, remembering his episode in the tree.

"But she never uses them, for she's so gentle."

"I don't think cats are as nice as dogs, do you?"

"I can't say. I've never had a dog. But I'm sure that I could never love another pet as much as Lady Sophia."

Jason, in all honesty, was somewhat bored with the prospect of playing with a silly cat, which he had never liked in the first place, so he said, "Does Lady Sophia like to swim? Perhaps she would like to explore the island?"

"Lady Sophia hates the water!" exclaimed Julia, looking up in amazement.

"But one mustn't keep a tight hold over an animal's curiosity, for they are born explorers and will become ill if you don't let them pursue their natural instincts. I've heard my tutor, Mr. Russel, say so on many occasions."

"But Lady Sophia has no desire to take any trips, for she is happy staying with me."

"But how do you know until you try?" said Jason, moving towards the cat.

"Lady Sophia has never told me about wanting to take any trips."

"I think we must--" started Jason as he lunged at the cat, which, though it had been watching Jason, was still taken somewhat by surprise. Jason grabbed the cat and flung it out into the pond.

"We must give it a chance to test its wings and explore!" said Jason as he threw the cat high in the air towards its aquatic destination.

Instantly Julia screamed and John, who was at this moment successfully standing on his head, rolled down in time to see the cat splash into the water. Without a moment's hesitation, he kicked off his shoes and ran into the water after the cat, forgetting entirely that he didn't know how to swim. This brought even louder screams by Julia. Rodney, too, joined in the fury as he saw Dow struggling in the dangerous pond. Very soon, people came out of the house and someone ran to get Mr. Vanderkamp. By that time, however, Dow was on the muddy bank, his wet clothes clinging to his body and his hair bedraggled so that his naturally thin frame was sharply accentuated. This made him look even more tired and helpless than he really was. The cat ran from Dow to Julia, who had its blanket. Julia hastened to Dow, who, she thought, looked half-dead.

Mr. Vanderkamp stormed quickly to the scene. "What's all the commotion?"

"Well sir," said Jason, who was anxious to be the one to relate the story. "I was just trying to see whether Miss Julia's cat could swim, and John thought that it was in danger and tried to rescue it by going into the water after it."

"Don't you kids know that the pond isn't for swimming?"

But John, still out of breath, was unable to reply.

"I don't know how many times I've told you not to go swimming in the pond and to only use the boat with life preservers. That is a dangerous body of water and it would be very easy for one of your limbs to become entangled." Mr. Vanderkamp, in his excitement, probably forgot that their boat had been inoperable for some time.

"But father," started Julia, not being able to bear the injustice to her little friend any longer, "Johnny was only helping Lady Sophia, who looked, to me, as if she would drown."

"Well, what's the cat doing in the water? Damnation, anyone should know enough to keep a cat away from the water. It's like letting mice around horses or putting a saddle on a cow, or cutting hay with a knife or—"

Mr. Vanderkamp stopped as his stream of similes had overflowed and flooded the banks of rational self-restraint. He was thus in a word: speechless.

"But father, it wasn't Johnny who put Lady Sophia into the pond. It was his brother, Jason."

Julia politely left out telling her father that Jason had not only put the cat into the water, but that he had done so against her own protestations, which Jason, for some reason, chose to ignore. This silence may perhaps be accounted for by the unwritten code among young people, yea, people of all ages, not to give testament against another—even when the other is at fault. This would open the witness to the charge of being a *tattletale* or in the case of adults, an informer.

"Jason, did you put the cat into the water?"

"Yes sir, I told you that, as you remember, in order to see whether it could really swim."

Vanderkamp turned to the nurse, who had been in charge of watching the children, but who, in fact, had taken the opportunity of the lazy afternoon to dream of a romantic suitor (for though she was married, she wasn't very pleased with her husband and never associated romantic thoughts with him). However, she had been awakened from her slumber by the cries of Julia and saw enough to be able to ascertain that Jason had commandeered the animal for his own purposes. "Mr. Vanderkamp, sir, I saw the whole incident. It seems to me that Master Jason didn't exactly have Miss Julia's permission to throw the kitten into the water."

"Is that true, Jason?" asked Vanderkamp.

"Sir, I saw the cat eyeing the water and thought that perhaps it would like a chance to swim and so I endeavored to give it that opportunity."

Mr. Vanderkamp became extremely agitated at this response as he found himself out maneuvered in the verbal duel by this little child. This didn't exactly ingratiate himself to either the boy or to anyone else for that matter. He simply said, "Well, I hope that'll be a lesson to all of you, and that it will never happen again." At which point he turned around, stamped his foot, and stormed to the house. It should be mentioned, however, that when Mr. Vanderkamp related the story to Mr. Beauchay later that afternoon, he told his neighbor of how he had severely admonished Jason for his part of the episode and hoped that Mr. Beauchay would meet out any other punishment as he saw fit. Mr. Beauchay, perhaps owing to his not being there, took it, after hearing Mr. Vanderkamp's account, that all the persons involved had been punished enough and so never said a word about the incident.

Chapter 2

"A Game of Baseball and its Unfortunate Overtones"

AS JOHN GREW TO BE A LAD in his teens, his visits to the Vanderkamp's were more often than not only to see Rodney, who John was beginning to cultivate as a friend. Dow was at that age when young men usually turn to primarily male pastimes and are so adamant about the exclusiveness of their company that women, as individuals, are almost never asked to participate. However, this does not exclude the acute awareness of the opposite gender as a general class, especially certain burgeoning physical features which their eyes were first examining.

Rodney Vanderkamp was the center of a group of such young men who would often gather at his estate and ride horses or throw around a baseball. Sometimes the activity was informal, but other times it led to a spirited game. Rodney's best friend was Victor Stuart II, who was next in the dominance hierarchy after Rodney. One day in the early summer, several of the boys were gathered on a field that Mr. Vanderkamp kept for the boys to use, and they were choosing teams for a game of baseball. There were only twelve boys and so there would not be enough to fill all of the positions, but this problem was solved by the elimination of the pitcher and catcher who were supplied by the team that was at bat. Also, there was no right fielder. A ball hit to right field was a foul ball.

The game had only progressed a few innings when John and Jason came rambling over the small hill that separated the two farms. John, knowing that some game or other had probably started as it was well into the afternoon, had persuaded Jason, who didn't like baseball particularly, owing to his poor hitting and fielding, to accompany him since no one wanted a single player to join the game after it had started and thus make the teams uneven. Though John was a skillful player, he was looked down upon by many of the other boys as being somewhat beneath them because of his birth and mixed racial features. He was not considered their social equal. Owing to his skill, however, he usually was quite welcomed during a ball game where he could easily turn the tide in a losing effort.

"Room for one more?" yelled Dow as they approached the area where the game was being played.

"Hey, there's Jason and that Dow kid," said Victor.

"We'll take Dow and let you have Jason," said Rodney, the captain of one of the teams.

"That's not fair," said Marcus Bordant, the other captain who rather liked Dow and wanted him on their team. "We had Jason last time."

"Shut up Marcus, you stupid thing, we don't want that little nigger on our team," said Victor.

"Okay, we'll take Jason. He can play right field," said Marcus and didn't make any further response, because he was so low on the dominance hierarchy scale so that anything he might say would make no difference anyway. The only consequence his further entreaties would have would be his continued slide on that all important scale. So Marcus, the shortstop, and second best fielder after Rodney, quietly let his superiors handle the intricate transaction of delegating the players to their respective teams.

"Dow, you're on *their* team; Jason, you're on *our* team," growled Victor.

As they played and the afternoon wore on, Julia and her maid, Marcia Coffman, came out to the field with large pitchers of lemonade to refresh the thirsty boys. Rodney, seeing his sister coming, gnashed his teeth in embarrassment that his sister would bring them something so fancy when the guys could have satisfied their thirsts by drinking from the lagoon. It seemed silly to make up pitchers of this delicate beverage. But when Victor gave a yell and started running toward the approaching refreshments, Rodney forgot his consternation and followed his friend in a mad dash to the drinks. It was not unusual that Julia would bring drinks to the boys, who all loved the break. But the frequency of her visits had, though unknown to anyone else, a direct correlation to the presence of young Dow, for whom she had a fondness; though to her displeasure, he didn't reciprocate in any noticeable fashion. The reason for this was not that Dow did not like Julia, his childhood companion and playmate, for, if questioned, he would probably express the highest admiration for her virtues and comeliness as a girl. It was simply that at the age of sixteen he was more interested in baseball and taking fishing trips alone in the woods than in the charms of any young lady. John's seeming indifference to the passions which were within her heart did not dissipate Julia's affection, for she was at an age when a man's visage alone was enough to feed romantic thoughts.

And so the boys crowded around Julia and her maid as the ladies began pouring out the drinks into glasses for the thirsty crew. Victor, who oftentimes acted as a clown, pretended impatience at the slow process of pouring out the liquid into the glasses. He grabbed a pitcher from Julia and lifted it to his lips as if he would drink the whole of it in a draught. In the wresting of the pitcher, Julia was startled so that she dropped her handkerchief, but before it hit the grass, John caught it with a graceful swing of his arm and in the same motion returned it to its owner. This slight action (in John's and the rest of the boy's eyes, whose attention was on Victor rather than on Dow, as the former was foiled in his mock attempt to down the entire contents of the pitcher by Rodney, who returned the pitcher to his sister) was seen by Julia in a much different perspective as she clasped the cloth tightly as a symbol of a much appreciated chivalrous action.

After the boys quickly satisfied their thirsts, they departed as quickly as they had greeted their Clara Barton. The young Miss Vanderkamp was left with little thanks and two empty pitchers of lemonade. As Julia strolled back to the house, her handkerchief was safely concealed in a place close to her heart, which beat feverishly over the action of her sweetheart.

When the game resumed, it was the eighth inning with Rodney's team coming to bat and down 20-17. John was up to bat with two out and runners on first and third. On the first pitch, he smashed a line drive to left center that went between the gap of outfielders. The runner on third easily scored and so did the runner on first as Dow was rounding second and heading for third on what would have normally been a certain homerun had not Harold Thompson been the center fielder. Since he was the fastest runner in the county, the ball was retrieved and relayed perfectly. So it was that Victor Stuart caught the peg at third just as Dow was sliding into the base. The throw had been perfect. John should have been out. But John made a clever hook slide around the glove of Stuart, avoiding the tag. So well did John avoid Victor's glove that the latter lunged awkwardly around trying to make the tag and fell to the ground, dropping the ball which rolled out from his glove into foul territory. Dow saw his chance and scurried towards the plate as Victor scrambled up and made a wild and hurried toss to the awaiting catcher. The game was tied.

Rodney's team made one more run and the score was unchanged until the ninth inning when Victor's team was at bat. There was one out and nobody on base when Victor got up and stroked a single. Harold Thompson was the next batter. He hit a sharp grounder which the second baseman tossed to shortstop Dow, who was approaching second base to make the pivot for a double play when he saw that Victor was coming in high to break up the double play. John brushed the corner of the base to avoid the collision that would prevent his being able to execute the throw and so end the game. However, even after Dow had made his successful throw, Stuart illegally veered away from the base path so he could ram Dow with his head and shoulder. John, seeing the body only at the last moment, tried to jump above the low moving battering ram, though with little success as his efforts only served to bring his knee against the underside of Victor's chin.

The force of the impact caused John to tumble over Stuart's head as both boys fell to the ground.

"Are you all right?" asked one of the boys rushing to the fallen Stuart.

But Stuart just lay on the ground holding his jaw, which was badly bruised from the collision. Quickly a crowd of boys gathered around to survey the situation, though no one actually offered to help. All that could be heard was the continued murmuring of, "Is he all right? Victor, are you all right?"

Dow, who also had been shaken up by the fall, got up quickly when he saw that his opponent still lay on the ground, and he gauged the reaction of the other boys as an indication that something must have happened to Victor. Only Marcus approached John and asked whether he had sustained any injuries from the altercation.

Finally, the inevitable happened: an accusing finger was pointed at Dow. "You really clobbered him." John tried to make his way through the others to see for himself what had happened to Victor amid the growing accusations of poor sportsmanship and cheating.

"How's your chin, Victor?" asked a concerned Dow.

"That was a mighty black thing to do."

"What are you talking about?"

"That knee to the chin. That's how the bush niggies play ball. If you want to play with us, you'll have to learn how to play like a white man."

John felt a growing disgust within him as he wanted to point out to his little rich neighbor that it was he (Victor) who had caused the collision behind second base and not the attempt, however futile, to try and avoid the impact of the collision. But instead John merely blurted out, "You don't know what you're talking about."

This comment, coupled with the action of Dow as he got up and started to walk away, inflamed Victor, who despite being so badly injured that he had writhed before his captive audience for several minutes, now instantly sprung up and ran after Dow and spun him around. Then Victor punched John Dow in the stomach.

John was taken by surprise and doubled over with pain. The "sucker" punch was quickly followed by a blow to the face, which knocked Dow to the ground. Had Victor stopped there, it is probable that John would not have continued the fight; however, seeing his victim on the ground made Stuart's appetite for total conquest become even keener as he jumped upon his disadvantaged opponent.

This proved to be a mistake, for Dow rolled over so that instead of landing on top of Dow, Victor hit the ground with a jarring impact, which was as effective at causing pain as Victor's previous blows to John's chin and stomach had been. Seizing upon this opportunity, John wrestled with great skill as he finally got his adversary into a choke-hold from which he could not escape.

"I'm going to get you, you goddamn son-of-a-" cursed Victor as he tried to force himself free.

"Will you stop fighting?"

"Let me go you little—"

"First you have to promise to stop fighting," said John as he tightened his grip.

"I'll die first," said Victor. "You little black, ugly, goddamn--"

Dow, who had no interest in prolonging the battle, only wanted to extract a promise from Stuart that the latter would cease and desist, as it would be foolish to let the other go and continue fighting. So John tightened his grip so that finally Victor begrudgingly said, "I'll stop. I'll stop; let go of me, you bastard."

With that, John released Victor from the hold. Young Stuart rose slowly to his feet sneering, "Did you see how he got me with his knee at second? He went out of the base path to do it, too."

Several of the boys nodded and one said, "Yes, I saw it. He played it dirty."

There were assorted grunts of agreement as Victor added, "That's how he fights too: dirty."

John had gotten up and started walking home. Jason was not watching Dow, but slowly nodding his head and mumbling concurring phrases with the other boys.

Chapter 3

"On Gaming and the Prudence of Jason"

IT SOON BECAME THE HABIT of the group of young men to frequent on occasion the gambling establishment in town (even though technically there was an age requirement of 18). Bill March, the manager, had instructed Miles Bon, the man who generally kept watch over the activities, to go easy on letting the older boys have a little action at roulette (which now was being run all afternoon) if they so desired. At night the regulations were enforced since the place was full with men, but during the afternoon there was little business and so the boys weren't in the way.

Jason and John had never been to the gambling place when one afternoon, as they were in town on an errand for Jefferson, Jason suggested that they go inside and see what the other boys had been talking about. John was at first reluctant, but quickly succumbed to the prodding of Jason and went inside. It was dark compared to the sun outside. The rose colored windows let in an off-color light that gave the place a queer atmosphere. At the back were some men who had come in to see what the odds were like on the town horse race, which would be held in two weeks. This was getting to be quite a large occasion with hundreds of dollars riding on each of the several entries. The prize was fifty dollars to the first place horse and ten dollars to the second place animal and rider. Anyone in town could enter if they had a horse that they thought could win, but usually it was the men around seventeen to thirty who would be the most active in the competition. This was because the race was too physically exerting for the older men and too dangerous for the younger. The two boys made their way, cautiously, towards the roulette table to watch the solitary player lose his money.

"It seems like it would be almost impossible to win," said Jason. "A one in thirty-seven chance isn't very good odds."

"I suppose they could make several bets."

"But where is the break-even point?" put Jason.

John had no response. The two boys watched. They were spellbound by the rolling marble and turning wheel. As they were about to go, there was some loud shouting in the back of the room.

"Get out, I said."

"But I jist wants some whiskey."

"We don't serve niggers during the day, and never inside."

"But I only--"

The man doing the yelling was Miles Bon, a tall, dark man with Negroid features.

"Get out, or I'll throw you out."

The other was a man about thirty-five. He had closely cropped hair so that his scalp shown in the dim light through the black curls. He was bending over and straining to reach the old bar.

"Ma wife, she's done left me. I gots ta have a drink."

"Not now," said Miles as he grabbed the other by his shoulder and shoved him violently against the back door. The body slammed with a muffled thud, the man hitting his head and sliding to the floor.

"Take him out back," Miles ordered the man running the roulette.

"Dump some water on him. He'll come to quick enough."
John hurried out, leaving Jason to fend for himself. Dow made his way to his horse, galloping the animal all the way home.

Mr. Russel saw John returning and reminded him that he had a lesson still to make up from the previous week. They waited to start the lesson until Jason arrived. The topic for the day was on the presidency of James Buchannan, the head of state just before the War Between the States.

"Mr. Buchannan was a lout and a fool," stated Russel flatly. "He didn't push the 1849 Compromise, which could have averted the War. The reason for this stupidity was his inability to listen to his advisors, who all favored the measure. It is a foolish man who can't listen to the advice of others. Many think this could have been due to his drinking habits which--"

"Mr. Russel," interrupted John. "I have a question. Do you think that perhaps both sides in Congress were in no mood for compromise?"

"That's nonsense. Everyone wanted compromise but the President. That bull-headed, strong willed lout caused the War between the States."

"If everyone in Congress wanted a compromise and if the compromise was a Congressional measure, then why didn't Congress simply act on its own?"

"What a foolish statement," said Jason, who hitherto had been silent. "What Mr. Russel is suggesting is that without the president's assistance, something that he was unwilling to provide, the Congress, who wanted a compromise, couldn't effect one."

Mr. Russel was delighted at this testimony from his prized pupil and would hear no further arguments on the subject. Now Jason, on the advice of Mr. Russel, was given some money by his father for a trip that they would take later in the month. Jason was delighted by the prospect and communicated his joy often to Dow, who was doing extra chores because Mr. Russel had reported that Dow had been especially lazy of late and this propensity might be reversed if some strong measures were taken. To this advice, Mr. Beauchay reluctantly agreed (for in all truth, his mind was at that moment occupied with other matters).

What was on his mind was the new owner of the hotel, Oscar Whren, who was emerging as a force to counter the Dodson influence. Samuel Beauchay had always been convinced that there were a considerable number of people who didn't like Dodson and would like to see him stopped if they could.

Whren was planning to expand the back of the hotel to hold conventions there, which he thought could become quite attractive to Atlanta and Savanna businessmen since prices were so much lower in Varner's Junction. Coming from Savanna, Whren seemed like a very decent fellow to Beauchay, and so he was happy to attend a meeting one evening to discuss a venture to counter Dodson.

The meeting began with a man from out of town who spoke briefly against George Dodson, "We all know that Dodson is behind the gambling establishment and that drugstore, though no one can prove it," started one man in an opening speech. "Now, what Mr. Whren suggests is to remodel the hotel. He would add an extra wing for an establishment to counter Dodson's place. However, as this venture would require quite a large outlay of money, a corporation would have to be formed with a board of directors to run the casino. Since real estate is such a good investment these days, I could see our investment consortium branching out to other areas in the state as conditions warrant."

"That's very good for Mr. Whren," said Samuel Beauchay. "We build a wing on his hotel so that he can attract more business!"

"I plan to pay most of the cost myself, Mr. Beauchay, which is why I would be the actual manager, but as to the profits, they would go to the stock holders, who would be you gentlemen and any others who want to keep our place free from the riffraff from Texas."

"Yes," said the out-of-towner again. "Have you seen how many niggers he's brought in to run all those places? Do we want our town turned over to the niggers?"

"I don't think we need to turn this meeting into an emotional outburst," said Beauchay, though the crowd was obviously behind Whren and the out-of-towner.

"It's now or never, gentlemen. What do you say?" put the out-of-towner.

There were roars of approval as most everyone was rushing up to pledge their money towards the new venture. But Samuel Beauchay didn't like the idea and stayed in his seat.

"Come on, Samuel," said Charles Vanderkamp. "It's a good way to make a dollar, and besides, it's a way to stop Dodson. You've always wanted to do that; here's your chance."

But something bothered Beauchay about fighting Dodson's gambling house (which probably wasn't legal) with another. He wanted to stop Dodson, but he wanted to outwit him and not overcome him by becoming baser himself.

It must be openly done, thought Beauchay to himself. Dodson is a proud man and the only way to defeat such a fellow is to duel him in the open. No, Beauchay thought, I must wait for my opportunity and then I'll out-maneuver him. Sometime or other it will have to come down to that. It will have to, or I'll lose any respect I've ever had for myself. If that ever happens I'll just give in and sell my birthright for a bowlful of stew.

Chapter 4

"Master Victor Comes to Call"

JULIA SLOWLY OPENED HER DRAWER and took out the linen handkerchief, holding it gingerly and laying it down on her bed; she took a nap still clinging to the piece of cloth.

Just then Marcia Coffman burst into the room. "Now Julia, what are you doing on the bed? This 'taint no time ta rest. Don't you remember the Stuarts are acomin' for tea and cakes this afternoon? You have ta be there ta properly receives them."

Julia had indeed forgotten about the visit. She had been lost in a dream about her sweetheart as she held the badge of his gallantry close to her lips. She conveniently ignored Mrs. Coffman.

"I don't know what's gotten into you, Miss Julia, but we has to gets going or your mother and papa will be fit to be tied. I can just hear your mother now," said Mrs. Coffman as she tried to wrestle the young creature from her resting place. "Land sakes, child; land sakes!" said Mrs. Coffman in imitation of Mrs. Martha Vanderkamp. "You know your mother will be so dreadfully upset at you not comin'. So now get a move on, child, we don't have until the judgment day." At these words, Mrs. Coffman took a hold of one of Julia's arms to try and move the lethargic young lady when she jerked free the handkerchief by mistake. Instantly, Julia sprang up and snatched the handkerchief from a dumbfounded Mrs. Coffman.

"Miss Julia," started Mrs. Coffman in surprise. "What's possessing you, child?"

"Excuse me, Marcia, but I will attend to my mother and whoever she wishes to entertain presently," said Julia as she pressed the handkerchief to her heart. Moving quickly across the room, she turned her back to the maid so that she might not see that water was issuing forth from her tear ducts over the interruption of her wonderful dream and the pollution of her cherished handkerchief.

"Miss Julia, you are acting strangely today. I would think that perhaps you were ill. For when I came in all you would do is scarcely move an eyelash when I tried to get you ready at your mama's request. Then you are activity itself, hopping around grabbing things out of people's hands. If I didn't know better, I'd think you were ill. Perhaps you are," said Mrs. Coffman on a moment's reflection. "Shall I call for the doctor?"

"I shall be ready presently, you may tell that to my mother who, no doubt, is anxious for the news."

"Yes, of course. Yes, but I'll say you are acting most peculiar today, most peculiar."

Then Mrs. Coffman continued the chamber mumbling to herself over and over again, "Most peculiar, most peculiar."

Julia, after a few moments of quiet reflection, resolved to go downstairs to assist her mother in any way she could.

"Julia. Land sakes, child. There you are," began Mrs. Vanderkamp. "I declare child, you gave us all a shock. Why, Mrs. Coffman has just told us about your odd behavior. I myself was just about to ring for a doctor. You know, Julia, you can never be too careful about these things. There is so much sickness going around; why, it's in the air." As Mrs. Vanderkamp delivered these lines, Julia was descending the stairs. When she reached the bottom, her mother fussed over her.

"Now, did you put any perfume on?' asked her mother. Julia shook her head.

"You go upstairs again child and put on some of Mother's Paris perfume. Young Victor is accompanying his father here this afternoon and land sakes; we must look our best for young Victor."

Julia was struck adversely by this news. She disliked Victor and dreaded the moments when she had to sit and pass conversation with him. There was something about his very nature she couldn't entirely understand. But whatever it was, it made her want to depart from her role as amiable, charming hostess and tell him that she was extremely bored by his company and desired to do something more interesting—like knitting. This imaginary conversation made Julia smile with satisfaction, which her mother took as an indication of her daughter's belated but appropriate joy at the prospect of such a fine young man coming to call.

Soon after the Stuarts came, Maria Vanderkamp suggested to her husband that they show Mr. Stuart the new garden that they were planting. This left Julia alone with Victor.

"Where's Rodney today?" asked Victor.

"He's gone fishing with the Beauchays."

"But Jason doesn't like to fish," said Victor, who was surprised that Rodney would have gone anywhere that might have put him into contact with the disagreeable Dow.

"I don't know Jason's personal habits," said Julia politely, "but what I know is that he said he was going to go fishing and that he was stopping at the Beauchay's first to see if someone wanted to accompany him."

"He's probably going with that little darkie," said Victor, as he began to launch into a Negro joke. But Julia interrupted him, which thoroughly surprised Victor. It was generally considered impolite for a woman to ever interrupt a man.

"I think it's strange that you should call Mr. Dow a 'darkie,' referring, I believe, to your conviction that he is a Negro, when you can ascertain as well as anyone that he has blue eyes and *no* Negroes are so featured."

There was a silence in which Victor felt somewhat indignant at having something he said questioned—especially by a woman.
"Excuse me for my inability to answer your statement immediately," began Victor, groping for words to express what he felt, "but I am unaccustomed to being interrupted while I am talking to a *lady*." This last word was given special emphasis by Victor, who hoped that such a rebuke on his part would silence Julia. For Victor believed that women often needed firm reprimands so that they might keep their proper obedience. Besides, with such interruptions, he would never be able to finish his little story, which, he confessed to himself, was one of the funniest stories that he had heard in a long while. He could hardly wait to relate it and make Julia laugh. But instead, Julia responded instantly and with a calmness that made Victor uneasy. "I'm afraid, sir, many of my sex have taken it upon themselves to open their mouths to articulate insights which we have impatiently waited for men to discover for many hundreds of years."

This retort smacked of Northern Suffragettes to Victor, who instantly felt as if he must counter the attack in some manner. However, he was unsure just how to do it. This woman spoke so calmly, and this circumvented the usual retort that they were just being emotional. One who spoke so clearly seemed as if she could handle a charge of being irrational. Having none of the normal replies that a man has at his disposal when confronting a woman, Victor simply muttered, "They certainly made a mistake giving women the vote; now they have an opinion about *everything.*"

"Perhaps sir, you are correct, but it is, as they say, a moot question now, *isn't it?*" Julia paused for an instant to allow Victor an opportunity to respond if he wanted to, but hearing no immediate reply, she added, "We have a lovely garden that Mother has started, would you care to see it?" Eagerly Victor took the opportunity to end discussion. To him it was an indication that Julia had given up trying to outwit him and was retreating to the out of doors so that they wouldn't continue their repartee. This conclusion, which was only a hope at first, soon grew into a conviction. Stuart thus grew confident and good-natured again by the time they had rejoined the others in the garden.

Julia, it should be stated, got no pleasure from arguing with anyone, man or woman. She did not feel a need to express herself whenever she was in disagreement. Indeed, she surprised herself somewhat at her verbal barrage. But there are occasions, she felt, when one must either talk or allow oneself to be crushed under the weight of another's personality. Whether the subject matter brought out this fierceness in Julia, or simply Victor's personality, was a question that she did not consider.

Jason was not around for Rodney to invite fishing as he, Jason, was in Atlanta with his father on a two week excursion, a reward for diligent study. Jason had been wanting to go to the big city for some time since he wanted to purchase some fine clothes. Now, it may seem strange to some that Jason would squander money on such frivolities as stylish clothes when frugality clearly dictated that the plain attire that he already possessed was sufficient to keep out the wind and rain and was no worse than the dress worn by most of his friends. But, sometimes, frugality is outweighed by other desires stronger than the love of money. In this case, the scale was tipping in favor of catching the eye of the lovely Julia.

Jason, for some time, had admired the beauty of Julia. But since he was unaccustomed to the company of women, he never knew quite what to say. He had devised many plans in his mind to make her his, but all of these were impractical. Being impractical, they were instantly rejected. Jason's mind only fed itself upon schemes which could actually be implemented. The first part of his plan was to change his image somewhat by becoming a fancy dresser. Nice clothing could draw the eye away from his pudgy frame. He was convinced that his father would also approve of this move. And, if Jason made his choices wisely, he might be kept in stylish clothes perpetually after his initial investment. As a result, the return on each dollar spent on this trip would, in the long run, be better for him both socially and economically. This was because his father, when he replaced his son's clothes, would buy him the same type of clothes. Thus the fancy attire he was purchasing now would be replaced by other clothes of the same quality in the future. This scheme delighted Jason so much that on the train ride to Atlanta, he could scarcely wait to go into the tailors' shops and pick out his finery. Jason also had an acute eye and did not flatter himself that he was presently the object of Julia's affections. But in time, if he handled his opposition well, he might win his esteemed prize. This goal, if achieved, would complete the goals that Jason had set out for himself: "To devise a plan for one's life," Jason told John one day, "is the proper course of action if one wants to be happy. The trouble with you is that were you never act as if there is any tomorrow." Mr. Russel had confirmed this opinion of Dow on more than one occasion.

"The difference between a wise man and a foolish one is that the wise man always maximizes his advantages and the foolish man never cares one whit about being happy until he finds himself in an unhappy situation."

All this Jason firmly believed. For that matter, John never gave any arguments against such sound admonitions. But what Russel failed to mention, though Jason was certain that it was in his tone if nothing else, was that an individual had to firmly understand that he was master of what he did and that a firm and solid plan would enable one to handle the difficulties that might arise and thus yield comparatively greater happiness. Jason thought that John was a quick enough boy when it came to thinking divorced from action. But Jason thought that Dow didn't understand the link between actions and resolves of the mind. This was because John seemed to treat resolves as being in a separate realm from the concrete actions themselves. Such an attitude, Jason was convinced, would make Dow always susceptible to any scheme that he or anyone else might devise to dupe John. In fact, Dow seemed to be governed by some set of imperatives that Jason could not fathom. For example, John would spend days on end fishing for the lame reason that "he liked doing it."

"Nice cast," said an admiring Rodney.

"Casting don't count for much unless I catch something," replied Dow lightheartedly.

"Just the same, it makes it easier to catch fish when you put the fly where you want it." John didn't say anything about Rodney's misplaced application of words. They were still-fishing and weren't using flies.

"It certainly is a nice day, isn't it?" yawned Rodney from his reclining position. "I don't know how you can lay there with a hat over your face; aren't you afraid of missing a strike?"

"I have my pole in the bank firmly enough. I won't lose it," replied John.

"No, what I mean is, aren't you afraid that a fish will bite and that you'll miss it?"

"I think I'll get most of them," said Dow as he shifted himself slightly to be more comfortable. "If I lose a few, well, then I lose a few. If they're that quick, they don't deserve to be caught."

"I don't think I could rest like that, I'd always be wondering whether something was nibbling at my line," said Rodney, who didn't understand Dow's attitude, but for some inexplicable reason wished that he, too, could be so relaxed about the whole thing.

As he lay there, Dow's thoughts drifted to the image of the black man that he and Jason had seen in the gambling house. What John remembered most about that man was his eyes. Those eyes seemed to convey sheer anguish to Dow's perception. What kind of history had produced such a debasement of the human soul to allow one to feel such pain? But what pain was he feeling? Dow was certain that he had never experienced anything that would compare to one's wife leaving with another man. Dow could only imagine what the man's feelings must be like. He had read books, of course, where desertion or adultery were part of the plot. But this was second-hand knowledge. Each instance had specificity. It wasn't like Othello's fury, though at some time such a reaction must have surfaced. He was not beaten down in the sense of being a pitiable creature like Hardy's Jude. But yet, the man seemed driven. He wasn't despairing, but perhaps he was driven by despair? What did it mean to be brought to such levels of suffering? Was it like Pip, who found that the world he had thought existed was in fact not the reality that did exist? The exquisite intrigue· of Miss Havisham's fortune was really the tainted money of a convict. John knew that such comparisons were only his grappling to fit feelings experienced third hand: from the author to his book to the reader. But what else had he to compare? Heaviness made him troubled. *A horse reared back from a loud car engine.* Why hadn't he helped the man? Certainly John could have offered the poor soul some of the candy that was in his pocket. Perhaps a kind word would have made all the difference to the fellow? A kind word, perhaps, that would have been all that might--Lord, *when did we see thee sick?*--Jefferson's voice rang in his head--those eyes imploring, willing to go to any depths for, for ----what? There was a gap that John could not fill. He didn't know the *what*. The solution could never become clear to him if he didn't even know what he was trying to solve. Everything swirled about. Nothing was clear except two eyes staring from within the darkness of the confusion. The two eyes were speaking to him, except he could not hear what they were saying. He strained to listen, but it was useless, for his blood was moving far too swiftly.

Chapter 5

"An Account of Old Reddy and the Price of Land"

THERE WAS SOMETHING about the golf course that appealed to Samuel Beauchay so that when it was known that the land might be up for sale, he decided to make further inquiries. The land lay between the Stuart's Farm (or what was left of it) and the old Rutherford Place, which was now occupied by the Dodsons. Perhaps it was for this reason that Beauchay, almost instinctively, felt that this piece of land would be instrumental in his effort to stop his brother-in-law's rise to prominence. For the Rutherford lands were now mostly split up so that the total acreage belonging to Dodson represented only a fraction of what the Rutherford Plantation had once been.

The decimation of the Rutherford Farm came as a result of the War. The estate which formerly belonged to Colonel Charles Rutherford and his brother, Randolph, had been inherited from their father, Lewis. Randolph, however, showed no interest in farming and allowed his brother to buy his share of the estate from him at a good figure. There Charles Rutherford stayed with his sister Cybil and her husband Edward Lee II. Charles was a man who enjoyed the prestige of having a farm, but who didn't want to be bothered with the task of running it, so he hired his brother-in-law as a sort of estate manager. Lee had no real skill at producing crops from the soil and soon made the land largely barren.

Charles Rutherford, being an astute businessman, quickly found this out. When Charles asked Phillip Beauchay to take a look at the entire operation, Charles found to his dismay that the plantation was in sorry condition and that nothing less than the removal of his brother-in-law would be necessary to save the lands from turning into worthless dust that wouldn't even hold grass. The task of getting rid of his manager was very difficult for Charles, as he liked his brother-in-law and didn't want to hurt him. Fortunately for Charles, the War came and such an action was indefinitely tabled to some future date.

When the War was almost over, in 1864, a tragedy occurred as Cybil and her four children were butchered by a detachment of Union soldiers at their home. In addition to this, Edward Lee was maimed badly. He had lost an arm and a leg while fighting in Virginia. All this made Colonel Rutherford (for so he was known after the War) unable to evict his brother-in-law from the land. Instead, Colonel Rutherford sold portions of his land to the Stuarts and the Thompsons, and decided to live in town and become president of the bank, leaving his bereaved and pitiful brother-in-law to stay on the estate--or what there was remaining of it. The land that Colonel Rutherford sold was largely worthless, but he got a good price for it primarily due to his imposing manner and good business sense.

When the house became vacated by the death of Edward, the Colonel had looked for someone to whom he could rent or sell the house and the small piece of property that went with it. The property was next to worthless because it was largely barren for farming. The house had been vacant for almost thirty years, with only a few tenants at infrequent intervals, when George Dodson bought the place at a low price. Such was Beauchay's recollection of the history of that land.

But Beauchay knew that in a county where holding land was a symbol of respectability, sooner or later George would enlarge his place, even if it was with the poor farmland on which the golf course now rested. There was something about the land that seemed to be imprinted with the very character and soul of its owner. In a part of the state where it was important to have some considerable land holdings, George Dodson was without such. Now as bank president, George would feel the need to expand. If he did not work the property as a farm at least he might enclose it with a fence so that everyone might know that George Dodson extended to impressive proportions.

Samuel thought about that entire portion of the county and how it had changed even since the time of his son's birth. The Lees had acquired some of the Jackson and Stuart Farms, and a newcomer had divided property that he bought from the Stuarts and sold a portion of it to the Thompsons (the northern parts) and to William Murdock, who had constructed a golf course. This, however, never caught on. Now Murdock wanted out.

Rumor had it that he wanted to move to Charlottesville where he would become manager of a large restaurant. Whatever the reason was, Beauchay didn't care. He knew that he must get that land. The entire future of the county might depend upon it. And so he entered the town on Highway Three (the old Plowman's Road) which turned into Main Street just over Sawyer's Bridge, and then rode into the rich neighborhood. It was "rich" because it was the only section where there were houses that were considered fashionable since they overlooked the river and were far away from the railroad tracks and the black section of town. He rode along Crescent Road to Murdock's place.

"Mister Murdock," began Beauchay when he met the other on a somewhat soiled front porch which badly needed some paint. "Beauchay, isn't it?" said Murdock without getting up from the chair. Samuel wanted to smile at this response. Everyone in the county knew who he was. This pose at ignorance was as suitable as the peeling gray paint which marred the appearance of the porch.

"I wanted to talk to you about some land that I heard you were putting up for sale."

Murdock's eyes blinked several times in rapid succession as he finally got up and offered Beauchay a seat and a cold drink.

--who is this Oscar Whren?--I don't know, is he the man who bought the house next to the Church?---no, that's John Oliver—Yes, I like that man, such a strong build—hello girls, what are you talking about? Did you hear that they are going to start a casino?-- what's a casino?--it's another gambling place—God forbid, -- amen--but why? Don't they have enough already? It's such a dirty eyesore, if you ask me I think they should do away with the one they have, it's not a good influence on the children—or the men folk either, why there are some men who lost most of their pay in that place--I don't see why—will you listen, I'm trying to tell you two hens why—Why, I never—two hens, indeed--oh, now don't get your feelings hurt, I was just--I don't think myself to be overly sensitive, but I don't enjoy being called--neither do I, you must have a little respect, after all we are both considerably more mature than you are-I'm sorry, but what I was trying to say was—You know

without a little respect for your elders, you'll be acting just like those niggers by the station—

"You know, Ike," said Jake as he scratched his head. "I think this town's going to the dogs."

"How'd ya mean, Jake?" put in Ed, who was setting up the checkerboard for a game.

"I think I know what he means," said Ike, coming out from behind the counter. "All these new faces around, makes a feller think he's in another town sometimes. Ain't that what ya meant, Jake?"

"Not exactly, Ike, I don't rightly know jist what I mean, I reckon when it comes right down to it. But, I don't know, things jist don't seem the same somehow."

***

"Why that's an outrageous price," declared Beauchay. "You didn't pay half of that amount when you bought it."

"Things have gone up since then, Mr. Beauchay," said Murdock.

"Not double they haven't. Now I know that you are losing money every day that you hold onto that land--"

"Doesn't make any difference, sir. For if you don't like the price, I'm sure there will be others who don't think my price is too extravagant."

"I don't know how you can baldly sit there and expect me to take your offer seriously. Now, if you like, I'm prepared to pay you exactly what you paid for that land, which is, I believe, a fair price considering that when you bought it the price was considered to be extremely high."

"The price of land, as I'm sure you know, Mr. Beauchay, is determined by how much money it will bring on an open market. Now, it is possible that the price that I quoted to you is not the price that I'd get if I opened the bidding to everyone. You understand that at this juncture in time I'm just kind of feeling my way around. I haven't made up my mind that I really want to sell--however, if I get the right offer . . . ."

"Nobody's going to pay you an inflated price for a small piece of land that is barren and won't grow anything except grass."

"I'm not so sure of that, Mr. Beauchay, I've already had one offer from a man who is very interested in the land as well."

"Might I ask who this other party is and what they offered you?"

"Mister Beauchay, I'm really very sorry, but as this is not really an open matter yet, I'm not at liberty to divulge his name, but I can tell you that his offer was somewhat below my selling price, and so I was forced to refuse him."

Samuel Beauchay was perturbed by the abrasive manner of the speech that this Murdock was using. Had it not been for his powerful motivation to stay, he would have instantly quitted this impudent usurer.

"Now Mr. Beauchay, I really shouldn't tell you this, but I gave this other party a first option of buying the land within a certain time period; however, as he hasn't shown the good faith of responding with a suitable offer, I will--partly because I like you and partly because I believe that we *gentlemen* have to stay together, know what I mean?--let you buy the land if you meet my price. Now, as you can see, I can't extend this offer indefinitely, as this other party has the technical opportunity to purchase my land any time within the period I mentioned. After the period is up, I put the land up for auction (if I still feel like selling). Then, I believe, I'll receive considerably more than the rather modest figure which I've just mentioned to you. But the option is yours, sir, to do with what you will."

So this fellow was going to play two people against each other. Who was this other party? Was it Dodson? He had said something about a landed class that he didn't want to be encroached upon, and that certainly fit Dodson, but this solved nothing. Perhaps there was some other third party and all this talk was simply a ruse that was directed at prodding someone to pay an exorbitant price for a worthless piece of real estate. And yet if there were a third party, how could Beauchay trust a man who is openly admitting that he has no business ethics? Might he just as easily take money from both sides in an attempt to exhort the maximum sale price? What was the nature of the game that this fellow was playing, and under what kind of rules was he operating? These questions persuaded Beauchay to take evasive action himself. "You are a most unusual man, Mr. Murdock. I will consider what you have said and at the same time repeat my offer of giving you exactly what you paid for the land."

"It was nice to have had the opportunity to talk with you, Mr. Beauchay, and I hope you find that you can do business with me." He extended his hand, which Beauchay reluctantly shook. Beauchay's hand was oddly cold despite the heat of the afternoon.

--did you hear that they are building a library?---who is? That religious press?--no, don't know, all that I heard was that Mr. Whren was starting a petition, which he was going to contribute the first night's earnings of his casino--what's a casino?--oh don't you know?--where have you been these past few weeks?--it's kind of a social club--yes, a social club, this town has needed one for some time--I went to a library once in Savannah--that's nothing, I saw the library at Georgia Tech--I had a cousin who went there, named Robert Lomas, you didn't--How would I know whether I ran into him, I was just on campus for a few hours, there were hundreds of people that I wouldn't recognize if they came up to me and kissed me--Margaret!--well, I did have one young man approach me and offer to give me directions--really--yes, just walked right up to me, I'm sure he would have taken me out to lunch if I had shown him the slightest encouragement, why he was such a fine lad, I'm not too skeptical that he might have been an engineer, or architect or something like that--probably studying for a big job in New Orleans or somewhere expensive like that-- imagine that, you might have married a rich executive--and lived in one of those wrought ironed houses--what happened---well, what would you do if some stranger walked up to you when you were in a different town; I walked right away from him without even talking, yep, that's what I did, just walked away

"If you don't like that Dobson feller, Jake, then I don't see why you don't like that Whren feller neither," said Ike as he put a new chaw of tobacco into his mouth.

"Yar Jake, especially as that Whren is so much agin' Dodson," added Ed as he set the checkers down onto the board.

"'Spose you two are right, 'cept I can't get it into me ta like the man."

"Can't say as it makes much difference to me whether he likes Dodson or hates him. But I thought--" started Ed.

"No, you've got it all wrong, Ed. I never disliked George Dodson as a man so much as jist *what* he was."

"Don't folla ya, Jake," replied Ike as he was working his jaws to mash the tobacco.

"You always said you hated Dodson and now you say ya doesn't. Sounds loco ta me," added Ed as he made his first move.

Jake was silent as he studied the board carefully. Both Ike and Ed stood by impatiently awaiting Jake's response, which was not forthcoming. Finally Ed said, "Well, Jake, how 'bout it--we're waiting."

"Yeah, I know," said Jake as he moved his black piece forward. Then he looked up at Ed and then to Ike and said clearly and distinctly, "There, how's that?"

Ike turned to walk behind the counter, relieving himself of some tobacco juice in the process. "You know when I was just a little 'un," began Jake as he leaned back in his chair, "I went with pappy out a huntin' in the woods jist west of Mitchel Evans'. Well, we used to go with an old coyote named Jimmy Tanner, 'cept folks used to call him Reddy, cause his skin was always so red that it looked like he had just gotten sunburnt--my pappy used to say that's how a man's skin gits after he drinks a lot of corn liquor over a bunch of years. Yep, his skin was real blushed all the time, which made the determinin' of his age pret near impossible, cause his skin was so wrinkled and he was bald as an egg. But still that red skin gave a kind of youthful look to him. Anyway, I used to like Reddy cause he would talk to me as if I was a man and not like I was some youngin'--which of course I was. But at that time the last thing I wanted to be thought of was as a little skipper. Sose Reddy and me and pappy used to go huntin', though I never got nothin' cause I was an awful shot, sose you might say that jist Reddy and pappy went huntin' and I tagged along with 'em.

"Well, Reddy was a good natured sort of guy, 'cept that he hated people who would set these weasel traps and baited them so that they had poisoned blocks of salt and meat which they would set where they didn't want no weasels to be. They was a bunch of Vanderkamp blackies who used to do it.

"I remember how Reddy would curse all of creation when he would find one of them traps. Ya see other animals would pick up and eat the meat or lick on the salt blocks and so would die. Was such a senseless death. Besides, with all the folks who had been living there for pret near hundred, two hundred years or so, why the whole balance of things wasn't really the way it should have been. In the wild woods, ya see, nobody cares none what they do, cause they figure that there's always more. Well, that's fine until you start adding up the years together and then you find that things ain't what they should be. They get a little off, know what I mean?" Jake looked at the others who nodded their heads. Jake rocked forward and put his elbows on the checker board. He propped his chin up with his hands.

"One day they caught one of the people who was doin' the poisoning. Pret near killed thirty animals, they figured, 'fore he got one weasel. They took him into town and they put him in the square. Sheriff Pete--who was also the judge—hog tied him in the center of town for one day and folks let him have all kinds of mischief. Only gave him one meal, if I remember right—jist afore he went in. After a day of that you can imagine that he swore up and down that he'd never set another trap."

Ike and Ed laughed at the thought, Nothing as exciting had happened since they had lived in town. "Pappy was real happy, but for some reason, Reddy wasn't. Pappy asked him why and he said that he didn't have nothing 'gain them blackies in person, 'cause what he was against was the poisoning of them animals. It's something that spreads, you know. Another animal eats a poisoned carcass and picks up a little of the poison and spreads it on to its babies and pretty soon a hunter kills one of the babies and gets some of that poison in him. The point is that the whole thing spreads. You can't stop it once it starts and has been going on for a spell. It keeps going by itself. Gradually it deforms the whole lot of them. The punishment of one person who was part responsible don't stop the transmission of poison. Don't stop others who might be doing it neither. I guess you can say that it's that poison that Reddy hated and what it was doing to the woods that he knew so well. It didn't have nothing to do with any person, really, but more to do with what was happenin'."

"Yeah," said Ed, "I remember people who used to talk about Old Reddy, didn't he live down where the dump is?"

"Wasn't a dump then. Was a real nice field with a marsh at one end. Lots of birds used to live in that marsh."

"Don't look at me," said Ike, "I'm a Tennessee boy, born and bred."

Jake didn't reply, but simply studied the checker board.

Chapter 6

"Catching More than Fish"

"HELP! HELP ME, Johnny, Dagnabit! Jeese! Holy--Johnny, come here, come here," yelled Rodney as the pain of the fishhook in his finger was making him dance about wildly.

"Come here, John, help!"

The cries were quickly heeded by John who was standing at the edge of the woods at that moment. He was attending to an urgent call of nature. Having finished, he rushed quickly to his friend's side and found that Rodney had a fish hook in his finger.

"Stop hopping around, Rodney. I can't get that out with you moving all over the place."

"But it hurts, it hurts, it hurts, it hurts!"

"Yes I know, but it will stop hurting if you sit down and let me take it out," responded John, patiently. Whether it was these reassuring words or John's forceful grip on the other's shoulder that pacified his companion, soon John was working on the task of extricating the barbed hook from the fatty flesh of Rodney's ring finger. The task of taking out a fish hook is not a simple one. This is because fishermen use hooks with barbs on them that are designed to hold the fish once the initial contact is made. The barbs cannot be pulled out directly without taking half of the finger with them, for just as they are efficient at holding fish, they are equally effective at containing any flesh that happens to come under their power in a most democratic fashion.

One must carefully move the hook back and forth as one applies gentle upward pressure in order to do the least damage. John was attempting to execute this task, which was not made easier by Rodney's fidgeting. Finally, however, the fish hook was removed and Rodney, elated over his freedom, jumped up as if propelled by a spring. "Golyadkins! I'm free!"

By jumping upwards in so sudden a manner, he pushed John backwards, causing John to cut himself on the same fish hook, though the hook did not enmesh itself in his flesh.

"Rodney, stop a moment," said John, a little irritated at the other's behavior and his own needless cut. "You've got to wash out that wound so that it doesn't get infected."

But Rodney didn't hear him. He was too busy dancing around in sheer delight after having freed himself from such a noxious pain. "Rodney," began John, this time a little more persuasive as he added a special inflection, taking Rodney by the neck and leading him over to the water. "If you don't wash that, you may lose that finger. Now you wouldn't want that, would you?"

Rodney was instantly sobered by the words "losing your finger." How could he lose his finger, he thought. Hadn't he just had the fish hook removed? And yet what if he did lose his finger? What horrible results would follow such an untimely disaster. All his dreams about becoming a big league baseball player would be dashed to ruins. He could never be able to play for the New York Yankees with Babe Ruth. He would be confined to the simple, rural life of Bella County for the rest of his days. What disgusting horrors! *--now at bat number eleven, batting four-twenty-four, Rodney Vanderkamp! The crowd cheered--Go Rodney, send it out of here, We love Rodney--Go Rodney--Give it a go Rod--Let her fly, Vanderkamp--*

But no. It now might never be. A life wasted on the barbs of chance!

Oh despondence; oh wretchedness; oh-- "Oh," said Rodney as the cold water made him start. John was putting Rodney's hand into the water and washing it for him.

"That water's cold."

"If you don't cooperate with me," said Dow jokingly, "I'll give you your Saturday night bath early."

Both boys laughed at this. The laughter seemed to bring back Rodney's confidence and his natural disposition so that John had no trouble dressing the puncture wound with cool river rushes.

***

Dear Julia thought that if she and Victor returned to their parents near the garden that Victor would become as quiet as he had been at the outset. She imagined that he did not like to talk around her parents. However, this didn't prove to be the case. When they joined the rest, young Victor kept up his chattering at the same (for Julia, incessant) rate as before.

"That's a lovely garden," said young Victor to Mrs. Vanderkamp. As he spoke, his hand wandered to Julia's waist where it attempted to tickle the young lady. But quickly Julia removed the hand with a patient smile. She really wanted to run back to the house, away from this bore, and lock the door. But good breeding won out over these immediate desires so that she merely, politely, removed his hand. Victor took the smile to indicate that the latter enjoyed his gambit, and he felt quite satisfied for the execution of it. So he took the next opportunity to try a further gesture, namely taking Miss Julia's arm in his as the group started to walk away.

Now, it was really of little consequence whether or not Julia walked arm in arm with Victor or not, as she had many times before taken the arms of visitors as a sort of courtesy to them and a sign of respect to her father. But for some reason, this action by young Victor did not in any way seem a trivial matter to her. It was a faux pas to take one's arm away from a gentleman (whomever it might be) so she found herself in a rather difficult situation, which she alleviated in a manner most discrete. She decided to trip and so lose her shoe. This afforded an opportunity to break the lock that Victor's arm now represented as she went to retrieve her lost shoe. Instead, however, Victor insisted on going back with her and helping her on with her shoe--during which she stepped on his fingers, which Victor attributed to the clumsiness of her being off balance.

But Julia was not clumsy.

Finally, with all other courses of action from her repertoire spent, she fell back on the old stand-by: the terrible headache. Because of this malady, she insisted that she had to leave the group immediately.

"I'll accompany you, Miss Julia," said Victor immediately.

"No thank you, Victor. Mother has so wanted to show you her lovely garden. I wouldn't feel right taking you away even for a moment. Excuse me, everyone." And with that she hastily made her exit.

Victor felt most satisfied with this encounter. He thought that Julia must have left because she was very impressed by him. Her departure signified something akin to a swoon over his gallant nature. All this served to increase the already very high opinion that Victor held of himself. It was for this reason that he felt no cause to look where Julia was going when she left. Thus, he did not see her when she changed directions from her path to the house.

What Julia saw was the sight of her brother and John coming from the direction of the road that ran between the two estates. It would be impossible to convey the high pitch of excitement that this sight occasioned. It is often true that an individual can reach extremely high pitches of happiness when a pleasing occurrence transpires immediately after an unpleasant one. This is so because not only is the individual brought from the normal level to this state of happiness, but also brought from the depths of unhappiness as well. This makes the complete ascent greater. Such was the feeling of Julia upon seeing the return of these two fishermen.

"Well, I see you've caught something," said Julia when she was in talking distance of the pair. What she didn't realize was that because of the accident, the two boys had decided to leave early and had, in fact, only caught three fish. This was a most unsatisfactory total in John's estimation so that this comment of Julia's, which was meant to be a compliment of sorts, was actually received in a much different manner by Dow, who usually caught at least a half-dozen fish when he went fishing for an entire day. But Julia had never been fishing in her life, and had never discussed the subject with her brother (though this would not have helped much) and thus didn't understand the effect of her comment.

"Hello, sis," greeted Rodney half-heartedly, for his finger had begun to sting some and he was not in the best of spirits. By this time, Julia was only a few feet from the two. She saw that her brother had reeds wrapped around his left hand. Then her eyes quickly saw the stains of blood on the pants of Dow. He had, in his effort to remove the hook, gotten more of Rodney's blood on himself than Rodney spilled on his own person. The sight of blood on her brother bothered Julia, but the sight of the stains of blood on Dow put her into such a state of disarray that she rushed to them crying, "What's happened to you boys?" (Meaning what's happened to Dow. Though she was concerned about her brother, she was guided by her passion to be more distraught by any possible injury to Dow.) "You must come to the house immediately and let me take care of you two. Really, men: you go on a simple fishing trip and then end up hurting yourselves so! I don't know how you could have gotten such terrible injuries, I--I--" Julia found herself at a loss for words. She wanted both to take care of John, and at the same time scold him for allowing himself to become injured. The conflict between these two feelings brought a resolution of seething quiet as she led the boys back to the house. When John tried to explain what had happened, she interrupted saying, "We'll have plenty of time to discuss all that, but first I want to examine your injuries."

In point of fact, Julia anticipated the role of nurse to her sweetheart with the fondest of human emotions, for she could imagine a no more satisfying role than to care for John in any way she could. She longed to relieve him of any distress he might have.

John, on the other hand, was thinking about how glad he was that Jason was not home to see how poor a day John had had fishing. He still would have to tell Jefferson why he didn't have any fish (for John planned to give all the fish to Rodney, even though John had caught them all. John thought that it might go better with Rodney's parents if they saw that their son had more than a fish hook injury to signify for his day's fishing.) The prospect of telling Jefferson didn't really bother John. He knew that Jefferson was a fair man. Jason, however, was different. John felt competitive with Jason. The teasing from him would be uncomfortable. Therefore, Dow was happy that the other was not home.

Rodney only wanted to get in the house and have a piece of apple and blackberry pie, which he knew would be waiting. When they got inside, Julia seated them at the kitchen table and looked at her brother's wound first, partly because she felt that it would be too forward to look at Dow's injury first and partly because after she had finished with her brother, she could spend as much time as she wanted with Dow's.

Rodney's finger was dispensed with quickly as Dow had done a very good job already. The only thing that needed administering was iodine and a gauze bandage. Rodney screamed when the iodine was applied and then set into applying all manner of polite curses at his sister, pretending that she was trying to poison him and that he could now rest in peace as the iodine had surely finished his life in one stinging blow. But soon Rodney's attention was wholly on the pie, which he was attempting to devour in its entirety.

Meanwhile, Julia was trying to attend to Dow. "I'm all right," said Dow.

"Now, be nice, John, show me your cut."

"I don't have a cut," said John, who was keeping his hands under the table. He, in all truth, didn't really care for anyone fussing over him, especially concerning such a small cut that he had sustained in the fish hook incident.

"Now you're being a naughty boy, I see blood all over your pants. Let me see your hand. I only want to wash it for you."

"I'm really fine," said Dow emphatically as he brought his hands up to gesture in his impatience at being fussed over.

The sight of John's hands gave Julia the opportunity to clutch one and to hunt for the cut. She found it quickly. And so Dow had to sit there while Julia carefully rubbed his hand clean of all the dirt with a damp rag and soap. Never was a hand cleaned so carefully and with so much deliberateness as Dow's hand. Julia reluctantly proceeded and applied the iodine and gauze bandage. After she was finished, Dow thanked her, donated the fish to Rodney and made his departure.

Julia was still sitting at the kitchen table, holding the implements of medicine in front of her when her parents returned from their jaunt to the garden. They were in a good mood, having just bid their friends farewell.

***

Jason sat contented on the train ride home. He held two boxes on his lap containing new clothes. These were the fruits of his trip. The holiday had been an interesting one. He was anxious, though, to get home. The words of Samuel Johnson rang in his ears: great things are never done at once, but are the result of prolonged effort and continuous diligence. Jason's plan was about to unfold upon his unwitting rivals. The wheels of the train clicked rhythmically in time with Mr. Beauchay's occasional snores as Jason smiled at the setting sun.

Chapter 7

"About a Chance Meeting at a Telegraph Office"

AS HAS BEEN MENTIONED EARLIER, John didn't get into town much. He rather avoided the excursion when he could. Because of this, he didn't know Cindy Pancroft, daughter of the barber. Cindy was known to a few by actual experience and to countless others through reputation, as a young woman who would (if the proper circumstances prevailed) endeavor to please a young man in any manner he wished.

This is not to imply that she was a professional (for she wasn't, and never would call that ancient trade her own--in fact, later in life, in another part of the South, she married a preacher and bore him three fine sons), but she was certainly more liberal with a young man who showed her a good time by his seeming sincerity or, lacking that, by his fancy presents. Several young men in town had covert relationships with Cindy that lasted on and off for many months. All this went on to the complete ignorance of Cindy's father, Mr. Pancroft, who was an immigrant that, for some inexplicable reason, shortened his real name from Krauftenheimer to Pancroft. He did so thinking that this new name was more American. There was never any "pan" in his name at any time, unless one wants to count the Pan-America, which was the name of the ship that brought him over from Germany when he was just a young man (though it is difficult to understand why anyone would want to name himself after a freighter that offered steerage accommodations).

Mr. Pancroft was a man who kept to himself. His wife was dead and he paid little attention to anything domestic, including his daughter. He figured that it was a child's place to look after herself. And so Cindy did, and brought a certain amount of business to her father's barbershop because some people felt a kind of obligation.

So it was one day that John was dispatched to town to pick up a telegram when who should be in the telegraph office but Miss Cindy. She was having trouble filling out a form for a letter she wished to send to an aunt in Tallahassee and asked John if he might help her. Now, it was no accident that many people found this woman attractive, as she had a figure that was full and pleasing in a most distinct way. This sight caught John's eye also as he was assisting the young lady with her cable.

"How many words do you want to use?" asked Dow.

"How many should I use?"

"Well, it depends on how much money you have and how complete a message you want to send. They charge you per word and that includes the address, too."

"I never counted the words, to tell you the honest truth," she purred as she moved an inch closer to Dow so that her skirt brushed against his leg.

"Maybe if you told me what you wanted to say I could help you phrase it using the least number of words possible," offered John in a most gentlemanly fashion. Actually, he did not find his task at all disagreeable as the comely appearance of Miss Cindy, was, in certain points, most inviting and distracting.

"Well, I would be most obliged to you, sir, if you would help little me with this awful telegram. You know, I don't have a head for such technical things as forms and numbers. And you seem to know quite exactly what you're doing. Why, I wouldn't begin to know how to start counting up these silly little words."

Dow smiled and Miss Pancroft indirectly delivered her real message: *I would be most appreciative for any time you might give to poor little Cindy.*

Meanwhile Dow cocked his head and considered her name: 'Cindy.' What a lovely name, thought Dow. It almost sang of its own accord. John stood for several moments saying her name in various ways to himself, and he stood in apparent daze, staring at the wall in front of him. His companion broke his chain of aimless musings as she touched his arm gently and handed him the form.

"What?" said John, startled.

"The form you wanted," sang Miss Cindy softly.

"What form?" replied Dow, who had almost forgotten about the favor that he had promised the helpless Miss Pancroft.

"Oh you boys can say the silliest things sometimes," laughed Cindy as she put the pencil into Dow's hand and brought him back to the telegraph office and mundane existence. It should not be surprising that Dow was struck by this young woman. This was due to the number of amorous volleys that were fired had under her command from the small but well-equipped garrison which she had directed towards the strong but largely green troops comprising Dow. There was no real way that Dow could, in any real sense, be any match for these weapons--highly efficient through much experience and expert handling.

As any field commander knows, it is better to have a lesser number of crack military troops who have had battle experience, than a larger number of non-experienced troops. The inexperienced troops are more apt to run into confusion the minute the loud artillery begins blasting away.

I am very anxious to know when you are coming. "How many words was that?" asked Cindy after her recitation. Dow, who was now in better control of himself as his eyes were fixed on the paper in front of him, quickly counted. "Ten exactly," said John offhandedly.

"Now how many do I have to cut off?" she asked in a timid voice. There was a minimum of ten words.

It seemed rather odd to Dow for a brief moment that this helpless tender thing should be able to hit the precise number of words needed for the telegram on the first try. The coincidence was unsettling, so he looked again at those innocent eyes of this young woman. Instantly all his doubts were removed as she pressed his hand on hers and began walking towards the clerk's desk.

"Yes, can I help you," said the clerk without looking up. He was writing something down on a piece of paper.

"This young lady," began Dow in a shaky voice that quickly found itself, "this lady would like to send a telegram."

"Where to?" inquired the clerk as he looked up. He smiled upon seeing Cindy with what he took to be another of her trophies, a suspicion which was confirmed, at least to the clerk's satisfaction, by the look on Dow's face. This look confirmed to him that this woman had Dow completely in her power, and also that Dow was not aware of this fact.

"Where do you want to send your telegram?" asked the clerk lightly as he looked at Dow and then quickly to Cindy with a look that said, I know what's happening, and I'm not going to ruin him for you.

"Ah, it is, ah," stammered Dow as he stumbled, trying to remember where Cindy had told him.

"The young man said she lived in Tallahassee, I believe," put in Cindy, as if she were somehow backing Dow in his vain efforts.

"Tallahassee, right--now what's the message?"

Dow read the message and paid for the telegram, insisting that he should be permitted the privilege of assisting a girl who had so fine a manner.

So done, they departed. Dow offered, and was accepted, the task of escorting Cindy back to her house, which was adjacent to her father's shop.

"I hope," began Dow, hardly knowing what he was saying, "that you will permit me to have the privilege of calling on you again."

"Oh the pleasure would be mine, Mr. Dow, if you cared to honor me with your company. Please feel welcome to call at my home any time."

This success buoyed John's spirits as he floated home on his horse. Only one thing struck him as somewhat peculiar. It was something which he didn't dwell upon, but it was somehow present in his mind about his chance meeting that day: Cindy called him 'Mr. Dow.' This was peculiar in that he never remembered telling her his name. "How did she know?" he thought. Perhaps the telegraph clerk called me by name, or perhaps he had written his name inadvertently on the paper, signing his name instead of hers. But to all these possibilities, John's memory seemed to be in direct disagreement.

But then Dow's contemplations were jarred when he remembered about the telegram that Jason had dispatched him to get for Mr. Beauchay. He had to go back. Jason had been very specific on John going immediately to town. John rode back, somewhat embarrassed at forgetting. He imagined that everyone would know the reason that he was re-entering the town.

Mister Beauchay, sitting at his desk, was unable to do the little paper work that lay in front of him because his thoughts were exclusively upon that little piece of real estate that now hosted a golf course. What was he to do? Should he accede to the unreasonable demands of Murdock? Beauchay knew that Murdock would not be able to get his asking price at any public auction. People around Bella County knew the price of land and would not be fooled by a fast talker who was trying to make a quick buck. What Mr. Murdock didn't know was that none of the landowners from the good families of Bella County needed a country club to let them feel as if they were important. They knew this from their history. Samuel Beauchay knew that even the Thompsons, relative newcomers to Bella County as they arrived after the war and split what was left of Thomas Garth's old place and taking pieces of the Stuart and Rutherford estates to form their farm in the northeast portion of the county, didn't need a country club to tell them that they were worth something. The wiles of Murdock were doomed from the beginning with his country club. Now he wanted to spite the landed class of Bella County. He wanted to play them against the disease which had infected them: George Dodson.

What Murdock didn't understand was the pride of Bella County. They had something to be uncommonly proud of--namely their families, which went back for generations. This lent a stability and way of life that the likes of Murdock could never understand. This was not a cutthroat existence. People built up upon their skills and not through tactics of undercutting the competition. Cutthroat competition was the way of the North, not the South. Here, there was a sense in everyone's minds that there was enough for all since the demand for raw cotton, peanuts, and soybeans far exceeded the supply. It was to everyone's advantage to team up and compete against nature and her allies, insects and blight, to produce the most abundant crop possible.

Everyone was united in a fight against the common foe. It was that land which could be so rich if it were managed properly, and if not, nature could take charge and make it barren in a few short years. So it was that each farmer had something common to contend with. No one had any pretensions about being any more than a single man fighting and guiding his fickle soil so that he could keep his bottle of whiskey filled and his wife in pretty clothes.

So long as everyone was doing the same thing, there was no problem. People often did things for each other. The Stuarts, for example, used to have a cultural evening on Thursdays. The Jacksons once had dinners or they celebrated the hunt that used to begin at Mitchell Evan's. But basically people held no illusions about themselves. They knew that as quickly as they had earned their fortunes, they could lose them again through poor managing. The times were grand because no one held any false pretensions-- well almost no one--but the few who did usually moved to town because running a plantation is not the role for someone who can't say to himself several times a day that though this land belongs to me, it will never be mine. I have to fight continually with nature to bring forth its bounty.

Nature never gives up.

All these things Murdock didn't understand. What he saw were a bunch of rich farms and some turkeys ready to be plucked. He must have come in expecting to make a bundle on the pretext of letting the large farmers puff up their conceits and join a country club. Now he was making the same mistake in thinking that they would pay any price for a piece of worthless land. Murdock didn't understand a farmer from Bella County.

Beauchay looked up at the sky. It was late afternoon. There was a sadness in the air. He wondered whether Dodson would get Murdock's land. I don't think he's interested at the moment, thought Beauchay, at least not at Murdock's price. Dodson's got too much respect for money to throw it away on a slimly creature like Murdock. Dodson understands Murdock best of all. They come from the same mold. He will be able to fight the other on his own terms. Yet, the longer I wait, the closer Dodson will be to cutting a deal with Murdock. If Murdock is the two bit operator I take him for, then he's going to accept my offer if I sweeten it by say 10 per cent or so. It's still too much to pay for that land, but not too much to pay for keeping Dodson off of it. Later on, that land may prove to be a valuable bargaining chip which I can use against the so-called bank president.

***

Jason was sitting in his study chair doing his lessons in economic history. He awaited the return of John from his telegraph errand to see how John had fared with Cindy Pancroft, who should have been able to handle the teen-aged boy with little trouble. Jason laughed as he put down the pencil. He had heard that Cindy would be at the telegraph office when he got his hair cut earlier in the day. It seemed to be an interesting play to put John into the way of mayhem. John was too simple to see the scheme.

Just now, Jason allowed himself to dream of his eventual ownership of both the Beauchay and Vanderkamp estates. The entire western portion of the county, save the small Mitchell Evans

Farm, would be his. He would be the squire with all the possessions a man could desire: Julia, farm hands by the score, and lots and lots of money.

Everything would be as it should be, as Jason would be a respected landowner throughout the state. Perhaps he would become a congressman or senator! Jason believed what his tutor, Russel, had told him: that industrialization and consolidation were the economic realities of the future and that if he, Jason, wanted to get a piece of the economic pie, it would be necessary for him to consolidate the small estates. This would afford economy by scale. If only he could get his hands on a few hundred dollars more, he could begin with a few investments now, before he came of legal age. Then he wouldn't have to go to college, a fate which he didn't especially relish, but would endure if need be. Mr. Russel said that there were a lot of potentially good contacts that could be made by attending the right school. Something in the northeast would be right, perhaps Harvard or Princeton or Yale--Jason was unsure about which to choose. But he was certain of his need to make contacts, which would aid him in his rise to money and power. Only the old schools full of Yankee money would do. This would be his ticket to fortune. The West was impossible for school because it was so backward. The South was impotent as an industrial center. He needed industrial contacts to diversify his financial position. Perhaps he could be on the vanguard of industry as it moved to the natural advantages of a warm climate. At any rate, such visions were beyond the scope of most small-thinking southerners. People tied to the land, like his father was, just couldn't understand. The future would be a time in which events would move swiftly and fortunes would be made and lost by the bold action of creative, imaginative men of opportunity. It was an age for men like Carnegie, Morgan, and Rockefeller. These men knew money and how to make all of it they wanted. These men of the northeast would be the leaders of the nation until other sections caught up with them. Each section of the country would have to groom its own giants. Jason hoped to become one of these.

The farm and other diversified interests would make Jason a man of the times. He would become a man of the future. Jason leaned back in his chair and bit the end of his pencil. What endless possibilities seemed to lie before him. There was a terrifying sense that he could be almost anything. His future was within his power, his will. Jason laughed as he snapped his pencil in two.

Chapter 8

"Presenting the Reader with Amorous Delights"

THE ROSE FINGERED AEGEAN −LIKE DAWN, child of the morning, stretched her hands across the sky over the forested hills that marked the eastern boundaries of Bella County. The early summer blooms were still on display, as the rich red earth showed forth its fecundity. George Dodson quietly rose and dressed himself as he mechanically prepared his body for another day of battle. There was a certain limpness to his shoulders that seemed to demonstrate a reticence over continuing in the pattern that he had repeated so often over the years, a limpness that seemed to be at odds with the armor: sharply pressed clothes and a sleek briefcase that bore the manufacture's name, *Tellum*, across the top in gold letters which were slightly faded from hours of use. George finished his preparation as he drained his coffee cup and finally mounted his automobile to drive the short distance to town. The noise of roosters crying in the stillness was almost drowned out by the sound of the motor car as George, comfortable in his soft leather seats, led the car into town. The wheels of the car, despite the morning dew, spun dirt on the sparkle, thus marring its dazzling display.

John also got up, though much later in the morning since he was rather fond of sleeping in. He had no chores to do until the afternoon so he decided to make the most of the warm softness of the sheets. In his mind he thought about his upcoming visit with Cindy, which he had arranged for that evening when they would attend a horn concert at the Baptist Church near the cemetery. John's imagination had never been so intensely captured by any girl before. His mind lingered upon his sweetheart in various situations and attire.

When night actually did arrive and they went to the concert, he couldn't help but feel a strange tingle. Perhaps this was due to the crowding of the church (the musicians had come from Savannah). Dow was obliged to sit very near Cindy so that he felt the otherness of her body next to him. *What if I said, "Kiss me Cindy!" I'm sure that she would instantly throw her arms around me and press her lips to mine. Right there in the chapel! But no, these aren't right and proper things to--after the concert, yes, after, that would be best, I will put my hand to her soft cheeks and gently guide her head towards mine and--* everyone started clapping as the last number before the intermission had finished. John began clapping very enthusiastically.

Afterwards as they were walking home John asked Cindy, "Are you tired?" The question was meant for a follow-up question of--why don't we sit down on the bench at the corner of Cumberland and Marshall Avenues?

But instead, Cindy responded, "I think it's a beautiful night, why don't we walk a bit?"

This confused Dow, who had everything worked out as to what he would do after they sat down.

"Isn't the moon beautiful?" said Cindy as they walked up to Main Street to make the big circle again.

"Yes, I suppose so," said Dow, still confused and trying to think of some way to get Cindy to sit down so that he could kiss her. Finally they arrived at her house and stopped. I suppose, thought Dow, that I could kiss her standing up as well as sitting down, but how will I do it?

"Well, thank you for a very nice evening," said Cindy, who stood perfectly still and was half-facing Dow.

"Yes, I liked it too. The--ah--orchestra was very good."

"The horns were nice," corrected Cindy.

"Yes," responded John, not realizing that he had made a mistake. His mind was totally occupied with the mechanics of just how his lips were going to traverse the seemingly insurmountable distance of two and a half feet.

"It was so nice of you to ask me," added Cindy, patching a long gap of silence. I'm running out of time, thought Dow. If I don't do something right now I won't have any time. But I can't go right up to her and kiss her. Why, it's only the first time I've officially gone out with her. Maybe she doesn't kiss on the first date, or maybe she'll be offended that I thought so low of her to try something like that when I hardly even know her. Why didn't I ask myself these questions earlier? I had all that time in the church but I didn't do anything really except dread this moment. This moment, which will be the only moment that I will remember from this entire night--whether I have the gumption or not to try.

What can it hurt to try? Won't she think it rather nice that I want to kiss her, even if she doesn't let me? Oh, I wish this evening were over. But there's no time to lose, it seems like I've been standing here for hours. I better say something while I--while I what?

"You have a nice fence," said John.

"Oh thank you, do you really think so? I don't care for it much really, it's old and hasn't been painted for years, see?" she said as she pointed to a section of the fence that was peeling badly. "It isn't much good, but then I suppose that can't be seen very well at night. I think you're right, it does have a rather nice shape to it."

"Yes, in the moonlight it's nice. I mean--" stammered Dow. Then he put his hand to her cheek.

"Oh," said Cindy as she jumped away from Dow's hand.

"What's the matter?" asked John.

"Nothing," said Cindy immediately. "It's just that your hand is so cold. Here," she said, taking his hand, "feel it yourself against you own cheek."

John was surprised as his hand was as cold as if he had been swimming in a mountain lake. He didn't know what to say or do-- why was his hand so cold?

"Now my hand is warm, feel." Cindy put John's hand in her own and pressed it to her cheek, an action which physically pulled John much closer to her.

Now the distance was only six inches, but John had long since stopped his careful analysis of the situation, which was now in complete turmoil as far as he was concerned. Then his lips touched hers and he felt the gentle firmness of her face. But as soon as it had begun, it was over with, John standing in front of the house and Cindy waving her handkerchief good-bye from the front porch.

It took many hours of reflection for John to understand the dynamics of the kiss. It must have been *he* who kissed *her*, though in all honesty, he had no real recollection of ever completing the act. But if he hadn't done it, how would it have occurred? The contemplation of this question, in time, convinced John that indeed he had boldly kissed Cindy and that she immediately retreated in her modesty to her front door.

This last (and for John, most reasonable, or the only reasonable explanation of what had happened) finally allowed him the soothing comfort of sleep as the fullness of night covered the sky in darkness.

***

"Ten percent more than my last offer and that's all I'm going to give you, Murdock. Take it or leave it. It's your choice."

"Well, now Mister Beauchay. I didn't expect to receive such a blunt offer from such a tactful gentleman as yourself."

"There are many signs of a gentleman, sir, but what we are discussing is land."

"Very true, sir, very true. I didn't mean to say anything critical about yourself. As you have expressed a desire to get directly to the matter at hand, I see no reason why we need engage in all the formalities that people of our station usually do. Though I must admit that I find such direct action disturbing in that it seems to detract from our own ultimate disinterest in such pecuniary matters. But since you insist, I must reply that such an offer is certainly out of the question."

"Does that mean you're rejecting it?" snapped Samuel Beauchay.

"It means, sir, that I quoted you a price at which I was willing to part with my land and that I mean to stick to that price."
"Then good-day sir," said Beauchay.

"Just a minute," put Murdock as Samuel reached for his hat and turned to go. "You're not leaving, are you?"

"I made you an offer which I will pay you, an offer which is more than fair. If you want it, then take it. If not, then I have no more to say."

"But you forget about the other bidder that I mentioned. Surely a man of your high station would not like to be outbid by someone of, say, a much lower one?"

"I have no interest in your competition or with any unnamed parties, Murdock. So if you will excuse me. . ." said Beauchay as he again started to depart.

"You forget about the public auction," said Murdock, rising slightly from his chair. But Beauchay never hesitated as he said over his shoulder, "You won't get two thirds of what I'm offering at any public auction. My offer is good for one week, Murdock, think about it." And with that Beauchay was gone, leaving Murdock half standing and gaping at the closed door.

*****

"Howdy, Ike," said Victor Stuart, Sr. as he entered the store.

"Afternoon, Mr. Stuart," said Ike. Jake and Ed didn't pay any attention to the customer. They were involved in a game of rummy.

"I'd like ten pounds of flour and four pounds of sugar and sixteen pounds of oats," said Stuart as he opened his wallet, almost as if an old habit made him demonstrate that he had the money to pay for what he was ordering.

"Yes sir," said Ike as he started weighing out the items requested into the sacks that Stuart had brought with him. "Nice day, isn't it?" said Ike. "Pretty good for summer, not too hot. There's a little breeze--I like that."

"Is your boy aiming to ride in the race this year?"

"I don't know, he's been in several smaller races; I'm not sure if he's ready, though he is a registered rider, you know."

"From what I hear, he's pret near the best horseman on this side of Georgia."

"Well, he's been working at it. I used to be a fair rider myself, but he's long since passed the stage where I have anything to teach him."

"Yep, well there'll be a lot of money ridin' on him when he does, I'll tell you that."

"Well, I know mine will, Ike," said Victor as he paid for the bundles. "But thank you for the compliment." Stuart began lugging the sacks outside. When he reached the door he turned and nodded his head goodbye.

"Much obliged," said Ike as Stuart left.

"That feller's got money these days, hasn't he?" said Jake.

"Yep, hasn't asked for credit for several months. Good thing too, 'cause I don't know how much more I could have given him."

"Funny how a guy can come into money all of a sudden like that, isn't it?" said Jake as he threw in his hand to start another game.

"Somebody said that he sold a few of his horses for over a thousand dollars, and that he's goin' into the raisin' of horses stead of farmin'," said Ed as he gathered the cards to deal.

"Thousand dollars for a few horses? You got to be kiddin', Ed. Why, those plugs of his weren't worth that," said Jake.

"All I know is what I hear," said Ed.

"They're okay for work, I'll admit, but t'aint that good," repeated Jake as he picked up his hand and began arranging the cards.

"All I know is what I hear," said Ed again as they started their game.

Chapter 9

"An Incident Concerning Samuel Beauchay and a Picture Sewn by Julia"

ONLY THREE DAYS had passed before Samuel Beauchay received the following note:

> *Dear Mr. Beauchay:*
> *Though I originally decided to reject your offer proffered a few days ago, circumstances have changed sufficiently so that I now believe that it is in my best interest to sell you my property. I have been offered a most advantageous position in Kentucky that I must accept immediately. Therefore, against my better judgment, I will sell you the land at your price.*
>
> *Very truly yours,*
> *F. Murdock*

The bluff had worked. Samuel Beauchay wasn't sure what he would have done if Murdock hadn't accepted his offer, but he had a hunch about the character of that little weasel and his hunch had proven to be correct.

It seemed to Samuel that things were beginning to work according to some as-yet unformulated plan that would allow Beauchay to use the land as some kind of weapon against his brother-in-law, though the precise way which he would do it was still largely undetermined.

***

It was very difficult for John Dow to kiss Cindy Pancroft that first night, but soon he overcame his fears and was a regular visitor at her door, stopping as often as she would allow, which was twice a week. As the months began to merge together, John became a frequent visitor of that area of catacomb paths in the woods near Sawyer's Bridge, which was a somewhat disreputable place. It was the haven for lovers who were seeking some privacy.

John congratulated himself at how successful he was with Miss Pancroft. He imagined her to be a pure, young thing, swept off her feet by his dashing figure. John's attention to Cindy did not go unnoticed by the town. Among the boys it was a regular joke how John would go strolling about with Cindy, taking her places and treating her as if she were a princess, while some of them were (or had been) simultaneously seeing Miss Cindy when she was not seeing Dow, for purposes alluded to earlier.

One day, after seeing Cindy and keeping her company for a few idle hours near Sawyer's Bridge, John decided to stop by the Vanderkamp's to pick up Jason, as John knew that he was spending the day there.

It was true that Jason was at the Vanderkamps, but the reason wasn't the one he had declared to John and Jessy at breakfast. He hadn't gone to talk to Rodney about horses or about the big county horse race in August. Rather, he had gone to see Julia and to show off his new clothes. The last shipment had finally arrived. It might be the case that he would do some talking with Rodney, but this was not his aim. So many of his expeditions had ended up without his being able to get Julia in private so that he might impress her. Jason made a firm resolution that this time would be different. He would isolate Miss Vanderkamp and let her see him in all his finery. When he arrived, however, he found the two of them in the game room busy with their own separate projects. "Why is it that every time I pay a visit, Rodney always he has to be hanging around?" Jason asked himself. "Why can't I ever find Julia alone?"

Rodney was cleaning a gun that his father had given him for a present on his eighteenth birthday and Julia was doing some embroidery when Jason came into the room.

"Hello, Jason," said Rodney without taking his eyes off the gun. He was carefully wiping the oil into the metal.

"Hello everyone," replied Jason, taking the advantage of Rodney's inattention to walk over to Julia.

Julia politely rose and greeted the young Mr. Beauchay.

"What are you doing?" asked Jason as he sat right down and leaned his head over her needle work.

"Something for a cushion in the salon upstairs," Julia responded.

"It's really beautiful," added Jason, trying to figure out just what the scene was that she was portraying. "It's a lake scene, isn't it?" ventured Jason at last.

"Not really," Julia said quietly, though she was a little perturbed at Jason for blocking her light and not allowing her to work. "It's a man on a horse."

"Of course, I see that now," put Jason as he slid closer to Julia so that his body was almost touching hers. "But it's by a lake, isn't it?"

Julia wasn't ignorant of Jason's movements, but hoped that if she remained as she was, determined to work, that he would desist and allow her to continue what she was doing. "I hadn't really considered that, but a lake might look nice, though I was planning to put in a forest instead." What she didn't tell him was that the picture was of Dow riding his horse into the forest as he so often did, being an excellent rider as well as a woodsman. It almost seemed profane that someone would go into such detail about trivial questions when she was engrossed in portraying an artistic rendition of someone for whom she cared so deeply. But still she clung to the hope that Jason would see her desire to work and take his cue to talk to Rodney, since she supposed that was why he had come.

But Jason was not to be denied, and persisted with a resolution that was formed in the long spaces of time that connect events of activity into some sort of cohesive unity. And so he moved even closer so that his leg barely touched hers as he asked, "Who's the rider, your brother?"

Rodney, hearing himself mentioned, instantly sprung from his chair to see what they were talking about. And before Julia had an opportunity to answer, he glanced at the embroidery and instantly declared that the horseman wasn't himself, as the style was far different than his own in the saddle and that the rider had black hair (Rodney's hair was light brown). "The rider must be Victor Stuart!" proclaimed Rodney, who, along with the rest of the Vanderkamp household, thought that Julia was deeply in love with young Victor and would one day marry him.

"Victor!" exclaimed Jason, who, though he had sensed that Julia had a fondness for John, never knew that she might also have some sentiment for Victor Stuart, too. This possibility proved immediately troubling for Jason—for though John was easy to dispense with, Victor was another matter. Not only was he well thought of by young and old alike, but as of late he was beginning to spend money more freely, which proved that his family's fortune was improving as well.

As Jason considered this new dilemma and Rodney was laughing over what he took to be his sister's embarrassment, Julia felt real consternation over the almost nightmarish situation in which she found herself. Her delicate feelings were being fiercely wrung by these dull witted boys, who had no idea of anything except those vulgar pastimes that boys and men seem inexplicably drawn towards, that leave them blind to the finer and more tender aspects of life. So Julia sat in anxious restlessness, which finally precipitated her rising and declaring in her well-modulated voice, "Did I hear mother calling?"

"Mother, no, that was me laughing. Mother isn't calling," declared Rodney loudly, as his own boisterous enthusiasm for the delightful confusion that he was causing pleased him to no end.

But Julia persisted, for though her voice was soft, it was not weak and again she said, "No, I'm sure I heard it. I'm not surprised that you didn't, Rodney, as you are laughing so hard that you couldn't hear your own name if someone shouted it across the room right now, which would be an extraordinary event at that, as it's something you rarely miss."

Rodney was perplexed as he sensed that his sister was trying to say something to him. Possibly she was even showing him some anger. This seemed completely odd to him as he was certain that it couldn't be over anything he had said, unless it could be the embarrassment that she was still feeling over his correctly guessing the figure in her needlework. This last explanation seemed perfectly delightful to him. Rodney felt a wave of protective fraternity for his younger sister and decided to let her leave if she so desired, for it was just like a woman to become fluttered over small things and she needed time to become unruffled.

So he responded most benevolently, "Well, if you hear mother, you better go see what she wants, but don't go dragging me into it. I'm cleaning my gun and I'm not to be disturbed, unless of course, it is for something to eat."

"Oh Rodney, you just ate, how can you still be hungry?" replied Julia as she gracefully made her exit.

"I'm always hungry, you should know that by now" returned Rodney proudly as his sister left the room. Rodney smiled and said to Jason, "Aren't women funny, Jason? Did you see the way she jumped when I mentioned Victor's name. You know she always denies that she has a sweetheart, but I know better. A girl doesn't jump like that over just anybody. Oh, I tell you, women are really a different animal. And that's the truth, Jason," declared Rodney in a suddenly quieter tone as he walked back to his chair, "yes, a different animal indeed."

Jason scarcely heard a word that Rodney said as he was still trying to sort out the events that had just recently transpired. There had been many times when he had noticed Julia give special attention to the group of boys, which he had always attributed to the presence of Dow. And hadn't she always preferred Dow when they were children? And yet, could it be possible that she didn't like Dow at all, but really liked Victor instead? This would seem more logical on her part, as Victor was a legitimate heir to a diminished but still substantial piece of property, and whose fortunes seemed to have made a shift for the better. Victor was handsome and a good rider (the best, many thought in their part of Georgia). He was respected and a leader among his peers. Yes, Victor would make a very logical choice—certainly a more logical choice than Dow, but would he be a better match than himself? I'm not good looking, he admitted. That's true, but then I'm not bad looking either, and the kind of good looks that Victor has will wear away very quickly, whereas my face will remain as it is until the day I die, which should comprise a considerably longer period than Victor as he is so immoderate. A woman has to consider where she'd be if the man of the house suddenly died and left her with no one to manage the money and look after the important affairs. And I'll certainly outlast Victor. I'm prudent and conservative, and not apt to make costly mistakes, as Victor probably would, or very likely *could*. My fortune will be quite a bit more than Victor's as well, which shouldn't be counted too lightly. I'm dependable and steady, and should the eventuality occur that I was to merge the two farms (as Rodney doesn't really like to farm anyway--he wants to be a professional sportsman or some such nonsense) I would be much better suited for the task than Victor. And how nicely our two farms would fit together! All things taken into consideration, I believe that if she were to be rational about her choice and if all things were presented to her in the proper light, that she must, as a matter of course, choose me over Mr. Popular.

So decided, Jason got up from where he had been sitting and moved next to Rodney. If Victor is my competition, then I've got him licked.

"Are you thinking about college?" asked Rodney, still working on his gun.

"Yes," replied Jason, still occupied with his own thoughts, but sufficiently free of confusion that he could easily carry on another conversation at the same time.

"Have you made applications?" asked Rodney in the same tone as before.

"Yes," said Jason.

"Where to?"

"Well my father suggested Harvard because he knew a fellow who went to Harvard and liked it. Jefferson suggested Cornell, and Mr. Russel, my tutor, wants me to go to Yale. He says that all the most important people in the country go to Yale and that if I really want to make it big, it would be most wise for me to go there."

"So where have you applied?"

"All three."

"All three?"

"Yes."

"But where will you go?"

"I don't know yet, and I probably won't decide until I get letters from the various schools so that I can examine their stationery and see which letterhead I like the best."

Both boys laughed at this, but Jason wasn't telling Rodney that though he was undecided, there was perhaps one favorite among the three: the one he thought would better his career.

"I don't think I could be so free and easy about it," said Rodney. "I think I'll go where my father thinks there is a good place for me on the football team. If you do well in college, then you have a good chance at getting a contract on a professional team."

"You want to play football?"

"Yes, I think so."

"But why, when baseball is so much more solvent? More people go to baseball games than to football. Besides, I think professional football will fold the minute times get a little tighter. Baseball has been around a bit. I'd stick to that if I were you."

"But Paddy Driscoll gets $25,000 a year playing for George Hallas."

"Yes, but just think about how much Babe Ruth gets! And it's not all in salaries either. There's endorsements and personal appearances and the like."

"Well, I don't know. I'll have to talk it over with my father and see what he says."

"The only game that people will continue to pay to see is baseball, because it is the only real American game. Football is so much like some game they play in England, I forget the name of it, but it's practically the same thing." While he was talking, Jason's spirits were getting stronger as he thought about Dow out with Cindy, and how John was making such a fool out of himself.

Suddenly Jason burst out laughing.

"What's so funny?" asked Rodney in a serious tone as he imagined that Jason was laughing at him or at something he had said in their conversation. This made Rodney feel peculiar (as he didn't feel confident discussing practical things around Jason, who always seemed to know more and be able to argue his point better than he, Rodney, could). Rodney felt a type of pressure building inside his chest: a pressure full of uneasiness.

"Oh, I was just thinking about John," said Jason after a slight pause. "He's out this afternoon with his sweetheart."

"You mean Pancroft?"

"Yes," said Jason, laughing.

Instantly Rodney felt the pressure transform into a wave of enthusiasm over the comical fate of poor, stupid John. "That brother of yours--" began Rodney, but was immediately interrupted.

"--He's not my brother," said Jason, rather seriously.

But Rodney was so keyed up over his own excited euphoria that he wasn't about to be deflated by this small mistake, or slip of the tongue. In fact he was so caught up in what he wanted to say that he didn't see the figure of his sister, who was standing just outside the door. Julia had forgotten her sewing in all the confusion of the previous episode and had brought the boys some sandwiches so that she would have an excuse for simply returning and leaving again. She didn't want to have to bear more of Jason's company than she absolutely had to, but upon hearing the name of Dow, she stopped to listen.

She had been entirely ignorant of what was going on between John and Cindy.

"Well, whatever you want to call him--" began Rodney again.

"How about unfortunate little bastard," suggested Jason.

This title only served to heighten what was almost a fit of nervous excitement so that Rodney went into new cycles of uncontrollable laughter, "Well at any rate, the way he goes around with that--"

"--Slut," added Jason, who was beginning to become caught up in Rodney's apparent gaiety, feeling somewhat complimented and satisfied in it.

"And he treats her like the Queen of Sheba. Walking around with her in the streets--in broad daylight, as if everyone didn't know what would happen once they got to the woods around Sawyer's Bridge."

Both boys laughed heartily at this.

"And the real clincher is that he thinks he's the only one!" exclaimed Jason as Rodney slapped the other on the shoulder to show his appreciation at this added hilarity. Julia, who could bear no more, stepped into the room and walked over to the boys, who were still laughing, and dropped the sandwiches in her brother's lap saying, "Here are your sandwiches, Rodney." And turning to Jason, she dropped the small bowl of egg salad in his lap so that it splattered onto his new pants, "And the egg salad." Then she strode briskly over to the couch and gathered up her sewing and exited as quickly as she had entered.

As she left the room, Rodney asked Jason in a speculative tone, "Do you suppose she heard what we were saying?"

But Jason was moaning in pain at catching the bowl of egg salad in his lap. This was partly due to the stain on his new pants but mostly because of the height from which the bowl had been dropped, which had caused the bowl to make a most indelicate and painful impression upon that part of his body.

"Do you think she heard?" Rodney repeated.

But Jason couldn't answer just yet and only moaned.

Chapter 10

"Showing the Reader the Fruits of Disillusionment"

NOW JOHN, it must be remembered, was coming over to the Vanderkamps to pick up Jason so that they might go home together. It was precisely at the conclusion of the aforementioned incident that he happened to be in view of the house.

As he drew nearer he saw Julia come out, and so John trotted over to say hello. When he got near enough and said hello, however, she stopped where she was and glared at him for a moment. The sun was starting to set behind some clouds, giving the illusion of twilight even though it was only five. But John could see that she was upset as her stare went through him. Those eyes, seemingly bigger than they usually were, enlarged by circles, circles of red, hot flaming crimson that seared him to the marrow of his bone and stopped him in his movement. She gritted her teeth and let out a laugh that was loud and hideous.

It was a laugh that seemed to echo in the chambers of his breast and evoked a tumultuous visceral trembling. As suddenly, the noise stopped and she stepped towards him and threw a handkerchief at his face, which brushed him on the cheek and fell to the ground. And then she turned and fled.

John didn't pick up the handkerchief because in all the confusion he forgot about it. Nor would it have mattered much if he had, for he wouldn't have recognized it as the one that he had plucked in the air and presented to Julia so gallantly a few years before. Instead he felt strangely as if he had done something wrong, yet search as he could, he could not discover what he had done or why it seemed to him that everything was his fault. He remembered what Jefferson had said to him once: sincere people are always feeling guilty for the sins of other wrongdoers because they imagine that their small guilt is as great as the other's large portion. Sincere people don't discriminate, because they find it hard to point the finger at someone else when they feel some sense of guilt no matter how insignificant in comparison.

And so John slowly made his way towards the house. Inside, Jason and Rodney were busily engaged in assigning the guilt for what had happened.

"These were new pants, you know," said Jason angrily.

"What do you want me to do about it?"

"I just bought them and they cost me twelve dollars. Twelve dollars for a pair of pants! They're the latest style and now look at them: mustard and mayonnaise all over them."

"Well, it's not my fault," said Rodney.

"It's your sister."

"But it wasn't me who--"

"It certainly was you; you started this whole mess," responded Jason.

"Nobody forced you to come over here, you know."

"Don't I know that, I only regret that I didn't have more sense at the beginning of the afternoon."

"You might have saved us all a scene," said Rodney with a sneer.

"You might save the air in the room if you'd keep your mouth shut."

Just then John shuffled in. He was no longer in the gay mood that had carried him to the Vanderkamps, but was now in a rather preoccupied mood. He didn't really pay attention to the cross words that were being said in the room before entering. Indeed, he hardly knew that a fight was in full progress when he offered his salutations, "Hello everybody."

"There's your brother, why don't you go home with him," said Rodney as both boys stared at the intruder in mutual animosity.

Jason turned to Rodney and said in visible fury, "How many times do I have to remind you, dunderhead, he's not--"

But at that moment, John, seeing a potential disturbance beginning, sought to avert it with some calmness, so he put his hand on Jason's shoulder and said, "C'mon Jason, it's time to go home. Dinner's almost ready and we have our chores to finish yet."

But instead of relieving the tension as John hoped that his gesture would, it acted to magnify it. Jason wheeled and screamed at Dow, "Stay out of this. You were the cause of all this. Now you get out of here!"

John didn't understand Jason's fury and instead of taking Jason at his word, he incautiously tried again to ease tempers with calm easiness. "Hey Jason, let's not get into a fight. It's the end of the day and--"

But John was never permitted to finish his sentence as Jason was beside himself and bellowed, "If I want to get into a fight, I'll get into a fight, so shut up--there wouldn't be any trouble if you didn't go about like an idiot with that town slut the way you do."

These words just burst from Jason's anger, as he would have never said them in a controlled state since it was to his advantage that John stay with Miss Pancroft and thus eliminate him as one of the suitors for Julia. However, this line of reasoning, which was once so artfully contrived to the click clack of an Atlanta rail coach, now seemed to be somewhat futile--or really more precisely: wasteful and inefficient since it turned out that Victor and not John was his real opposition. It didn't really matter whether John stayed with Cindy or not. So the ultimate outcome of his statement held considerably less import than if the original, the illusory picture or situation, was the actual state of being. This illusory state had been predicated upon ignorance of Victor's influence, an influence that once pointed out, made perfect sense. For how could anyone, logically, like or have any real affection for an illegitimate child with no money, who may even have enough black blood in him to be considered a Negro? The entire idea seemed utterly absurd to Jason and in the back of his mind he was still laughing at himself for his foolishness--a foolishness that made him feel like a dolt. Such humiliation didn't sit lightly with Jason, even though it was only humiliation before himself. These feelings swirled and thrashed about in those sparks that sputter in the dark grayish pink folds of the brain. They were going on separately in ignorance of or in defiance of what was presently happening--events so trivial—all that they wanted was time: time to rethink the entire situation; time to rewire the circuits, to make yet just one more fold.

"What did you say?" replied Dow sharply. He was willing to be good natured about almost anything in an attempt to get Jason home without a fuss, but there were certain things that he could not abide—one of which was slander on those he loved. Dow would have been able to withstand any remarks about his parentage or anything degrading about his appearance, intelligence, or any other natural ability. But to degrade someone who he highly regarded and thought of so tenderly was an offense that he could not excuse, for it was not in his power to excuse. It was not an offense against *his* person, but against someone else's, and to be silent or passive in the midst of such remarks would have been to give at least implied support to what was being said. If he did or said nothing, it would be as if he were making the remark and slandering a loved one who was not present to defend herself. The impropriety of such accusations, as well as the outrage which they evoked, along with the resulting pain that occurs when one imagines that someone who is loved is being injured in some fashion, all served to thicken John's voice as he repeated his demand, "What did you say, tell me!"

"You heard me," said Jason, who now had regained complete control of his voice, contrasting it in quality to Dow's loud, uncontrolled braying. "I said that you were making a fool out of yourself and the entire Beauchay Family by going around with that town slut."

Immediately upon his uttering the word 'slut,' Jason felt a sharp jolt in his midsection, followed by another as his head flew back, sending him to the ground with Dow close behind. John and Jason had rarely fought in their childhood since Jason was never any physical match for the much stronger and quicker Dow. And John had never wanted to take advantage of his comrade by using an obvious superiority to bully him. John, in fact, didn't like fighting out of anger and usually disliked himself for it later, though he did enjoy an occasional wrestling match when the contest was all in fun. But now he had lost all control. He was defending the honor of the woman he loved.

Rodney instantly called for help as he tried to separate the two. It was fortunate that he intervened. Because of Rodney's action, Dow was only able to land the two original punches and was restrained from landing any others. Immediately Mrs. Vanderkamp was down the stairs and sighed when she saw the boys fighting.

For even though she knew that she must break up the fight (since it was her responsibility), and even though she did not like fusses and commotion and the damage that it might cause to the furniture in the room, still, Mrs. Vanderkamp rather liked the sight of two boys fighting. It reminded her of when she was a young girl and boys used to fight each other over the privilege of walking her home from town. Those were grand, happy days when the War was over and everyone was building up again.

"Land sakes, boys, don't tussle. Rodney, stop them."

"I'm trying, Mother."

Mrs. Martha Vanderkamp walked over to John and put her hand on his shoulder, "Now John, you know that you shouldn't fight indoors--and least of all with Jason. Why, you two share the same roof."

As she spoke, John suddenly got control of himself and put his hands to his face so that he covered his eyes. He hadn't wanted to hit Jason and it wasn't Jason, really, that he wanted to chastise. It was--something else. All of the anger that was previously directed towards Jason was now thrown back upon himself with savage intensity, *the bright car, bright bright bright—Jefferson* I need, he told himself, I need--a *glass of cool lemonade, prepared by slender fingers the grass; where was the grass? Why was it all so dirty? His greatness, his potency—was only a hole in the ground. Instead of building a fortress, he had only dug a hole and now the dirt was falling in.*

"That's right John, now let Jason up. I declare, you really punched him hard."

Dow turned his eyes to Mrs. Vanderkamp for a moment and then he slowly stood up, aided by Rodney and his mother.

"That's right, now just stand up there and we'll help Jason."

Jason lay on the floor. He was more shocked than anything else. The blows had been sharp, but the worst he would get was a little swelling under his left eye.

"Now get up Jason, everything is all right. It's going to be all right, child. My, but you're going to have a little shiner under your eye."

Jason put his hand to his eye to feel.

"No the other eye, Jason. The other eye."

Jason touched the other eye and squinted. It was sore, but he had gotten worse bruises before, he told himself, simply from riding a horse.

"My my, what on earth could you boys have been fighting about?" asked Mrs. Vanderkamp as she knew, or thought she knew, that the only subject that would makes boys of that age fight with such ferocity was female. How wonderful it was to be fought over, she thought. How magnificently primitive, she sighed, to be sought after by two men so intensely. How really stimulated it made her feel to think about it. She experienced a kind of admiration and peculiar longing for the victor, almost as if she had been the object of their fight—that they had been fighting over her and now she was ready to submit to the victor. How very much like animals it was to fight. It reminded her of what she imagined life as a Negro must be like.

"Now you two boys make up," she said, not letting Rodney speak. He was eagerly waiting to respond to her question of how and why the fight had started, but her second statement followed so quickly that he didn't have time to make his reply. Mrs. Vanderkamp turned to bring John over to shake Jason's hand, but he was gone. "Now where's John?" said Mrs. Vanderkamp.

"He's gone," said Rodney perceptively.

John's departure made Mrs. Vanderkamp strangely sad, and so she walked over to the door, but seeing no one said, "You look after Jason, Rodney, darling. I'll just have a look outside and see if I can see John."

And so Jason was put in a chair and Rodney lay a cold cloth to his swelling and listened to Jason tell him how little control John had and how he could be capable of anything with such a hot temper. And Rodney listened to it all, even after he heard his mother return, alone, and shut the back door.

***

"Say Jake, you hear 'bout the golf course?" said Ed as he got up to put the checker board away.

"'Taint nothin' new about that Ed," said Ike from across the counter as he was putting things away for the night. "The country club closed months ago."

"Yep," said Ed, "but nobody knowd' who bought it."

"Wasn't much mystery to that," said Jake as he blew his nose.

"What ya mean, Jake?" asked Ed.

"Think most people in this town know who bought that land," said Ike.

"Who then?" asked Ed.

"Why our fancy-dan-bank president, George Dodson. Who else?" said Jake with a gesture of his hand.

"Nope," replied Ed.

"Nope?" repeated Ike in an amazed tone.

"What do you mean, *nope*?" asked Jake after a short silence.

"Jist what I says, n-o-p-e."

"You don't have to spell it our fer us," said Ike, a little perturbed.

"Tell us what you mean," prompted Jake.

"Samuel Beauchay."

"What?" replied Ike and Jake in unison.

"Yep, that's it," said Ed smiling.

"You mean a tell me that Beauchay bought the old golf course, and not Dodson?" paraphrased Jake for clarification.

"Well, I'll be," said Jake.

Ike came out from behind the counter and interrupted his routine to ask, "How'd you find this out?"

"From Murray Finngate over in the record's office."

"You went fishin' with him the other day, weren't you?" asked Jake.

"Yep."

"What did Murray say?" asked Ike.

"Jist that the deal had finally gone through," said Ed.

"How was the fishin', Ed?" asked Jake.

"Pretty good, got a dozen carp and three--"

"What about the deal?" interrupted Ike.

"Nothin', jist the land deal tween Beauchay and whatever the other feller's name is--"

"Murdock," supplied Ike.

"Yar, Murdock."

"You go up to Silver Lake, Ed?" asked Jake.

"Heck no, we jist went in the old Maria pond, a little north of the point tween Jackson's and Lee's place."

"Is there good fishin' there--?"

But before Ed could answer, Ike put in, "C'mon Jake, stop askin' questions 'bout fishin' when I'm talkin' bout this land deal."

"He's already done told us 'bout the land. I want to know where he went fishin'."

"Well that's fine, but can you let me ask a couple a questions first?" Jake's silence meant, 'yes,' and so Ike inquired, "How come it's taken so long to go through?"

"Don't know, must have been some tamperin' with the records or somethin'."

"Murray tell you that?" asked Jake immediately.

"Well, now, not exactly," admitted Ed.

"Did Murray tell you anything about any tamperin'?"

"Well, no, but how else could the records have taken so long?"

"How do you know that they took a long time? What's long? I haven't bought any land recently, have you?" returned Jake again. Then Jake said to Ike. "See, he don't have no more ta tell, let me ask him 'bout his fishin'."

"Just one last question, Jake. Did Dodson know about the deal or have anything to do with it?"

Ed looked at Jake and then shook his head. "Can't rightly say, Ike." Then Ike turned around and went back to his routine and Jake pressed on about the fishin'.

--are you going--what do you mean am I going, going to what-- why the big party at the social club--when is it--Saturday night-- are they going to have a good band--I hear it's a band from Atlanta—really, all the way from Atlanta—hello girls—hello Margaret--what are you talking about--there's a party on this Saturday night—where, at that casino of yours--social club--really Margaret, you shouldn't be such a prig, after all most of the town belongs--and the rest belong to that rougher one down the street, you know--really Margaret it isn't anything like the old saloon. why it's got carpeting and pretty lights--and the tables are so nice—so nice that you hardly notice the gambling room, eh—listen Meg, if you don't have anything nice to say--oh, I'm sorry girls, but you know how I hate gambling and drinking--but there's no drinking at the social club--well I've never been there you understand, but I was told by Basel Amstead that they have a place to buy alcohol—oh, you know Basel, she thinks there's a witch under every bushel basket--why don't you come along sometime Meg, I think you'd like it--sorry girls, but I think I'll just stay home with the family, they're plenty for me--

In the twilight, Julia started for the house. The silhouette of the structure against the darkening horizon seemed frightening. It was hardly the same house that she was used to seeing in the brightness of the daylight. The western sun had set and now the recant of light that always followed its wake was quickly disappearing.

Julia knelt to the ground and searched about with her hands, being unable to see plainly. Then she found it, and she lifted the handkerchief to her face and kissed it gently, and then put it into the palm of her hand so that she could caress it. It felt as if it were still quite the same except for one of the edges which felt slightly soiled and damp. Julia rose and walked slowly back to the house in the darkness.

Chapter 11

"Speculation and Investigation"

"YOU KNOW ED, I've been thinking about that land," said Ike as the three friends walked home along Robert E. Lee Street towards the older section of town.

"Which land is that, Ike?"

"You know, Ed, the land that Murdock sold to Beauchay. You remember--we talked about it a week ago."

"Oh yeah, really was a queer deal wasn't it?" said Ed, scratching his nose where his long nose hairs were tickling him.

"I was just wonderin' a why Beauchay would want to buy that land unless he knew something about it that none of the rest of us did."

"What you drivein' at, Ike?" asked Jake.

"Don't rightly know myself, 'cept that it jist seems mighty strange to me, that's all."

"Maybe he didn't want Dodson to get it," offered Ed.

"Don't think so," began Ike as he rid himself of his wad of tobacco. "I thought that myself, 'cept it don't make no sense, cause if a feller's got money to spend, there ain't any way that no one's goin' ta keep him from havin' some land, and Beauchay's smart enough ta see that."

"Suppose it's part of a feud or something 'tween them. After all, the two never see each other and it's no secret that Beauchay tried to stop George from becoming vice president."

"Could be, Jake, but I don't know. I jist wonder if there's something else there. Some other reason why Beauchay wanted to get that land. And so secretive, too--you know all that records mumbo-jumbo and all. I jist get a hankering that there's something else there sides jist a trying ta git back at his kin, even if he does dislike 'em."

The three men walked further down the road, neither talking nor looking around when finally Ed suggested, "Why don't we go out there and see for ourselves?"

"What do you mean?" asked Jake. "Go out there when--and do what?"

"Tonight, and just look around."

"What good would that do?" asked Jake.

"Don't know, but what harm would it do? Might be something."

"Might tell us more about that piece of property," added Ike, who rather liked Ed's idea.

"I don't know who's more a fool, you for suggestin' this ding burn scheme, or me for going with you. But I'm willing to tag along with you two if you want to go."

And so they got Ike's cart and hitched up his mule and started out along Highway #1 towards the golf course. When they had passed the road that leads to the Stuart's house, they tied up the mule and walked the rest of the way cross-country so that they wouldn't be seen by anyone who might be on the property. They weren't exactly sure what it was they were looking for, but whatever it was, they wanted to be certain that they weren't noticed.

"Tit's a mighty hard way to travel, like this when thars not much moon," said Ed.

"Shhh, twas yourn idea, so be still," said Ike as he pushed a branch from out of his face. Finally they made their way to a point where they could see the golf course. The visibility was not very good because the moon was hidden just then behind some clouds, but there was just enough light coming through so that they could make out the dim outlines of the series of mounds that constituted the former course.

"Don't see how anyone ever farmed that," said Jake.

"They didn't," laughed Ike in a whisper, "that's why they went broke."

They all chuckled at this and finally sat down to wait. What exactly they were waiting for, none of them knew. Ed poked Jake in the side after a long interval in which Jake had shamelessly fallen asleep. "I see something."

"What?" said Jake, a little too loudly, for he had just awaken and had forgotten that they were supposed to be very quiet.

"Shhh," the other two hissed at once. And Jake instantly knew where he was and felt a bit chagrinned, not at having talked a little too loudly, but for having been convinced that he should give up his good night's sleep to lay on the damp ground in the middle of an old field waiting for hell to freeze or something of the sort.

"What da ya see?" asked Ike as he strained his eyes but saw nothing. Jake, too, was trying to recognize the source of Ed's excitement, but with similar results.

"There ain't nothin' out there, Ed," began Jake, "you're seeing things."

"Nope. I saw something all right."

"Well then where is it? I don't see it."

"I don't see it right now neither, but I saw it just a moment ago. I know I did. It was over by that sycamore tree."

"Where?" asked Ike. So Ed pointed.

"That's no sycamore tree," said Jake.

"Well, then, what is it?"

"I don't know, but I know that it's no sycamore tree, that's for certain. If you ask me, I think we should pack it in and head off. A nice bed would sure beat this prairie grass."

"Go home if you want to," said Ed. "No one's stopping you. But don't take the cart. Ike and me will need it to get back."

"And walk all the way back at this time of night? No thank you; I'm not a kid anymore, you know."

"Well then stop talkin' like one," added Ike, who was getting a little disturbed at all the noise that they were making.

"I'm going to go a little closer," said Ed.

Ed started ahead as Ike went with him. Jake stayed where he was at first, but when his comrades were only twenty or so yards away, he got up to join them. Then he heard a rhythmic pounding. It was a metallic sound.

When they were a hundred yards closer, Ed stopped. "See it now?" he asked. But he needn't have asked the question for now both Jake and Ike could see what appeared to be a figure moving up and down. The motions seemed to correspond to the metallic pounding.

"There's someone there all right," said Jake. "Let's circle around the other way so that we can get a better look, unnoticed."

The other two took Jake's lead as they painstakingly made their way through what proved to be a very muddy section of low ground.

"This soil doesn't hold the water, that's for sure," said Jake.

But the other two didn't care to discuss the topography as they were more interested in seeing who the mysterious person was and what he was doing. Finally, ankle deep in mud, and with their shirts full of cockle burrs, they got to a point where they could see better.

"Who is it?" asked Ike, as his glasses were muddy and so he could not see much of anything.

"I can't tell, can you, Jake?"

"No, but I know that he's hitting some metal thing into the ground. It's long and thin and he's driving it in with a sledge hammer."

"But why would he--"

"Let's wait and see," said Jake whose interest was somewhat keener than it had been before, but who soon, as before, fell asleep. Soon, though, he was poked again by Ed who said, "He's stopped."

"What?" began Jake, but this time Ike put his hand over Jake's mouth so that the sound barely escaped.

"He kept driving in things. Would knock in a pipe and pull it out again. Did it again all over."

Then the figure lit a lantern and they could see him clearly. It was Samuel Beauchay.

"Well, don't that beat all," said Ike on the way home as he drove the old mule cart with a steady hand.

"What ya 'spose he was doing?" said Ed.

"People use pipes like that sometimes when they are trying to reach water or--" he paused for a moment as if he were trying to fathom the real import of the words he was about to utter, "--trying to take soil samples."

"You mean for farming? That land's no good fer farmin', Beauchay should know that," said Ed as he scratched his nose.

"No, he doesn't mean farming. Anyone in this county knows that it's worthless farming land. What Jake means is,--ah, ah--what do you mean, Jake?" asked Ike.

"I mean maybe Beauchay thinks that there is some sort of mineral deposits in that land, and maybe he's takin' them samples of soil to figure out if he's right. Alls you have to do is send them in to some agency and they tells you whether or not the land's any good."

"You mean like gold?" asked Ed as his eyes flashed.

"Well, like gold, but it probably wouldn't be gold around here. Can't say jist what it might be. But one thing's fer certain, he ain't trying to dig no well."

All three men laughed at this joke as the wagon rolled slowly into town.

For the next week or so, each of the men would take shifts watching Samuel Beauchay going into his field to pound the metal pipe into different sections and then take it out again before retiring. For a week they watched him as he went through his methodic ritual. And for a week, each of them tried to formulate ideas about what in the blazes he was doing out there all by himself and what minerals he might be looking for.

"Couldn't you get your friend to ask a few questions in the records office?" asked Ike.

"What good would that do?" said Jake. "They don't handle everything. All they is concerned with is legal documents, like deeds, marriage licenses, birth and death certificates. Ed wouldn't get anywhere questioning Murray."

"But still, don't you think that they might be able to find out something?" asked Ike.

"How could they? Sides, we don't want too many people to get in on this. Could cause a panic, you know."

"Yar," added Ed, "and anyway, if it's for real, then we want to be able to get in on it before anyone else does."

Both men looked at Ed and smiled. "I don't know what it is, but one thing's for certain, we've got to keep our eyes wide open these next few weeks."

All three men nodded their heads as if in agreement.

Chapter 12

"Night Thoughts"

AS AMBROSIAL NIGHT lulled itself into its stillness, Jefferson John Brown sat with a notebook on his lap that he was not reading. There was a kerosene lamp in front of him which he did not even smell. He sat there staring at the flame while he held an oddly shaped cross that hung on a chain around his neck.

He had already stayed at the Beauchay farm much longer than he had anticipated. Only a year or two, he had told himself-- until things quiet down a little. Then I will go back. But somehow one year had a way of sliding into another and at every projected point of departure, there would always be some reason why he shouldn't go just yet. And now he was almost sixty and no longer the young man with promise, but an old man who had little realistically to look forward to except death.

But how could this be? I don't feel old. I can still work and think as well as I ever could--well almost as well. It's really that I can't work as long anymore. Not as long as I could when I was young, but when I do work, I can remember things sharply. I can analyze as perceptively as I ever could, maybe even better. This is because I have had so much of life behind me that I can see all the mistakes which I used to take for truth. I can see that all the simple answers in which I used to feel such comfort and conviction are only broad, misconstrued labels that, in themselves, mean nothing. It no longer seems as if there are any foundational, unifying principles, as each principle seems to be defined in terms of itself so that it must be examined only on its own terms. But where is the connection?

Plato talked about the Forms as if they must, of necessity, be transcendent, but that this couldn't be as he shows in the refutation found in the Parmenides. The argument never seems to have been adequately answered. How does one connect a Form (such as God or the Form of the Good—which may or may not be the same thing) with the world? The only way seems to be through some kind of connecting material. But what connects the connecting material---more connecting material? But what would connect that . . . and so on. There is no end to the connecting materials. The result is that transcendent Forms or a transcendent God never gets connected to the world. On the other hand, God (or any other Form), in this model, must be transcendent. But perhaps the model is incorrect as it assumes a transcendent God and then asks the silly question: how does one connect a completely transcendent God with the world when the answer is initially prejudiced in the formulation of the question? That is, when one assumes a transcendent God to begin with. Then it is impossible to connect it with anything since it is defined from the outset as transcendent.

The other case is that God must be immanent. Let's consider a wholly immanent God. This type of God must either be the whole the material universe (of which we are a part) or else we must be the whole of which God is a part. In either example, God is dependent upon us because He (it, she, etc.) is either included in us or we in Him. He is not completely omnipotent because He depends upon us in either mode for some of his His divine satisfaction.

But what ontological role does that leave for God? Is He not the same as we are or we as He is? Are we to take the Biblical passage, "we were created in His own image," to mean that God and Man are existing on the same level of reality? Surely not. But what is there left to say?

Jefferson picked up the chain and twirled the cross so that it wrapped itself around his index finger. His thoughts spun around to his life in Baltimore. He had so wanted to be a great man. He had wanted to be a model for children to look to when they grew up. Both black and white children would hold his name as cherished: the man who showed to the world that Blackness and Whiteness, yea all cultural distinctions, meant as little to the realm of the ethical as the ethical meant to the realm of the spiritual. *There was no connection. Blackness and Whiteness were psychological states and as such created psychological problems which were never relieved by employing short-cut sociological stereotypes.*

A group of people living with certain common neuroses could possibly be able to cope more easily if they assigned guilt to some other entity or group which was completely unrelated to their problem (in a logical sense). Because of mutual reinforcement, the acceptability of this short-cut might be affected. It could become evident to the people that there was a "quick" solution to their problems. This "easy" answer could be rapidly accepted so that it might be adopted by some group as a solution to their psychological difficulties. The problem is that this solution is no solution at all when scapegoats are employed. The neurosis is not really helped at all. At best, only a few symptoms are affected. Soon it becomes inadequate to a future need. Then the individuals in the tribe turn to their familiar source for the answer and find it suddenly lacking in its ability to meet this new group need. This produces added hostility towards the surrogate solution and further alienates the scapegoat.

When one adds to this that the oppressed group has neuroses of its own apart from the added ones brought on by the oppressing group, then one can see a very complicated matrix of hate and resentment arising from both groups. This matrix is what separates whites (in general) from blacks (in general) and blacks (in general) from whites (in general). Individuals, of course, need not be tied to these group patterns, and may establish successful relationships apart from group thinking.

The best way for a black person to form an individual relationship with a white is for him to resist allowing himself to play the role that the white person expects that he will play. He must doggedly maintain his individuality. If he is confronted by a situation when this becomes practically impossible, then (if some defense role must be employed, as indeed there must be at times as we all feel threatened) he should always jump into the role of the superior party. Hopefully a superior party who is so far above his adversary and can offer quiet logic in return for any accusation or threat, no matter how emotional.

Assuming a superior position is preferable to one of inferiority because that is the role that the oppressor expects. When one thinks himself as inferior, then he can act in only two ways: 1. He can attempt to assert himself physically in order to show the adversary that even if he (the adversary) is better, that at least the oppressed individual is stronger in body, or 2. The oppressed party can roll over and lick the shoe of the adversary. Both of these alternatives are self-defeating. The latter defeats the self, because soon he has made himself an object so often for so many "masters" that he can never be anything but an object. The former defeats the self as it denies that the oppressed party is human by relying on a non-human (viz., bestial) response to a social conflict. The person who is forced into employing this defensive guise habitually also loses the ability to return from being an animal and resume his role as a homo-sapiens. Thus, when one assumes a role of inferiority as a defense mechanism, it is necessarily self-defeating.

The alternative is for the oppressed to assume a role of superiority. The better one can play this role, the less the adversary can query whether the oppressed party really thinks himself superior. That is, the essence of this role is assuming a self-control that surpasses that of the adversary so that the oppressed party can be in the position of power and, as a result, minimize the chance of experiencing serious pain. For any pain that the adversary inflicts, he will be inflicting it from the lesser role of one who has lost control. Thus, the attack can be seen in its proper perspective (i.e., that it has resulted from some paucity or defect which the adversary has been experiencing, and thus is indicative of the adversary's weakness and not pointing to some innate inferiority in the oppressed party).

Thus the resultant pain is mitigated. In order to assume this superior role, one must understand the dynamics of just what is happening in a human encounter. This means accustoming oneself to the hidden language of social intercourse, e.g., when someone says, "You black people certainly have ugly, flat noses." What they are really saying is that, "I have some facet of my make-up that I feel deeply inferior about, perhaps it is my own face. I have anxiety over whether people find it really attractive or not. I think that if I can make some depreciating remark about your appearance, then in a competitive sense, I'm at least one up. I'm trying to alleviate my own inadequacy (at least in part) by criticizing you." The individual in the superior role sees that the first statement really means the second and therefore doesn't feel offended, but rather sorry for the adversary who feels so badly about himself that he has to try to build himself up at the other's expense.

However, it must be emphasized that to play this role

responsibly, one must belong to a truly oppressed group (and it should be emphasized that this role is only to be assumed when a party feels oppressed and defensive). It is not a role to be assumed all the time, for this would breed a false sense of power and would make one lose touch with what it means to actually exist on the same ontological level as those people who are relegated to the "lesser level." This means understanding the artificial nature of this solution.

This path is temporary at best, and at worst, it can lead to an accelerating cycle of recriminations. To assume the superior role all the time is to fall prey to the same artificial solution that the bigots (one example of the above phenomenon) do. It is to fall prey to the same problems and worsening cycle that they experience and--since our goal is to become authentic people--we want to avoid any path which might destroy this opportunity. We must analyze each item of criticism that is offered to ascertain whether, in fact, there is any justification in it: any thread of truth. This analysis should occur in a period of reflective equilibrium, when one is not confronting the adversary, but when one is by one's self. This enables the oppressed subject to maintain an objective view of himself, so he can accept the good criticism and reject the bad. It makes him susceptible to becoming defensive about the same subject in the future. In short: it allows the subject to maintain the maximum amount of openness, while minimizing his chances for pain by offering a constructive program for self-betterment.

Now, many of my brothers will say, why should I have to do all of this when whites don't do a thing about their personalities? The only answer to this is that an individual can never do anything about anybody else except himself. To do otherwise is imperialism, among the worst of interpersonal crimes. If, by example, others watch you and ask you how you seem to be able to keep your head and remain so calm when others can't, or why you always seem to know what to do, or why so many people, white as well as black, respect you as yourself, then maybe you can share with them what you have found to be true for yourself. And further, how you are able to cope psychologically with a very difficult world, and that you don't expect anyone else, black or white, to do the things that you do, because one cannot. This is not because you're some kind of superman, but because you have such a reverence for life that you want to react to each person *the way you would ideally if there were not any such things as psychological blocks, which arise because the world is so damn frightening. To act in any other way would be to commit imperialism. To merely hope would be to engage in a futile exercise.*

It takes work and desire to want to obtain this type of objectivity over one's self, but the rewards are great. Human relationships take on a new depth, and a greater order will become visible to the mind's eye. This order is what's inspired by the Divine, and to act truly from this impulse is to try and to do the best one can.

Jefferson put his head down. These notes had been intended for a book that he was going to write when he had some time. After Baltimore--after the successful intimidation which left him a widower without children. He had abandoned the project. He left the life of conflict, in which he tried to carry out his ideals, for the old life of rural Georgia. The notes, however, never quite died. He kept them out of some feeling for the past and had added to them at irregular intervals until they required a new storage box to keep them.

He had planned someday to put them all into a book that might be printed. But all he had were notes. How cold it was in the Baltimore jail. The remembrance of that numbing dampness which pervaded everything made him shiver. He had aspired to be an organizer of his race. He had envisioned a union of black laborers. So many black men worked on the docks and in the factories that he would have had plenty of members. But the USA didn't like unions. Even Debs was clamped away during the war. And he was a white man.

What do they want a union for? They should be happy they ain't slaves—them niggers gettin' pretty uppity for my taste. They lucky to work. What they want a union for?

Jefferson remembered Peabody and his voice reading the Bible after supper to his admiring feline crowd. What a simple man he was, yet what tremendous courage—the kind of courage that Jefferson had wanted to be able to display so many times, but never had to his own satisfaction. It seemed to him that the more one tried to be courageous, the more difficult it was to achieve. For when one contemplated whether he should do something in terms of it being "courageous," then the act lost any potential it had of being a courageous action. Because when one wants to be brave and selfless, then one is faced with a self-referential context. These contexts operate this way: "Epimenides the Cretan says, 'All Cretans are liars.'" Is Epimenides speaking the truth? If so, then his statement becomes false. If he is lying, then he is speaking the truth. The self-referential situation belies the intended outcome.

In the same way, if one *intends* to be selfless and courageous, then he is undercut by the selfish attitude. These two properties can be a part of one's acquired character but not the outcome of some instantaneous action because the conscious decision to appear selfless and courageous would make one a phony for the true virtue in question. Instead, he's be selfish and using a dangerous situation only as a career builder.

Yet the action appears to others as having some value. The action when viewed by others does not reveal the sordid selfish motivations which one harbored in his breast. Yet these are integral to the action, for without them human behavior would be nothing but a series of accidental "happenings." The spectators applaud with much emotion, yet the agent knows. He understands what it was really all about.

Then Jefferson put down his notes and got up, left his room, and ventured outside. The night air felt pure in his breathing. Still, he felt incomplete. There didn't seem to be any way that he could be the kind of man that old Peabody was. Peabody seemed to be driven simply by the motive of doing what was ethically right, because it needed to be done, and unless someone else stepped in who could do it better, he would try to do his best for as long as he could. *But with me it is hopeless. I always try and decide whether I'm doing something for myself or for others, and the 'others' always lose.*

There may be some sense that an action is judged by the spectators, as all actions are within the realm of the ethical, and the ethical only deals with human action. But the impulse behind that action is spiritual. God doesn't care what we do. What is important is that given a certain set of actions, do we feel that they reflect that unity that we feel as the Divine impulse? If our actions can fit into a coherent whole, which is consistent when applied to everyone within a given subset, then that system, and all actions therein, is divinely inspired since the Divine principle is the impulse to ultimate order.

But again I'm getting off the track of what I am to do. It's so easy to get off track from following a particular argument to its conclusion when it inspires another question to be explored ad nauseam.

Then there's John. Haven't I tried to do well for him? But where have I been when he has really needed me? What have I done? He is such a basically good boy. He's a little thoughtless at times, but then all boys are at his age. He's got something, though, that I deeply respect: his simple good will. I remember once when I—

In his hand he held the chain. It used to be the cat's (John's) chain; the one she wore around her neck. There was an inscription on it; he stopped to read it. "They shall be satisfied." It was the short form of "Blessed are those who hunger and thirst for righteousness for they shall be satisfied." That inscription had once intrigued him. He was only now beginning to understand. Why had he failed to become the kind of leader that he had wished to be? The crisis had come, and he had been defeated. What does one do in defeat? What does one do when his wife and baby are slaughtered? He had gone back to Georgia for a rest before continuing, but he had never been able to resurrect himself from his defeat. The murder of his family had taken all the drive out of him. He had wanted a refreshing rest and all that had resulted was a death-like sleep.

Jefferson knew that it was late at night. He was walking in the fields. He was seeking nature. But he had hit an impasse. Now he had to stop. He should turn in, as he had a busy day ahead. But somehow sleep seemed impossible. His mind just refused to rest. He looked up to the moon. It was a waning crescent. Then Jefferson returned home. He lit the candle stub in his room. Jefferson put his head down on the table next to the candle and tried to cry, but couldn't. When the candle was out, he was asleep in his chair. His hand was still clutching the chain.

Preview of Georgia—Part Two

The book begins on an idyllic note: it is late summer and time for the Bella County Fair. This is an annual event with many activities: pie baking contests, needle point competitions, daily events in tents from clown shows to some exotic dancers (carefully supervised by a Christian women's group) to games of skill and chance. At the end of the week is the rifle shooting competition, the cross-country horse race, and a dance. Behind this façade of normalcy lies a growing criminal element that began with moonshine and gambling but is now branching out. This cancer strikes the calm rural scene and creates change through violence and deception.

Other Novels by Michael Boylan

Rainbow Curve (2014) Fans of baseball's history will appreciate this compelling tale about race, politics, and corrupting power and one's man's courage to stand-up. *De Anima #1*

The Extinction of Desire (2007) What would you do if you suddenly became rich? *De Anima #2*

To the Promised Land (2015) Are there limits to forgiveness: personal, corporate, political? *De Anima #3*

Maya (forthcoming) Follow the fate of an Irish-American family through three generations. It's the story of immigrants. *De Anima #4.*

Naked Reverse (2016) There is a backdoor to the ivory tower. Find out what happens to one college professor who escapes. *Archē #1*

Georgia: Parts Two and Three (Forthcoming) A novel told in three parts. Explore racial identity through a murder mystery set in the early 20th century. *Archē #3-4*

T-Rx: The History of a Radical Leader (Forthcoming) An epistolary novel about radicalization in the Vietnam-era. What is and what is *not* legitimate tactics for social/political change? *Archē #5*

The Long Fall of the Ball from the Wall (Forthcoming) A novel set in the investigation of the JFK assassination that connects it to larger social phenomena. *Archē #6*

www.ingramcontent.com/pod-product-compliance
Lightning Source LLC
Chambersburg PA
CBHW030628030726
47497CB00006B/1686